THE GENTLE INSURRECTION

VOICES OF THE SOUTH

DORIS BETTS

THE GENTLE INSURRECTION

AND OTHER STORIES

LOUISIANA STATE UNIVERSITY PRESS
Baton Rouge and London

Library of Congress Cataloging-in-Publication Data
Betts, Doris.
    The gentle insurrection and other stories / Doris Betts.
       p.   cm. — (Voices of the South)
    ISBN 0-8071-2224-6 (pbk.)
    1. Southern States—Social life and customs—Fiction.   I. Title.
II. Series.
PS3552.E84G46   1997
813' .54—dc21   97-14746
                                                                     CIP

"The Sympathetic Visitor" appeared in *Mademoiselle* magazine in March 1954; "Mr. Shawn and Father Scott" appeared in the August 1953 issue of *Mademoiselle*. "The Sword" and "The Gentle Insurrection" were first printed in *Coraddi* at the Women's College of the University of North Carolina.

The paper in this book meets the guidelines for permanence and durability of the Committee on Production Guidelines for Book Longevity of the Council on Library Resources. ∞

FOR LOWRY

Contents

THE GENTLE INSURRECTION

The Sympathetic Visitor

MISS WARD pulled her car over to the side of the road and stopped where three little black boys were shooting marbles. They had their backs to her, squatted on thin haunches like dark and patient toads, and their voices came up soft and pleased when the colored marbles clicked against each other.

"Ain't none of the rest of us usin' a steel," said one of the boys sullenly, and another took it away agreeably and thumped a bright red crystal towards the center.

A pig's eye, Miss Ward thought to herself, watching them from the car window. That's what you call it. You draw a pig's eye and try to shoot the other marbles out.

"Can you tell me where Nettie Sue Morrison lives?" she said.

The little boys giggled nervously and jumped up onto brown bare feet and glanced at each other. They looked down at the ground and followed it with their eyes along the dusty road. One of them touched her car fender with a reverent finger, leaving a little circle in the dust. They did not look at her.

"No'm," they said, almost in unison, like a badly rehearsed chorus.

3

They giggled down at the bare feet and at the dusty road, but none of them looked at her.

The bravest boy, digging a fist into the back of his neck, explained it for her. "No'm," he added, squirming. "We don't know where she lives."

Miss Ward put the car in gear automatically, not even bothering to send them a stern glance for the lie. It must be the heat that made her feel so tired. "Thank you," she said vaguely. Of course they knew where Nettie Sue lived. Every nigger in Rabbittown knew where Nettie Sue lived, especially now. But they didn't want her to know. Miss Ward sighed.

The road, unpaved, crunched under her car wheels as if to slow her down, and it seemed to Miss Ward that window shades moved in the houses she passed and quiet eyes observed her and measured her, and perhaps signals were passed along from cramped back yards—She just went by my place. They were all hiding Nettie Sue, banding together in a warm, living wall of brown flesh, and even their children were in on it. "No'm," they had all been told to say. "No'm, we don't know where she lives."

Miss Ward felt tired already. Niggers always left her feeling tired. She looked back at the three little boys, who stood in an excited brown cluster staring after her car.

Frowning, she turned down another unfamiliar road. None of the streets in Rabbittown were marked and there was nothing to distinguish one from the other; they wound in squares and circles and came back upon themselves and quit abruptly at dead ends. The niggers knew every foot of the section but no one else ventured very far; it reminded Miss Ward of someplace in an old Charles Boyer movie, but she could not remember what it was. All these streets were alike, narrow and dusty roads with slightly higher paths on each side, and lined with rows of tired, unpainted houses that seemed all to have slumped at the same moment and in the same direction. They rested against one another like a row of dominoes and all of them were leaning in the direction Miss Ward was driving; it gave her a sense of nagging guilt as if she had unwittingly pulled a string at each corner and tipped them that way, clumsily off balance, for the whole block.

Chinaberry trees grew in some of the bare yards, and the kinky heads that stuck out from between some of the branches were like brown burrs; it was as if all the trees had some common disease and were full of darkly parasitic growths. I'm awfully morbid today, thought Miss Ward. Several houses down the street ahead of her there would be giggles and shrill talk from the children in the trees, but whenever her car drew alongside, everything was silent and not a green leaf moved. Only after she had driven past did the dark heads come slowly out to look after her.

It seemed to Miss Ward that where the hidden children's eyes touched her, small gentle bruises rose up under the skin. She shook her head angrily; this was no time to be fanciful and imagine things. Not today of all days.

Ahead of her, an old man was walking down the middle of the road very slowly, as if he had come a long way; a wind pushed by him and his arm wavered like an empty sleeve. Miss Ward touched her horn slightly and then wished she had not; it screamed out angrily at the old man and there was something personal and insulting in the sound of it. His shoulders jolted forward and he leaped into

5

the ditch and stood there, looking back at her car, waiting.

Miss Ward bit nervously at her lip and stopped the car beside him. He stood without moving, his mouth slack and faintly trembling, his eyes quiet—he was like a bird surprised in his nest, and—having no wings yet—waiting for what might come, food or wing or claw, watching and waiting without even the luxury of resignation. The old man looked at Miss Ward with his eyes that were like a bird's and his look banged against her face.

She cleared her throat. "Can you tell me where Nettie Sue Morrison lives?" she said.

The old man wiped his mouth against the back of his hand, wiped that on his trousers, looked blankly down at his trousers as if he had never seen them before. There it is again, thought Miss Ward, fighting down her irritation. They're all like this. His eyes wandered on down one leg, examined the ground for insects. He said finally, "Yessum, I can tell you that."

There was a pause, as if he were giving her a chance to spare them both this whole experience by withdrawing the question, while he moved his feet, watching them with faint surprise.

He said then, "Nettie Sue lives down the road a piece. On this side. Her brother's crepe is up."

He bobbed his head, not looking up, not seeing the grateful smile Miss Ward was giving him. She let it fade, swallowed, and tried to transfer it to her words.

"Thank you so much," she said pleasantly. "I've had such a time finding my way. None of the streets are marked." He looked up at her then and she knew suddenly

6

that it was all her fault about the streets and she drove away, seething with anger.

I hate these niggers, she thought grimly, clenching her teeth. They have no right to be this way.

It had always been like that with her, she reflected, even when she had been a little girl, and toothless old Aunt Mag had come in to do her Mama's washing—cumbersome, awkward Aunt Mag, with her swollen feet in the dirty cut-out oxfords.

She remembered the day she asked, "How come the city cut the water off Sunday afternoon?" and Aunt Mag, shuffling through the kitchen, answering her, "I don't know, we ain't got no water, Child," and the queer feeling in her stomach, like little angry wings.

Then later she had asked about Aunt Mag's husband and learned he was off on the chaingang for stealing; a "good man," Aunt Mag had called him then.

There had been eight or ten of Aunt Mag's kids, looking all alike, like so many brown peas out of the same pod, and one day she had brought her little girl to work; the two were about of an age and Jean Ward, trying to be kind, had said to her, "That's my dress you've got on. I gave it to you," and then listened with horror to the little girl's quiet answer, "Yessum"—just the way Aunt Mag answered Mama, but with some secret hid behind the eyes until she knew sharply that she ought to apologize for the dress and did not know why.

Miss Ward sighed, pulled her mind back into the present, shut it in between the staggered rows of houses by the road. A little wind, she thought, would flatten them out, slap

7

them down in a row like little cardboard fronts for houses. The houses seemed to her then just like Aunt Mag's little girl, and the three little boys and the old man; that was the reason niggers didn't fix up their houses, paint or clean or plant geraniums; it was to keep them just the shabby way they were, something to affront, to startle, to blame the passer-by. Miss Ward lost all patience with her thoughts.

In front of Nettie Sue's house (just like the others except for the death wreath, she thought—the same yard and porch and probably the same step broken), Miss Ward stopped the car and sat for a few minutes. The dark crepe against the front door was like some festering sore on an old tired body. It was for Nettie's brother, the old man had said. How odd. She shook her head, wondering.

Then she got out of the car and put the keys in her purse, clicked it shut, remembered, and took them out again, angry at herself. It was a gesture of profound mistrust somehow; she thrust them back into the ignition and slammed the door with a frown. That's not right either, thought Miss Ward, but she turned her back on the car and went up the front path.

I'm embarrassed and scared, she realized with some surprise. The chinaberry tree in Nettie Sue's front yard was an old one, twisted and bent, and the wrinkled yellow fruit lay thickly in the yard and smelled a little where feet had crushed it. I'm overdressed. I don't know what to say. And then she was at the front door, rapping sharply and keeping her eyes away from the faintly quivering wreath.

It was ridiculous that she should care what these niggers thought of her. Nettie Sue was floor maid up at the store; she swept and ran errands, and on Thursdays she took soapy

8

water and washed out the dress bins. And Miss Ward was the store manager. Miss Ward always called on her employees when there was a death in the family.

She had a sense of purpose now, a feeling of having fitted this whole visit into a pattern; she knocked more firmly on the door and it was too loud, like the car horn had been. The door swung inward before she could knock again, and Nettie Sue stood there, framed starkly in the screen. For a minute Miss Ward did not know who she was, this taller black woman not wearing a uniform but neat and starched in some cheap Sunday dress. I thought she'd have the uniform, thought Miss Ward foolishly, and she felt strange, as though the absence of the uniform made both of them different.

After that, nothing went as planned. It was Nettie Sue who sensed the other's confusion, who said the right thing in a soft voice, "How good of you to come" (gently, as a lady might say it), and it was Miss Ward who felt awkwardly grateful to her as she came inside, finally stammering, "I was so sorry to hear, Nettie."

"Yessum, we all was," said Nettie Sue calmly, and added, "Won't you sit down?"

Miss Ward sat hastily, feeling she might otherwise stumble and fall headlong across the floor. The sofa was cheap and without springs; she sat down hard and the jar ran up her spine. Nobody sits here much, she thought, and looked at Nettie Sue, sinking into a straight chair now, quiet and unsmiling. Her features seemed to be delicately carved from some polished wood, the nose and the eye-hollows and the long curve of cheek cut just so, burnished to a high luster. Miss Ward moved uneasily on the hard cushions.

"I only heard about it yesterday," she said, and jumped at the sound of her voice, raucous and harsh and strange. She searched for another register where the tones would be smooth and sympathetic. "It's a real tragedy," she added. There, that was right.

Nettie Sue inclined her carven head gravely. "Yessum," she said, and Miss Ward looked down at her own feet and crossed them and then put them flat again. The whole house smelled of death, she thought, smelled as no uptown house ever would. And it was not the quiet coolness touched with scents of carnations and talcum; there seemed to hang in this room the warm sweetish smell of drying blood, of little cakes of shattered flesh. She swallowed and her face was suddenly cold.

Unexpectedly a low moan rose in the house; it came from the timbers and oozed out of the unpainted board walls and seeped through the cracks in the floor; the house wracked and writhed with grief, primitive and unrestrained. Miss Ward started, clutched at her handbag.

"They're helpers," said Nettie Sue, watching her with—was it satisfaction? "They're women from down the street, helping with the mourning."

"I see," said Miss Ward. Involuntarily her long tight breath relaxed in a sigh. This, she thought, was savage and obscene; for a minute naked black women swayed in front of straw houses and splatted at drums with the palms of their hands. From somewhere in the house and still seeming to come from everywhere, the voices chanted, nasal and singsong, and the back of Miss Ward's neck prickled as she made out the words:

He won't come home no more, Christ-God.
He won't come home no more.
And if he come, won't nobody meet him in the door,
Won't nobody lay out his supper in the evening.
Everybody dead in this house, Lordy.
Everybody dead and gone away
And won't come home no more. . . .

She swallowed as the voices faded to a hum, rose again in the wail. Nettie Sue sat across from her, watching. Watching, thought Miss Ward wildly, from a thousand miles away, a thousand years ago. There was a brown-edged gardenia wilting on Nettie Sue's shoulder, and she could smell it for the first time, mingled with that nearly perceptible smell of blood drying. It's hot in here, thought Miss Ward. I'm going to be sick when this is over.

She reached for words, the well-worn words stored away against such a case of bereavement, the sallow flaccid words. She said, "Don't you worry about coming back to the store, Nettie Sue. You just take as long as you need."

"Thank you, Miss Ward."

Won't come home no more, Lordy.
Never be here no more. . . .
Never come home singing at night
Or get up early in the morning.
Done laid down and won't get up
And won't get up no more. . . .

"The salesgirls wanted me to give you their sincere sympathies," said Miss Ward, her voice quick and nervous. The words were hollow when she spoke; there was not warmth nor sympathy to fill them, only the nameless horror. Sooner or later I've got to ask her about it, thought Miss Ward. I've got to hear it from her, just the way it was.

The strength of the compulsion left her weak; it was hideous, the way some quivering delighted part of her *wanted* to know how it was, *wanted* to smell blood and flesh just the way they had been; the desire rose from something in her that was older than the chanting native women and she shivered, deliciously and with revulsion.

Suddenly she was terrified that Nettie Sue's quiet dark eyes could see it all, read all her thoughts; she said in a rush, raising her voice above the chanting women, "We were all sorry to hear, all of us at the store. The girls wanted me to tell you."

"That's kind," said Nettie Sue thoughtfully, nodding her dark head. "That's very kind of them." There was a silence. She added finally, "The flowers are pretty. You tell them how I 'preciate the flowers."

"Yes," said Miss Ward. "I'll tell them."

"The bodies ain't back yet. They'll be here tonight," she said, and Miss Ward nodded. There was a throbbing in her throat to hear Nettie Sue speak this way, so casually. She looked around her, wondering if the coffins would go in this room, against that wall perhaps? She clenched her jaws to hold back the shudder.

"It takes a long time with Mama, you see," Nettie Sue explained.

Miss Ward nodded. "Yes. Yes, I should think so." Her voice sounded weak, breathless, as if it were not really her own.

Involuntarily Miss Ward felt her eyes wander around the

room, taking in the tinseled motto *God Bless Our Home* on one wall (something caught in her throat at the sight of it), the stiff upholstered chair with crochet spreads on the back and arms. Miss Ward stiffened, knowing suddenly that old Mrs. Morrison had made those spreads, bent over her work with twisted brown fingers like the roots of bushes, going in and out, chaining and double crocheting, in and out, hook and pull. She forced her eyes back to Nettie Sue with an effort.

"You try to sleep tonight," she said irrelevantly. "You try to get it out of your mind."

"Yessum," said Nettie Sue. She looked down at the hands folded in her lap, smooth and dark with the sickly blanched palms. Miss Ward thought, I must go. I really have to go now.

The sound of her own voice struck her with horror; it seemed disembodied, not really having come up and out of her own throat—the voice said, "You found your mother's body, didn't you?" and Miss Ward started at the sound of it. Hush, oh hush, she thought frantically.

"Yessum, I found her. I come home from work after the neighbors called and she was laying like that in the kitchen."

"Oh," said Miss Ward. "In the kitchen."

"She was just laying there," said Nettie Sue thoughtfully, as if she were recalling this to her own mind, having already forgotten Miss Ward was there. "I bent down and touched her arm, but it was already getting cold when I touched it."

"Yes," said Miss Ward. It really is too hot in here; I'm going to be sick in a minute.

13

Nettie Sue looked at her. "You'd like to see, wouldn't you?" It was a statement of fact. "You'd like to see where it happened." Was that a smile that flickered on her face?

Miss Ward jerked her hand to her mouth, stammering some denial, but Nettie Sue—unperturbed—had risen, was leading the way out of the front room and down a dark hall to the kitchen. Miss Ward followed her numbly, not daring to protest. This is awful, she thought, still pressing her fingers tightly against her mouth. What is she punishing me for? But she followed silently, her whole stomach tightening and loosening in violent waves.

"She was laying right here in the kitchen with her head shot off, and the whole floor was red," said Nettie Sue over one shoulder. Was there bitterness in her voice? Miss Ward could not tell. She came on into the kitchen behind Nettie Sue, who added softly, "She was already getting cold when I come home," and Miss Ward coughed so she wouldn't have to say anything.

The kitchen table was full of food and flies buzzed on top of it—sticky banana pudding and shriveled pieces of fried chicken and two fruit baskets; the heat was thick. Then she saw the big hole in the kitchen plaster and her stomach went soggy and dank.

"That's where?" (Her voice was a croak.) "That's where it was?" and Nettie Sue nodded, putting up her hand impersonally to touch the ragged edges of the hole.

"How terrible," breathed Miss Ward, staring at Nettie Sue's hand. "How simply terrible." And it seemed to her that bits of bloodied hair were embedded in the plaster. "She must have been standing right where you are."

Nettie Sue looked at her with eyes that seemed to be

faintly mocking and again she nodded. "She must 'a been calling up to him, asking what he was doing in the loft. And then he come to the top of the steps with the shotgun. That's why it's taking so long with the bodies; it just blowed off Mama's head like that."

Miss Ward stared, fighting back nausea, looking unwillingly up the narrow steps where the shotgun had appeared —a short flight of steps. (So close, she thought, and with both barrels . . .)

"She couldn't have felt nothing," said Nettie Sue.

"That's good," said Miss Ward vaguely. (Here the old woman had stood, calling a question up the steps to her son, and then he had come and looked down and shot her, just like that. Horrible.)

She added without thinking, "She probably didn't know what hit her." But that wasn't right either. She must have known something, just in that split second of time before death came rushing down the stairs with a roar at her. What had gone through the old woman's mind then, looking up the steps into the hungry pair of barrels and knowing for an instant that her son was going to shoot?

Nettie Sue was watching her, probably reading her thoughts, and Miss Ward grew suddenly embarrassed. She looked away from the steps and from the great hole in the plaster, but she couldn't look at Nettie Sue either. She forced her eyes back to the kitchen table with its neglected food, its clusters of houseflies, and her stomach moved and twisted. Suddenly Nettie Sue leaned up against the wall, and Miss Ward saw that she was tired and very sad.

"He was a good boy," Nettie Sue whispered. "He was always a good boy, Miss Ward. He just went out of his head."

What will I do if she cries now? thought Miss Ward desperately. Should I put an arm about her shoulders, or not touch her at all? Oh, this isn't fair; I have no business here! She wished one of the women would give up that senseless mourning chant and come out into the kitchen. It was suddenly loud in the silence that followed Nettie Sue's words:

> Everybody dead in this house, Lordy,
> And won't come home no more, Sweet Lord,
> And won't come home no more.

"Of course," said Miss Ward, as gently as she could. He had just gone out of his head. She had already heard the story; how the boy had come out of the house in broad daylight after the neighbors had heard that first terrible shot; and how he had stood on the porch and screamed at the children until they ran home, fearful. He had stood there watching them scatter (some said he snarled, and some said there were flecks of foam on his mouth, but nobody could be sure of that), and then he had gone out, up and down the now-deserted streets, throwing rocks at windows and pumping the shotgun—loading and shooting it off at trees and clouds and stones, and screaming. Everybody agreed he had been screaming.

"It was the war done it," Nettie Sue was saying. "He was always a good boy before that. But after he got out of the army, he got sick in his head from the war."

> And won't come home no more, Sweet Lord.
> Won't never come home no more. . . .

"The war was a terrible thing," said Miss Ward. Platitudes, platitudes. Shut up, she told herself, but she couldn't seem to keep still. "A terrible thing."

16

When the police had come from uptown, they couldn't catch him, and nobody would open the door and say where he had gone; it was a sudden ghost town, and the shiny police car went up and down the nameless streets, but he was always ahead of them, loading and firing at nobody knew what.

"It was the war done it," Nettie Sue repeated dully. My war, thought Miss Ward. That's what she means. It was my army, and somehow I made him murder his mother, all because I run a dress shop and Nettie Sue works for me. It's not fair! It's not fair!

Nettie Sue was shaking her head back and forth. "But we never thought of nothing like this," she added. "We never thought he'd really go out of his head and shoot anybody."

"You never know until it's too late."

He had gone to a church where the news was not yet known and a choir was practicing for Sunday, and he had stood in the back, waving his shotgun and screaming at them to sing! sing good! sing loud! And they had gone on singing for him, rolling their eyes, hitting the wrong notes, but paralyzed beyond motion until he went away, closing the door and leaning against the outside for a long tired moment—some said he was sobbing for his mother and some said he was cursing God, but it probably didn't matter.

"Mama was just laying here," said Nettie Sue sadly, looking at the floor, and Miss Ward found herself staring, fascinated—a fat woman she would have been, lying headless and bloody in her own kitchen. Nettie Sue looked around the room and then she seemed to come out of her sorrow and grow tall and straight and proud again. "You can't tell

17

it now, can you, about the floor? That was one of the first things I done, right after they took her away—I scrubbed the kitchen. I didn't want it like that for the funeral."

"No, of course not," said Miss Ward. Under the soles of her shoes the floor seemed suddenly sticky, and again the warm wet smell of dying flooded her nostrils, stuffed them, and she breathed harshly, tasting it on her tongue.

"The law couldn't catch him, neither!" snapped Nettie Sue, fixing her with beady eyes. "He went up and down the streets shouting and shooting off the gun, but couldn't nobody catch him." The fierce pride ebbed, and her eyes grew dark and sad again. "I wish I'd 'a been here. He'd 'a come to me."

She was working that day, thought Miss Ward wildly. It was my fault because she was working in my store.

"He'd 'a come to me," said Nettie Sue again, and it was almost a whimper the way she said it. I've got to go home, thought Miss Ward. I've got to get out of here.

Aloud she said, "Where did they finally find him?" She knew she had to hear it all. She had to stand there in the bloodied kitchen with the old nigger woman dead at her feet until Nettie Sue had said it all. Miss Ward wanted to get it all over quickly, so she could walk out the door and by the chinaberry trees and drive home; and the tiredness would go away and she would feel good again.

Nettie Sue was not looking at her. "The next morning. It was the next morning in Hampton's pasture."

Yes, Miss Ward had read that in the papers. She remembered. ("The body of the killer was found early the next morning by Officers Kent and Sigmon in the pasture of Keener Hampton, Negro.")

"He just leaned over the gun and shot hisself," Nettie Sue was saying, slowly and gravely. "He kind of fell forward on the barbwire fence and it made a line of holes across his chest and there wasn't nobody there but the cows."

Miss Ward saw it sharply—the yellow edge of sun lighting him where he fell, a limp rag doll over the fence, and the shotgun at his feet perhaps—in a pool of blood that had first gushed, then slackened, and finally dripped slowly and thickly; and around him there would be the faintly puzzled cows, watching with deep wet eyes. She jerked her thoughts away, heard Nettie Sue dimly . . . "A good boy . . . just went out of his head. . . ."

She cleared her throat. That was all; that was the end of it; she could go home now. "I must be going," she said. "It certainly is tragic."

Nettie Sue, dismissed, led the way down the hall again, out of the kitchen with its terrible hole in the wall. "Thank you for coming, Miss Ward," she said.

Miss Ward, following her, fumbled for the formalities, reaching gratefully for old, familiar words. "I just wanted you to know how sorry I was. How sorry we all were."

> Won't sing no songs no more, Sweet Lord,
> But he never meant no harm.
> Won't eat no more or sleep no more,
> Cause he won't be home no more, Sweet Lord.
> But he never meant no harm, Sweet Lord,
> And he won't come home no more. . . .

"Yessum, I 'preciated you coming. And the flowers are pretty. That was real kind. You tell the girls how I 'preciate the flowers."

"Yes," said Miss Ward. "I'll tell them."

They stood at the door where the black crepe hung. This was the moment of severing, the last word, the turn of back to back and two pairs of feet going finally from each other. Then it would be over, and what one knew now could be forgotten, and nothing more would remain to be said. Let me get through this and be gone, Miss Ward prayed. Everything was flat now and used up; it had all come full cycle.

"He just went out of his head," said Nettie Sue. She touched the wreath gently as if it were something living that could hear and understand. Then she looked up and down the darkened little street.

"Everybody was scared," she said abruptly, her words quick, loud, having a sense of nakedness about them, as if for the first time she herself were really speaking and as if the other had been only something recorded, something appropriate for the occasion. "When he walked down the street shooting off his shotgun, everybody run inside and locked the door. And all the time the law was looking for him, didn't nobody go outside. Didn't nobody in all Rabbittown set one foot outside their house."

In the shadow her eyes took on a brittle shine; they were like a pair of metallic cartridges embedded in her skull, and the light touched them uneasily, went away, came back again. She said, "I hear that even all the way uptown the doors was locked. The big doors and the apartment doors and the rich doors and the store doors. I hear everybody was scared up there and didn't nobody go outside." She looked expectantly at Miss Ward and her dark eyes were shining in the shadow.

"Yes," said Miss Ward. Now the tiredness was all over her, hanging on her limbs the way moss hangs on trees in a swamp; she felt herself slumping, flattening. "Yes, we were all scared uptown, too."

"Yessum, that's what I thought," said Nettie Sue, and her voice was full of acceptance, of satisfaction. She kept nodding her head over and over again, as though—once started—it would not hold still again.

"You stay out of work as long as you need to," said Miss Ward dully. "And if there's anything we can do, you let us know."

"Yessum, Miss Ward, I sure will. It was good of you to come."

"Good night, Nettie Sue."

"Good night, Miss Ward."

Miss Ward went to the car as fast as her heavy legs would carry her. (Niggers always left her feeling tired.) She slammed the car door, reassured by the sound it made, groped for her keys and finally started the car. The motor ran smoothly and somehow that surprised her, that it was still all right.

She drove down the dusty, darkening street, anxious to be home, and on past the little black boys who were putting their marbles into their pockets, going home for supper, and watching her shyly after she had gone past. She thought about Nettie Sue and the boy and his mother and her eyelids were stinging, but the tears were not for them.

A Mark of Distinction

NUMBER 209 Millwood was just like number 207 on the corner, or the house directly above it, number 211. In fact, all the grayish houses on both sides of Millwood Street were exactly alike—just so many identical, dingy boxes lined up at exact intervals all up and down the street, with exactly the same number of windows showing the same green window shades, and exactly the same four porch posts and the eight green steps that went up from every dusty walkway.

Mr. Orlon found this uniformity very depressing. Every time he walked down Millwood Street (that was a silly street name, he thought, it sounded so elegant) he would discover afresh that his own house was no different from a dozen other houses, and no matter how cheerful he had been before, this left him very grumpy.

"I wish you'd plant some flowers." Mr. Orlon had told Sarah that just last spring.

"I thought you didn't like flowers," she said. That was just like Sarah, as if his liking them had anything to do with it.

"I don't," he'd answered shortly. Besides, no self-respecting flower would take root in the thin dust along Millwood

Street, and even an experiment with grass had proved a failure. Henry Orlon's house continued to be an exact duplicate of Si Parker's which stood next door on the corner, and George Blane's, number 211.

Once Mr. Orlon had thought about knocking off the unsightly front porch, but after he crawled around under the house looking at timbers one Saturday afternoon, he found that as nearly as he could judge, this would bring the whole house down.

He was especially angry that night at supper. "You'd think from common sense, wouldn't you," he complained to Sarah, "you'd think it was downright impossible to build a house so that every board was nailed to every other board."

"Yes, I would," said Sarah. That was one thing about Sarah; she was long on common sense.

Mr. Orlon grunted. "Well, as far as I can tell, if I take a brick out of the foundation, the roof'll fall in."

"Really, Daddy? Will it really?" This was from Martha, the youngest, aged seven.

"Pass the potatoes," Sue said. Rachel ate her supper quietly, not saying much of anything.

"You've a spiderweb in your hair," Sarah added.

When you came right down to it, the only thing that made number 209 Millwood any different from the corner Parker house or the Blanes' next door was that Henry Orlon and his family lived in it.

This was no small distinction. There were Henry and Sarah Orlon and their three daughters, Rachel sixteen, Sue thirteen, and Martha seven. Besides that, Mr. Orlon had the reputation of being a smart man. It was he who generally represented the other millworkers when they had a grievance, which wasn't very often, since they were fairly easily contented. The Kyles family, which had owned and operated the mill for the last fifty years, tolerated no talk of unionizing the workers, which, they said, "sowed the seeds of unnecessary unrest."

The only member of the Kyles family who was very active in the mill any more was Charlie Kyles, a plump bachelor of about forty, who was always walking around trying to be friendly with the men. He'd once taken a college course on personnel relations and had never gotten over it. The workers were, as a body, contemptuous of him.

"Charlie Kyles is a half-wit," Mr. Orlon was fond of saying, and in the evenings the other Orlons would hear whether or not "that half-wit Charlie Kyles" had been "bungling about the mill today."

Still, Charlie Kyles seemed to consider Mr. Orlon some kind of "diamond in the rough," and was always being very friendly to him, which embarrassed Mr. Orlon greatly. Sooner or later he was always forced to make some subtle remark that would put Charlie Kyles in his place at every interview, and all day long the word would be passed by grinning workers from loom to loom. "Hey, did you hear what Henry Orlon told old Kyles today?"

Mr. Orlon was a hero. There was really no question about that; he was a man among men; he did his work quietly and well; and in the Millwood community he was liked and respected by everyone.

That's why the house bothered him so. He never came home from work in the evenings but what the sight of it was a nagging annoyance to him, and over supper he would be still and moody.

25

"I wish we could move uptown," he'd mutter.

"Away from your work and at three times as much rent?" Sarah would demand. She was such a practical woman. There was no argument to use against a practical mind like Sarah had, and Henry Orlon knew it. But that didn't mean he accepted her point of view; he simply let it wash over him and pass by and then he went back to thinking about a distinctive house somewhere uptown, maybe even with a telephone.

As far as Mr. Orlon could tell, his three daughters were completely undisturbed about the appearance of the house. This, he felt (almost bitterly), was because he had given Sarah such a free hand in the raising of them, and she had turned them out very reasonable girls, but without a sense of values. If there had been only one son . . . ah . . . that would have been a different matter.

Of course (and even Mr. Orlon realized this dimly, although he could not have put it into words), the trouble with Mr. Orlon was that he had been misborn. His allegiance was to another and more vivid age, where a man's honor was something to duel about, and the questioning of a man's rights might set off a nationwide revolution. Yet, here he was, Henry Orlon, aged forty-four and rapidly losing his hair, without banner, sword, or Crusade to ride forth upon. Here he was, stuck incongruously in Lincolntown, S. C., at 209 Millwood Street, along with four placid women in a house that was just like every other house, and for eight hours daily running a machine that was like eighteen other machines. It would have dampened the soul of King Arthur; it would have bored Thomas Paine to tears.

Their life on Millwood Street was quiet. On summer evenings, Mr. Orlon and his wife and the two younger daughters would sit on the green front steps (Rachel was always out with some boy; she was too young, thought Mr. Orlon) and they would speak pleasantly to some of the people that passed, or maybe they'd go over to the Parkers' for a beer and a radio program. (Mr. Orlon had taken his own radio to the mill where everybody could hear it while they worked, a generosity which Sarah had accepted quietly but did not wholly approve of.)

There had been some difficulty with Charlie Kyles about the radio, but Mr. Orlon had been well prepared for that. As a smart man, he was a great reader and his mind was always swarming with facts and statistics. Of course, sometimes his memory wasn't too good, but everybody admitted Mr. Orlon was a smart man and nobody doubted his word; so when he became forgetful he just made up some statistic that would do just as well. It always made his conversations very impressive.

That morning when that half-wit Charlie Kyles approached him about the newly installed radio, Mr. Orlon was ready and waiting for him.

"Now see here, Henry" (Mr. Orlon always flinched when Kyles had the audacity to call him by his first name), "about that radio . . ."

Mr. Orlon shut off his machine with an impatient frown. He always did this when Charlie Kyles addressed him in the mill, and it gave the impression that Kyles was a troublesome fellow who was always holding up production in his own plant by disturbing his efficient workers. Several of the other men grinned and dug each other in the ribs when Mr. Orlon switched off his machine.

"Statistics say," began Mr. Orlon thoughtfully, "that music creates a definite rhythm and increases efficiency by 87 per cent."

"That so?" blinked the half-wit.

"Yep. That's what statistics say."

From Mr. Orlon's reverent tone of voice, Statistics was conjured up as being an infallible, rather ill-tempered old man—a kind of second lieutenant to God—who had been let in on the secrets of the universe. Charlie Kyles had a vast and growing respect for statistics, which had been carefully fostered during his acquaintance with Mr. Orlon.

Still, Kyles tried to shift the victory to himself by putting on a patronizing smile. "Well, anything that keeps our workers happy," he said blandly, laying a friendly hand on Mr. Orlon's machine. At this time, Mr. Orlon flicked the switch and Kyles snatched his hand away barely in time as the wheels whirred into action.

"That's right," said Mr. Orlon politely. Kyles searched his face for a smile or a sneer, but there was none; and finally he stalked off—the personification of a wicked and ousted archduke, the oppressive Redcoat army, or the defeated Huns of World War I.

All day the men grinned to themselves about Mr. Orlon's mastery over that half-wit Charlie Kyles, and in that way, the radio became a permanent fixture of the Kyles Textile Plant.

Still, Mr. Orlon had never been in serious trouble with the management. He went quietly along, undermining the Kyles superstructure with deft little nips at the most vulnerable places, but there was no open clash between them. Mr. Orlon was respected as a shrewd but restrained leader of the mill's employees, and the Kyles family felt that if he should be cast down, some less civilized rabble-rouser with communist leanings would spring up to take his place.

All this was before Mr. Orlon decided to build a fence.

April was always the most dangerous part of the year for Mr. Orlon. During that month his very blood and bones seemed to awaken and vibrate within him, and he would take to baiting Charlie Kyles more openly out of nothing but pleasure. It was as if he had been suddenly set upon by violent spirits—Joan of Arc and Sir Galahad and Paul Revere, for instance—and as if any minute the submerged centuries might break loose in him and set him to nailing theses to the door of the Kyles Textile Plant.

It was one April afternoon as Mr. Orlon was walking home from work, averting his eyes from the rows of monotonous little houses, that the idea came to him. He stopped before 209 Millwood and examined the house thoughtfully, turning his head first on one side and then on the other. Yes, it would do perfectly. It was just what the place needed. Mr. Orlon wondered why he had not thought of it before.

When he came in to supper that night, he was humming happily "The Battle Hymn of the Republic," and Sarah and the three girls stopped their talking and looked at him. He grinned and broke suddenly into song while washing his hands:

I am trampling out the vintage where the grapes of wrath are
    stored,
I have loosed the fateful lightning . . .

29

"Sit down, Henry," said Sarah. "Everything's getting cold."

He sat down docilely. After all, he had no time to argue about trifles.

"I'm going to build a fence," he announced, smiling.

Sarah stopped with the dish halfway to the table and stood there eying him. "A fence?" she said.

"Where?" said Martha.

"What kind of a fence?" put in Sue.

Rachel didn't say anything; she just sat looking at him, waiting. Although she was the oldest, she didn't talk very much. Mr. Orlon still had hopes for her.

This was the sort of moment Mr. Orlon loved. "We got any butter?" he asked.

"No," said Sarah shortly.

Mr. Orlon put beans on his plate, picked up a fork, examined it, moved it in the air unnecessarily. "Just a fence," he said.

"Out front?" asked Rachel. This was the first sensible question of the evening. It showed the girl could think. Mr. Orlon looked at his oldest daughter with some interest, and showed his respect for her direct question by giving it a direct answer.

"Yes," he said. Sensibly enough, he observed, Rachel began quietly to eat her beans.

"What for?" asked Sarah. Mr. Orlon was profoundly irritated at that—what was a fence usually for? He did not even look at her. "Where's the pickles?" he retorted. It was an expression of obvious disapproval. Sarah, never very sensitive, put the jar on the table in front of him.

30

Mr. Orlon looked at his daughter Rachel with a new warmth and addressed himself to her as if they were alone. "What do you think of a white picket fence?" he asked pleasantly. She looked up at him (that's good, he thought. Always look squarely at people you talk to) and he noticed with pleased surprise that her eyes were pale brown too, very like his own.

"That'll be handsome," she said.

Content ran smoothly throughout Mr. Orlon's body like syrup. Now there was an answer for you. It was somehow just right. He sighed with pleasure.

Sarah brought in the jarring note. "I thought Mr. Kyles didn't want the outside of the houses changed."

Mr. Orlon got up from the table. He suddenly felt three inches taller. "I've finished," he said stiffly, "excuse me," and went to read the paper.

The next day was Saturday, and in the afternoon Mr. Orlon went uptown to pick the lumber. He was so outraged by the prices that he very nearly decided to cut his own, but something of Sarah's sensibleness saved him.

"That's much too high," said Mr. Orlon, fingering the boards, "to pay just for a picket fence."

"All wood's high these days," shrugged the man. "It's good lumber."

"I know it," said Mr. Orlon shortly, who had never bought lumber in his life before. He tapped a board thoughtfully with his forefinger, having some idea that you tested its greenness as if it were a watermelon. He added, "Lumber's 78 per cent higher than it was in 1939."

The man squinted. "How's that?"

"Nothing," said Mr. Orlon. "Give me enough to make a picket fence."

"How big of a fence?"

Mr. Orlon was startled. He had not realized how exact a science this could be. He looked at the man in annoyance. "I'll let you know," he said.

In the end it was Rachel who went back and ordered the lumber after Mr. Orlon measured how many feet of yard he was going to fence. There was nothing to use for this but an old tape measure belonging to Sarah, and crawling around at three-foot intervals was a long process.

"You're getting it dirty." Sarah kept coming to the front porch to watch the measuring operation.

"Yes," snorted Mr. Orlon. It didn't seem to him that hers was an observation worthy of his notice.

They bought white paint too, and the fence was due to be started the following Saturday afternoon.

"I still don't see what it's for," Sue said.

Rachel silenced her. "To keep the grass in the yard," she said. Mr. Orlon grew even fonder of his oldest daughter.

During the week, Mr. Orlon was cheered daily by the prospect of his yard being surrounded by a trim white picket fence. Maybe Sarah could plant blue morning-glories; they said morning-glories would grow anywhere.

He couldn't resist mentioning it at the mill, and the men immediately accepted it as his right and privilege, just as in an older age they would have accepted without question the chieftain's having a more durable tent. It was inevitable that news of Mr. Orlon's venture should eventually get around to that half-wit Charlie Kyles, and on Thursday afternoon, Mr. Orlon saw him coming. One of the workers was tiptoeing along behind him, imitating the mincing movements of Kyles' plump buttocks, but Kyles never looked behind him and probably wouldn't have believed it if he had. He was sure all the men adored him.

Mr. Orlon switched off his machine with an air of patient resignation. "Yeah?" he said.

Kyles was jovial. "Hear you're planning some building over at your place." Mr. Orlon, his face expressionless, looked at him and waited. "Gonna put up a fence, I hear."

Still Mr. Orlon waited. These preliminaries he brushed aside without interest. He believed in a man saying what he had come to say, and then moving on.

"Well, I wish you wouldn't do that, Henry," said Charlie Kyles finally, putting on his best one-man-to-another expression.

Mr. Orlon winced at the first name. "How come?" he said.

"Well, you know how we feel about changing anything on the outside of the mill houses. Leads to competition that all the workers can't afford. Makes the men unhappy, you know."

Mr. Orlon watched him.

"Now I let you paper the hall, didn't I? I mean, the inside —now that's your business." He dropped a friendly hand on Mr. Orlon's shoulder and Mr. Orlon looked down his nose at it as if it were an open sore.

"Afraid we're going to have to ask you not to build that fence, Henry. You understand. . . ."

"That all?" said Mr. Orlon.

33

"Why . . . why I guess so. I just wanted you to understand how it was. . . ."

"Well, I'm getting behind then," said Mr. Orlon, and the machine came back to life noisily. Kyles blinked a few times and then walked away, nodding affably to the other employees, none of whom responded.

Mr. Orlon was seething. He worked at a furious pace all day, and the other angry men who were friends of his did the same. Production climbed, but Charlie Kyles was uneasy. He hung around all afternoon until the shift changed, and was standing at the door when the men filed out.

"Gonna build that fence Saturday, Orlon?" one of the men called, as they were leaving.

Mr. Orlon squared his shoulders. "Sure am," he said firmly. He did not even look at Kyles.

On Friday, Rachel went to work in the women's section of the mill, in one of the sewing rooms. On Friday too, Charlie Kyles came through the mill with two of his relatives that nobody had seen in years and handed Mr. Orlon a long blue piece of paper. It was the rent contract, and one of the paragraphs forbade exterior changes to the mill houses without special permission from the owners.

"You see that, don't you, Orlon?" said Kyles. He looked very angry. Mr. Orlon nodded quietly. The two old men with Kyles nodded their heads too, more vigorously. Looked like everybody's neck was loose, Mr. Orlon said later.

Just then Tod Clan walked up, not paying any attention to the three representatives of the Kyles family. "Just wanted to tell you me and my brother Sam'll be over to

34

help with the building tomorrow." Tod and Sam were the tallest men in town.

"Fine," said Mr. Orlon. "Thank you."

Charlie Kyles had gotten red in the face and his plump lower lip had begun to tremble with rage. "Now see here, Orlon, you'll be violating the law if you put up that fence."

Mr. Orlon studied him thoughtfully.

"The way I figure it," he said quietly, "a man's got a *right* to a fence."

The three Kyles men walked away. Every line of their backs said that Henry Orlon was no longer a man to be tolerated, patronized; he had become a quiet kind of menace. He must be fought. Charlie didn't even speak to any of the workers when he left.

It was probably just as well. By quitting time, nearly everyone on Millwood Street had cut himself in on the fence building.

Sarah didn't understand what all the fuss was about. "It ain't as if we needed a fence," she protested at supper that night.

Mr. Orlon tried to explain it to her. "It's just that we got a *right* to a fence," he said. "It's just that I can put up a fence if I want to be different from my neighbors."

"So who wants to?" argued Sarah. "Have the Blanes next door got a fence? Have the Parkers got a fence?"

Mr. Orlon tried to be patient. "They don't happen to *want* a fence," he explained seriously.

"But they're still gonna help us put up ours," put in Rachel.

Mr. Orlon smiled. "That's it. They're going to help us anyway. You see, Sarah?"

"No."

Mr. Orlon sighed. You just couldn't do much with a practical woman. They couldn't understand about things like fences.

That night a truck pulled up in front of Mr. Orlon's house, and it turned out to be the man from the lumberyard. He came up on the front porch and stood on one foot and then the other as if neither of them were his, he had just borrowed them for the evening and they didn't fit very well.

"Uh . . ." said the lumberman, "we're running kind of short up at the yard on material. Uh, thought you might sell that lumber back at a nice profit to yourself."

"Rachel," Mr. Orlon called sharply. When his oldest daughter appeared, he nodded toward the door. "You go set out on that lumber pile and keep an eye on it," and she glanced at the lumberman and went.

The man from the lumberyard came on into the house to discuss the business over a glass of beer, and Mr. Orlon found the price had gone up about one third over what he paid for it. He told the man all about the fence and about Charlie Kyles, and by the fifth glass of beer, they had both gotten very angry about it.

The lumberman ended up giving Mr. Orlon the check for the wood anyway. It was made out to cash and it had Charlie Kyles' signature on it.

"If I was you, I'd cash it pretty early in the morning," said the lumberman.

"And what're you going to tell Kyles?"

36

The man giggled. "Don't nobody but me look after small lumber. I'll say I bought it, just like he said, and dumped it back on the pile at the lumberyard. Guess you must of bought some more someplace else."

Mr. Orlon was so pleased that he wouldn't let the lumberman go home. They went out and sat on the lumber pile with Rachel, and the three of them sang all the verses of "The Battle Hymn of the Republic" several times.

The lumberman had a good tenor.

On Saturday afternoon, the fence went up. Half the mill was there to help, and it took shape as if it had been altogether prefabricated. Midway in the afternoon, the lumberman drove over with a barrel of apple cider, and Rachel let him kiss her.

All in all, it was a very gala affair. Once the three Kyles men drove by, just to see if it were true, but they didn't stop their shiny car anywhere on Millwood Street. They had evidently decided in the face of such unanimous support that it was better not to openly cross Henry Orlon.

"After all, this is better than some cooperative workers' union," said John Kyles hopefully. John was seventy-nine. Charlie just glared at him.

As it turned out, not even morning-glories would take root in the dusty Orlon front yard, but this didn't dim the glory of the fence. You could tell which was his house from blocks away. And strangely enough, not one of the other workers built a fence. It was like Mr. Orlon said, "Some folks want a fence, and some don't." Sarah never did. She said it took half her time putting down packages to unlatch the gate.

A Sense of Humor

THEY STOOD without moving in the doorway, wiggling their noses like a pair of curious, but timid, rabbits. Then they came into the room and closed the door behind them, shutting out the sound of people whispering in the parlor.

The smaller one said, "But how do you know he's asleep?"

Evie stepped on his foot. "Hush," she said.

They came on tiptoes into the half-dark room, their shoes making rapid tick-tocks against the rug like a clock with its insides all wrong. It seemed as if the noise of their feet would call some watchful adult out of the parlor to stand grimly in the doorway and say What-Are-You-Children-Doing-in-Here? They almost waited for the sound of the door opening behind them and the sharply impatient voice of an aunt or a cousin or one of the strangers.

Evie frowned at the noise they were making. "Pick up your feet," she said. She looked down at a limp flower which lay whitely against the rug; then she put the heel of her patent shoe against it and ground it out, thoughtfully.

She said aloud, "I just know he is, that's all." The flower made a white glue under her shoe heel when she took her foot away.

"It's just what he'd do, that's all," she said, looking at the place where the flower had been.

Mark had begun to whimper as he watched Evie's foot go round and round on top of the flower. He looked up at her.

"Who told you?"

Evie took her foot completely away from the dead flower and put it down on Mark's, but softer this time—more as a warning than a punishment.

"Nobody has to tell you everything," she said. "You all the time think somebody has to tell you. Some things you just know, that's all."

Mark had stopped his whimper and was staring at her. "How come he'd want to do something like that?"

"'Cause that's the way he is, that's all," said Evie. She thought, Mark isn't but seven. Mother says I've got to remember Mark isn't but seven. She said aloud, "You're not but seven," because that made her feel better. She added, "Let's look at him."

Mark made a sound in his throat like a rubber mouse squeezed too hard. He said, "Evie, I don't want to. . . ." and trailed off into a softer squeak, when the mouse is thrown against the door and falls there.

Evie frowned. "Hush, crybaby. I'm not scared. I tell you, he's just asleep, that's all."

Suddenly she took three loud steps against the linoleum and stood beside the gray box which sat in a nest of flowers, but Mark—who was only seven—took one step backwards and stood watching her.

Evie said over her shoulder, "Baby!" and put her hand out and rested it against the box, feeling how cool it was to her fingers and how she left swirling fingerprints on the shiny rail at the side. She was not tall enough to see into the box; she began to look for a chair.

Mark was tugging at the straight chair across the room before she got there.

"I help," he said hopefully, but she did not answer him. They dragged the chair up against the flowers and Evie climbed up and looked inside the box.

The head on the satin pillow looked as if it had been cut from soap. The eyes, blue-lidded, were closed, and the mouth was a thin line left by pink crayon on his face. Two hands made a white cross-mark against the front of the coat. Everything smelled funny. Evie didn't feel very good.

She looked down at Mark, who watched her with big eyes, and whispered, "I don't think it's him."

Mark pulled at her skirt. "I want up there. Let me see, Evie," he said. "I want to see him too."

Evie leaned down and hit him in the face.

She whispered fiercely, "You'll make me fall. Don't pull on me, that's all. Now step up—" she took his hand—"but don't you make me fall."

Mark climbed up on the chair beside her and stared into the box. Then he looked disappointed.

"Who's that?" he said. He was whispering too. "Evie, is that Uncle John?"

Evie had reached out a finger to touch the man's nose but she took it back quickly and curled it with the others into a fist at her side. She said aloud, "I don't know. I said I didn't think it was him."

Mark blinked and took a small step backward and the chair wobbled under them.

"Then who is it?" he said.

Suddenly one of the man's eyelids twitched. Evie was sure of it. One minute they had both been down like small gray flaps and then a little flicker had stirred under one of them. She caught her brother's arm.

"Did you see that? Did you see that, Mark? He moved. I saw the man move. Did you see his eye, Mark?"

Mark was already halfway to the floor, pulling loose from Evie's fingers. He said hurriedly, "I want to go back in there. I don't like him. I want to go, Evie," and pulled away from her and got off the chair.

Evie got down too, but she caught his arm again and shook it over and over, like a dog playing games with old rags.

"Don't you tell," she ordered. "Don't you tell them what we saw, that's all."

Mark jerked his arm loose and began to hiccough and head for the closed door. Mark said, "He looks all scary. Whoever he is, he looks all scary and I don't like him. I don't care if it is Uncle John."

He began to cry before he had finished and two tears popped into the corners of his eyes and started down his face on both sides. Evie pulled the chair back into its place, not looking at the gray box.

When the chair was back, she, too, left the room—but less hurriedly—keeping her eyes away from the box where the soap-man was. On the way out she stepped on the crushed flower and it slid a little under her foot.

Aunt Margaret glanced up at them when they came into the parlor and then got up from the sofa and came to kneel by Mark, looking very much like a giant squatting toad, Evie thought. Aunt Margaret was very fat. She put one of her flabby cheeks against Mark's and began to push at his still-wet eyes with one finger.

"Poor Mark," she said, poking her finger on his wet face. "You're unhappy too."

Mark's eyes slid into one corner where he had an alarming view of Aunt Margaret's nose. He said agreeably, "I'm unhappy too," and Aunt Margaret began to cry with great snuffling sounds, reaching down her dress for a handkerchief. Aunt Margaret was married to Uncle John.

Evie sat on the sofa watching Aunt Margaret fish for the handkerchief. It's stuck, thought Evie. The handkerchief is stuck down there between all that fat and she won't be able to pull it out. It's just stuck there forever and ever.

She was still smiling about Aunt Margaret and the handkerchief when the Strange Man bent over her and nodded his head several times as if it weren't very well fastened on his shoulders. He had pale eyes that weren't quite blue, and a long face that went on down into his collar without stopping. Evie looked up at him. She thought, I will not blink my eyes until he does, and made her eyes big and stared up at him.

The Strange Man said, "And how old are you?"

She was cautious. "Ten," she said.

He nodded as if she had given the correct answer to a question, and she wished she had said something else.

The Strange Man said, "And have you seen him, Dear?" and smiled at her. When he smiled, his teeth were like little cakes of soap set into fences. Evie thought, I will not blink mine either, and she picked out an inch of his forehead and began to examine it closely.

Aloud she said, "Who?"

The smile closed up around the white fences and immediately the Man blinked his eyes twice.

He said, "Your Uncle John, of course," and Evie smiled triumphantly because he had been the first to blink his eyes.

She said, "Yes"—still smiling—and the Strange Man wrinkled the inch of forehead she had been watching and moved away from her, looking back at her once with the wrinkles still showing.

Someone had finally given Aunt Margaret a handkerchief and now she stood up and spread it wetly over her face while the Strange Man came over to her and patted her shoulder.

The Man said, "Mr. Perry and the children were very close, weren't they?" and when he said it he looked back at Evie and frowned again. Aunt Margaret's tall hairdo and the handkerchief wagged back and forth. "As if they were his own," she wailed, and began to cry again. "They played so much together."

Mark, left alone by Aunt Margaret, pulled at the coat sleeve of the Strange Man. He said gravely, "I'm unhappy too," and the Strange Man put both hands on Mark's shoulders and patted them up and down as if he were bouncing balls. Evie put her mouth tight together. He was only seven.

She waited until Mark was nearer to her before she whispered to him angrily, "You are a piece of vomit," and Mark stopped looking unhappy and got mad at her.

All around them in the parlor, people were whispering back and forth about Uncle John. Evie thought, if he was in here instead of in there, he'd be putting electricity in the chairs—and for once she smiled about it. Once Uncle John had put electricity in the dining-room chairs before one of Mother's parties and everyone had said later what an informal air it gave the whole evening.

Evie turned to a thin woman who was sitting behind her and said, "I wish Uncle John would fix *these* chairs," and the lady pulled her glasses to the end of an extraordinarily long nose and looked at her through them.

"Aren't you young Evelyn Perry?"

Evie shook her head. "I'm Evie," she said. "Just Evie, that's all."

Just then Mother came in, standing in the doorway and looking around the room anxiously, a thumbnail propped behind her front teeth; then crossing over to Evie, she got between her and the woman with the long nose. Daddy hadn't been out of his room all day. Mother said Daddy was prostrate with grief.

Mother said softly, "I know this is tiresome for you and Mark, but you can't very well go play or anything. It's not much longer." She put the thumb back into her mouth and bit off the nail with a jerk.

Evie didn't say anything. Mark came across the room and sat down on the floor at Mother's feet and she put one hand against the back of his neck.

"Tired?" she said, and Mark said no, he wasn't tired. Mother lifted one finger rapidly after another until they were galloping against the back of Mark's neck and he moved his head away.

Mother leaned over to talk to the woman with the long

nose and Mark screwed up his face and said in a low voice to Evie, "I am not."

She looked at him without interest.

He raised his voice a little. "I am not a piece of vomit," he said to her, pulling small brows forward into a line over his eyes.

Evie did not even bother to look at him. "A green piece of vomit," she said with emphasis, and Mother turned around just in time to see the expression on Mark's face. She put her fingers against the back of his neck again and began to draw small circles with one of them.

"There now," she said. "We mustn't be too sad. Remember all the funny jokes Uncle John used to do. He wouldn't want us to be too sad."

No, thought Evie, he wouldn't want that. She could remember Uncle John coming in on Saturdays to see her daddy, standing in the kitchen door and waving his arms like they were flags.

"Hey! Why so quiet! Who's dead here?" and he would come on in and goose Mother under the arms and pull Mark's hair.

"Hey, Evie, cat got your tongue?" he'd say, poking at her where she sat watching him from the kitchen stool.

"No," she'd say thoughtfully, not taking her eyes off him.

"Let's have a party! Good old Betty, pretty as ever," he'd say, tickling Mother again and she would turn red and push feebly at his hand.

"Now, John," she'd say with a smile. "Now, John. . . ."

"Hey, Evie, what your eyes so big for?"

She'd eye him from the stool, braced to evade his big red hands when they came out for her.

46

"Nothing," she'd say slowly. "Just watching you, that's all."

No, Uncle John wouldn't want them to be sad. Evie half expected him to come banging in from the other room saying in his big voice, "Hey! Why so quiet! Who's dead here?"

She giggled when she thought about it.

The Strange Man came across the room and took Mother's fingers as if they were strips of macaroni and said, "I don't believe I've spoken to you yet. My sympathies to you and your husband, Mrs. Perry," and Mother said thank you. She found a loose piece of hair among her reddish curls and began to pull it out and coil it up, over and over, while she talked with him.

"They say that Mr. Perry was such a jolly person," said the Strange Man.

Mother turned down the ends of her mouth. "Always joking and carrying on. Everyone always said John was the life of any party," she said. "John was my husband's brother, you know."

"Yes, I know," said the Strange Man. "How is your husband?"

Mother sighed. "Well, it was such a shock. I mean Friday John came by to show us some souvenirs he'd bought in Chicago—there they were, laughing about John's trip—and the next morning he was gone."

"It's always a shock for someone so full of life," said the Strange Man slowly, as if each word were important.

Mother nodded. "He'd been over here laughing and playing with the children that very Friday. That's one thing he always did—played with Mark and Evie. And then so suddenly . . ."

47

"Enjoying life right to the end."

"Oh yes, that's one thing. John enjoyed life so."

Evie remembered the electricity in the dining-room chairs. She remembered Uncle John hiding in the dark places in the hall at night, and then leaping out at her—screaming—until she ran down the long carpet with her stomach soggy from fear and the big pounding in her head, and lay stiff in her dark room, praying to sleep without dreams. She remembered the lizards he had hidden in Mark's box and the buzzer in his hand and the flower that squirted salt water.

Mother was saying, "John forever entertained the children, didn't he, Evie? Just one laugh after another, wasn't he?" and Evie said yes, he was, and began to play church-and-the-steeple with her fingers. Uncle John had played that game with her once, but his hands had been full of something white that burned your nose and throat and eyes and made you cough and want water.

Mother caught her hand then and said it was time for them to go to the church.

That night when the house was cleared of people and their noises and the flower smell had sifted out open windows and lost itself, Evie and Mark talked across their dark room in small whispers.

Mark said, "Evie, was it really Uncle John? Was it really Uncle John in the box?" and Evie said she didn't know.

"It didn't look like him," said Evie. "But it looked like something, that's all. It just looked like a something."

Mark made soft swishes against sheets when he turned in

bed. "Was it a joke of Uncle John's? Like the rubber bug and Mama's dress and all the noise?"

Evie looked up at the ceiling which she could not see because of the night in between and thought about it seriously for a minute.

Then she said, "I guess so."

Mark didn't answer that, so Evie turned on her stomach and looked out the window.

She said suddenly, "Uncle John isn't nice. I don't think he is nice."

"What did they do with the box?" said Mark.

Just then Mother came tiptoeing into the room to see if they were asleep. She sat down on Evie's bed and straightened the covers and pulled at the pillowcase.

"Poor children, it's been a hard day, hasn't it?" she said. "So many people and so much to understand. Are you very tired?"

"No," said Evie, which was the truth.

Mark said, "Mother, what did they do with the box?"

Mother said to Evie, "Daddy told me to say good night for him too. You know he isn't feeling too well. He thought so much of John." She sniffled.

"What did they do with the box, Mother?" said Mark.

Mother found a stray piece of hair and put it around her finger.

"They buried it, Mark. They took it to the cemetery and put it with other boxes."

This was news. "In the ground?" said Evie. "Did they put Uncle John in the ground?" and Mother made a noise that was like a cough. The hair wound and unwound on Mother's finger.

"Well, yes. . . ." she said slowly. "Only not the real Uncle John." She stopped for a minute, frowned, and turned the piece of hair around and around her finger. "Not the real Uncle John. Not the laughing and the jokes. You see, Evie, that part we call the . . ."

Evie interrupted. "And covered it up with dirt?"

Mother got up suddenly and sniffed as if she had a cold. She pulled at one hand with the other. "Yes," she said. "Now you children get to sleep. I'm tired too," and she went out the yellow square of door and closed in the dark again.

For a long time they lay in the dark without saying anything and then Evie began to giggle.

Mark said, "What are you laughing at? What's funny?" and Evie went on giggling.

Mark sat up in bed. "What's funny, Evie? Tell me what's funny." Mark was only seven.

Evie said, "He can't get out, that's all. They put dirt on top." She rolled on her stomach to muffle the laughing. "Mother said they covered it up."

Mark began to laugh too, hesitantly—mostly because Evie was laughing.

Evie had to put the pillow corner into her mouth where she choked and gagged on the taste of starch.

"When he wakes up tonight, he can't get out," she said between laughing. "He can't ever get out again, that's all. Isn't that funny?"

Mark laughed out loud then. "He can't get out!" said Mark delightedly. He lay back down in bed and giggled.

When they finally went to sleep, they were still smiling.

Mr. Shawn and Father Scott

M R. SHAWN was a man with a mission—which was
unfortunate—thought Father Scott.

He put down his book and looked out the broad window
behind his desk. Mr. Shawn was going down the sidewalk, stepping carefully on each line. During the day, Mr.
Shawn wore a gray wig and carried a mayonnaise jar
full of pennies, although at night he looked like any other
man in the parish. Mr. Shawn had appeared in the town
about two years ago; he had climbed off the eastbound
train one winter morning with his wig and his pennies, and
no one had ever gotten enough courage to ask him about
them. Almost daily Father Scott would see the townspeople
talking with Mr. Shawn—smiling and gesticulating and not
taking their eyes off Mr. Shawn's face, as if to convince him
that they found nothing strange about his jar of coins and
the gray wig which made a pigtail down his back. Father
Scott rocked back in his chair and reached for his book
again.

Lord! He was coming in!

Father Scott sat up straight in his chair and squinted.
There could be no doubt about it; Mr. Shawn was swing-
ing open the white gate and starting up the sandy path—

51

tall and fat and red-faced—with the pennies in one hand and the gray pigtail rising and falling a little when he walked.

It was not as if Mr. Shawn had not been there before. Father Scott directed his eyes wistfully toward the ceiling but there was to be no deliverance. The bell rang. Father Scott put a bookmark at page 96 and went to the front door.

"Well, good day, Mr. Shawn. Won't you come in?"

"Yes, I will," said Mr. Shawn, which pretty well disposed of that. Father Scott smothered a sigh and followed the big man into the study. Mr. Shawn put his pennies down on the desk with a clunk and sat in a great leather chair with his hands crossed patiently on his stomach where there was plenty of room for them.

Father Scott scurried behind his desk and put his fingertips against the heavy oak just to make sure there was something between the two of them. He thought angrily, I am like a mouse hiding from the house cat.

Aloud he said, "And how are you today, Mr. Shawn?"

Mr. Shawn lifted his two hands and patted his stomach as if he were very fond of it. He said, "I am annoyed with you, Father Scott."

There! He had done it again! Once again Mr. Shawn had put the Father on the defensive with a phrase. All this has happened before, thought the Father grimly.

"Now, Mr. Shawn." Father Scott waved his hand before him, feeling rather shamefacedly that it looked like a flag of truce. "What have I done now?" He pasted a thin smile on his face.

Mr. Shawn frowned. This was truly a terrifying process. First he wrinkled up his forehead so that the gray wig slipped forward slightly. Then he turned the corners of his mouth down almost to the edge of his face and his eyes began to bulge a little. And then—as if to crown the whole terrible procedure—he would (without taking his eyes off the Father), lift one red forefinger and gently nudge the wig back into place.

Altogether it was too much for Father Scott. He moved uneasily in the swivel chair.

Mr. Shawn said, "You spoke to the Citizens Committee last night." He paused and looked at the Father as if to say, Go ahead, deny it!

Father Scott felt his arteries harden, one right after the other. He tried desperately to remember what he had said in City Hall last evening. There had been only a fair crowd of the so-called "progressive" young adults of the community, and he had been asked to speak on world problems.

Mr. Shawn leaned forward and reversed one by one the physical steps which had led to the frowning.

"Problems," said Mr. Shawn. "You talked about problems."

The Father nodded. I wish I'd included you yourself, you old goat, he thought grimly. But he only nodded and waited for Mr. Shawn to get on with it. Sometimes Mr. Shawn was very tedious about getting to the point.

Mr. Shawn took a folded piece of paper out of his pocket and began to spread it painstakingly on his broad stomach, and Father Scott felt the floor of the study collapse beneath his feet. He closed his eyes while the debris smashed down about his ears and the last bit of plaster shook itself from the walls and fell into a splash of dust. Then he opened his eyes again and looked at where Mr. Shawn sat in his chair

—carefully spreading out the paper—in blissful unawareness of the catastrophe which had just come upon Father Scott's study.

Mr. Shawn said, "I have your talk here."

"Of course you do," said Father Scott politely. It was some especial and perverted cosmic injustice that Mr. Shawn should be the only man in the entire county who could take shorthand. Furthermore, it was incongruous—big, beefy Mr. Shawn making neat little symbols on a pad every time the Father opened his mouth. Father Scott sighed.

"Of course you have my speech," he repeated. He was resigned. This was the way the Christians had felt in Nero's Rome, when they waited gravely in the Coliseum for the lions to fall upon them. Father Scott looked across at Mr. Shawn, who shook his shaggy mane and finally smoothed out the page with one great paw.

Mr. Shawn said, "Did you write this speech yourself?"

Suddenly, even to Father Scott, it seemed an unforgivable speech to have made to the Citizens Committee. He cast about wildly in his mind for someone else to blame and was debating between his housekeeper and Becky Ruth, a neighbor, aged nine, when Mr. Shawn swept on by without giving him time to answer. It was a habit Mr. Shawn had.

"Now here," said Mr. Shawn, stabbing at the page with a vicious forefinger.

Father Scott leaned across the desk anxiously. "Where?" he said.

"Now, just what do you mean by this sentence, Father?" Mr. Shawn began to read aloud from the paper. " 'What is

54

needed in our age is not new weapons, but a deeper spiritual appreciation of the powers at our fingertips'?"

Father Scott, to his dismay, found himself scattering wildly in the Coliseum arena and exhibiting no bravery at all. He swallowed. Now what had he meant by that?

"Why, it means," began Father Scott, "It means . . ."

"Yes?" prompted Mr. Shawn.

Father Scott said weakly, "It's out of context. What did I say before?"

Mr. Shawn waved the paper and seemed about to stand up. "Don't you *know?*" he roared. "Don't you *know* what you said before?"

He's going to charge, thought Father Scott.

But Mr. Shawn settled back into his chair again and took the paper out of the air.

"And listen to this," said Mr. Shawn. " 'We are faced with new and challenging questions which demand answers as vital as themselves.' "

"Well, don't you think that's true?" said Father Scott. He cleared his throat and said it a little louder. "Isn't that true, Mr. Shawn?"

"But what are these vital answers you talk about?" said Mr. Shawn.

Father Scott thought, I am going to stutter. If I answer him now, I am going to stutter. I wish I had an aspirin. I must be calm. I must think of Mr. Shawn's immortal soul. It was always a help to do that—to look all the way through Mr. Shawn to where his soul was curled up whitely, sleeping. Or dead, thought the Father.

He said slowly, "Well, the Church . . ."

Mr. Shawn looked utterly disgusted.

"And all the Church stands for," Father Scott finished defiantly. He had made his last stand. He was backed against the wall now, and the crowd of Roman spectators had risen to its feet.

Mr. Shawn smiled. "And what does the Church stand for, Father Scott?"

I will not stutter, thought the Father. I *will* keep my mind on his eternal soul.

"Well," he began, speaking slowly and deliberately so his tongue would not get left behind and begin to go into contractions, "that's a question that will take some time to answer adequately. . . ."

"Perhaps it's one of those new and challenging questions you told the Citizens Committee about," interrupted Mr. Shawn.

"I haven't finished," said Father Scott stiffly.

"Excuse me," said Mr. Shawn.

"Well, it involves what we believe about God and man's need of Him." Father Scott cleared his throat again and thought firmly of Mr. Shawn's soul until he thought he could go on. "It is the necessity for salvation. That is, I think, today's question—how shall we be saved? And the Church's answer is through the sacrifice of Christ and the life lived in the light of that sacrifice."

Father Scott drew a deep breath. He felt a little proud of himself. I must remember that phrasing, he thought.

Suddenly Mr. Shawn sighed and the wrinkles went out of his face so that the lion turned back into a pussycat, and he looked like nothing but a kind and somewhat sad old man.

Mr. Shawn said slowly, "I am going home now."

This was the worst thing about these arguments with Mr. Shawn. Just when the Father felt he had made an especially good point and vindicated himself at last, Mr. Shawn seemed to utterly despair of him and would go away—shaking his head so that the gray string of hair wagged behind him like a misplaced tail. It was very confusing to Father Scott. He stood up now, as bewildered as if the lions had suddenly gone off in a corner of the arena and begun a quiet game of handball among themselves.

"Oh, don't go," he began awkwardly, putting out his hand, but Mr. Shawn had picked up his jar of pennies and started for the door, shaking his head and muttering to himself.

Father Scott almost ran from behind the desk to get to the front door before Mr. Shawn did.

"Sometimes he's so close . . . so close," Mr. Shawn was muttering.

He went out the door and down the sandy path without saying anything else.

"Good-by, Mr. Shawn," called Father Scott hopefully.

But Mr. Shawn went on up the sidewalk, not even bothering to step on the lines, and Father Scott watched him until he turned the corner.

When he came back into the house, he met Mrs. Grimes, the housekeeper, who was leaving for the day.

"Good day, Father," smiled Mrs. Grimes.

He said to her, "Mrs. Grimes, I am a harassed man."

"Yes sir," said Mrs. Grimes, who hadn't the faintest idea what he meant.

She went out the door and up the walk after Mr. Shawn.

57

Father Scott went back into his study and sat down wearily behind his desk. He began thumbing hurriedly through his Bible until he came across St. Paul's passage about the Thorn in the Flesh. Father Scott read it over and over, moving his lips around the words, until he was somewhat comforted.

Just before the Father went to bed that evening, he found Mr. Shawn's transcript of the speech he had made the night before to the Citizens Committee. He burned it.

The following night was the first Thursday in November and this made it the regular meeting time for the Association of City Churchmen. The Association was composed of all the preachers and some lay-Christian workers in the town, along with the one Rabbi and one Catholic priest, Father Scott himself.

It was originally to have been called the Ministerial Association until some of the founders remembered Rabbi Lipstein and Father Scott.

"Well now, that's not exactly an appropriate title," they had said then. "And it isn't as if we want to give the impression of being prejudiced or anything."

And so it had become the Association of City Churchmen. Its membership was predominantly Methodist, and at these bimonthly meetings, the young Methodist ministers would come striding briskly into the hotel dining room, faultlessly attired in blue serge with automatic pencils in their shirt pockets. And there we sit, Father Scott would think—the Rabbi and me—like two monstrous carbuncles on the belly of an otherwise magnificent steed.

This thought had come to him at one of the regular meetings, and the Father had been so impressed with the comment that he had written it upon the napkin then and there and passed it across to Rabbi Lipstein. But the Rabbi had merely looked confused.

On this particular Thursday, the Father set out for the meeting at his accustomed early hour, smiling to himself. Two monstrous carbuncles, he thought with pleasure. It was sufficient armor against a thousand Methodists.

As usual, Father Scott arrived at the hotel earlier than the others. He always managed to come early because it gave him a comfortable feeling that was sure to counteract the rest of the evening.

Rabbi Lipstein was there before him—probably from the same motive, thought the Father.

"Hello there, Meyer," said the Father, feeling benevolence spread out over him like melted butter. "Nice fall weather, isn't it?"

The Rabbi said it was as nice as could be expected.

Father Scott sat down. "What's on the agenda for this evening?"

Rabbi Lipstein pushed a menu toward him that was headed Roast Pork, which probably accounted for his moroseness.

"Oh no, I meant in the business line."

"I don't know," said the Rabbi. "Something about a city-wide canvass."

Father Scott shivered. He knew about these brisk blue-suited city-wide canvasses. Suddenly Mr. Shawn loomed up before him and waved a jar of pennies under his nose. Father Scott blinked and the image went away.

"I am not feeling well," said Father Scott thoughtfully.

59

"The strain is constant," said the Rabbi.

Father Scott took a bottle of aspirin out of his cassock and swallowed two, hurriedly. It was his one vice. Sometimes he would stop before the rows of empty aspirin bottles in his bathroom and see in them the manifestations of Original Sin. They were liquor and gambling and strange and wicked women to him, he supposed.

"Shouldn't take too many of those things," said the Rabbi.

"No," said Father Scott. He replaced the bottle, feeling greatly reinforced.

Then the Methodists came.

They came in nice substantial Ford automobiles, disembarking noisily at the curb and clasping one another's hands affectionately. Then they filed into the hotel dining room and settled at the long table where they began immediately to move their chairs restlessly and fiddle with the silver. Rather like a Harvard rowing crew, thought Father Scott.

Dinner was tedious. Rabbi Lipstein sat next to the Father and ate several pear salads while his main dish went untouched. It was a shame, thought Father Scott. He traded his pear salad for the Rabbi's roast pork. Yes sir, it was a shame there couldn't be more open thinking in the Church these days.

Dr. Herbert Myers, of Park Elm Methodist Church, president of the Association of City Churchmen, finally tapped on his water glass and stood up at the end of the table.

"I am, uh, glad to see so many of you present this evening, since we, uh, wish to discuss a most important problem in our community." He had a sharp Adam's apple that consistently banged against his collar. And they think *we're* uncomfortable, thought the Father. I wonder if he wears gaiters.

"It is the problem of the non-churchgoer," said Dr. Myers.

Father Scott glanced at Rabbi Lipstein, who was stealing a final bite of pear salad. Yes, it must be true. A city-wide canvass. Well.

"You know and I know," said Dr. Myers, leaning forward confidentially so that Father Scott thought for one wild moment he was going to go head foremost into the flower bowl, "that the problems of our age are, at base, problems involving the human spirit."

Somebody clapped.

"And how shall these problems be met except by a spiritual solution?" said Dr. Myers, straightening up.

It all sounded very familiar, thought the Father.

"Our problem, it seems to me," continued Dr. Myers, "is to channel the people of our community into those havens of the spirit where these problems can be confronted by the power of God."

He banged his fist gently on the table, so that not even the china tinkled.

"That's right," said Reverend Forbes.

"Yes," said Reverend Russell Kerr, who was a Presbyterian.

"Now we wish to consider this in the democratic manner," said Dr. Myers with a smile, "so I wanted to bring this problem to the Association tonight and see what you, as a body of thinking Christians, thought of it. What suggestions do you have for achieving this end?"

Father Scott leaned forward and tapped the Rabbi on the

shoulder. "How did you know about the canvass?" he whispered.

Rabbi Lipstein raised his eyebrows mournfully. "The Methodists had a separate meeting last night at Park Elm Church," he said.

"Oh," said Father Scott. So that's the way it was. The whole thing was already planned.

Everyone sat quietly at the long table while Dr. Myers shifted from one foot to the other and continued to smile. A few men looked at each other and shrugged with their eyebrows. Someone seemed to have missed his cue.

Dr. Myers cleared his throat and chuckled. "Well, now, just anyone. . . ." he said.

Father Scott stood up. Dr. Myers looked at him doubtfully, took his glasses off, put them on again, and finally— seeing the Father was still on his feet—said without much encouragement, "Yes?"

"I think we should have a city-wide canvass," said Father Scott, and sat down again.

Dr. Myers looked as if he had been picking his way gingerly through a wading pool and had suddenly stepped off over his head. He took his glasses off again and stared at them as if he wondered where they had come from. Then he pulled his eyebrows together and looked expectantly at Reverend Forbes, the vice-president.

Finally he said, "Would you mind repeating that, Father Scott? I don't believe everyone heard what you said."

He bent down to whisper to the vice-president while Father Scott got to his feet again. "I said, I move we conduct a city-wide canvass among nonmembers and find their church preference."

"I second the motion," said Rabbi Lipstein sadly.

Something like this had never happened in the Association of City Churchmen before.

Reverend Barker, one of the younger Methodist ministers, got hesitantly to his feet, which he proceeded to shuffle back and forth. "Well," he began doubtfully, "as a matter of fact, I was going to suggest the same thing. . . ."

Dr. Myers looked at him sternly through his glasses as if to say, Well, why didn't you? and Reverend Barker moved his feet hopelessly and sat down again.

Reverend Kerr said, "I don't think we ought to put any pressure on anyone during this canvass. It ought to be conducted sensibly and rationally. No emotionalism or high salesmanship."

Dr. Myers nodded. Reverend Forbes stood up on his right, and Dr. Myers sat down gratefully as if he were tired and took a long drink of water.

"Of course, this project is going to bring up many problems, which is why it must be discussed here—with this group," said Reverend Forbes. He sent a frown down the long table that was probably intended for Father Scott but was absorbed by some innocent Methodist somewhere along the way. "For instance," said Reverend Forbes, "suppose we find a non-church-member who has been attending one church for some time, but when asked for a preference, indicates some other church?"

Dr. Myers nodded. "There are several occasional attendees of Park Elm," he said, "who come from Baptist families."

"And then," said Reverend Forbes, "there is Mr. Shawn."

Ah yes, thought Father Scott, there is always Mr. Shawn.

63

Dr. Myers looked thoughtful. "Oh yes, that's the rather large man with the . . . ah . . . has gray hair, doesn't he?"

"That's him," said Reverend Russell Kerr.

"Strange fellow," interrupted Reverend Barker. "Sent me a comic valentine last year."

Father Scott smothered a giggle.

"He doesn't really seem to belong here," said Reverend Forbes. "It's as if he's just stopped in for a while. No friends, no ties, seems to have no family."

"Doesn't he attend your services, Father Scott?" said Dr. Myers.

"Yes sir," said the Father. "Mr. Shawn is rather faithful." He tried to think of some tactful way to assure them all that there was nothing he would like better than to see Mr. Shawn "channeled" into some new haven of the spirit.

"But I believe Mr. Shawn once said that he was by training a Presbyterian," said Dr. Myers, smiling at Reverend Kerr.

Rabbi Lipstein leaned forward to whisper to the Father. "Told me once he was the son of an Arab camel driver," said the Rabbi.

Reverend Kerr said, "Mr. Shawn's mother was a Presbyterian, I believe."

"That's what I thought," said Dr. Myers.

Father Scott raised his eyebrows—both of them, at identically the same moment. Somehow he had never pictured Mr. Shawn as having a mother. Mr. Shawn ought to have sprung full-grown from his father's head, dressed in armor and bearing the wig and the pennies. Father Scott had always supposed something similar to that had happened. So

Mr. Shawn had a mother—a normal ordinary mother who was furthermore a Presbyterian. It did a great deal to make Mr. Shawn less awe-inspiring, thought Father Scott.

"Well, that's the sort of problem I mean," smiled Dr. Myers. "We must agree beforehand, in the privacy and solemnity of this room, that there is to be no self-interest involved in a campaign of this sort."

Everybody looked appropriately horrified. Self-interest? Among the clergy?

But just to make certain that no evil serpent lurked in any breast among those assembled, Reverend Forbes led the group in a special closing prayer.

"And Lord," he concluded, "give us unanimity of purpose, a spirit of brotherhood, and open love for our fellow creatures in this, Thy Great Enterprise. Amen."

Altogether it was a very impressive prayer and had probably been smoldering in his consciousness since last night's meeting at Park Elm Church.

Father Scott took two extra aspirins as he went out the door.

Walking home that evening, down the thin sidewalks which went under open-armed maple trees—almost bare now, and showing a few stars here and there—Father Scott wrestled with his spirit.

This, he told himself, is not Christian love. This is not even Mr. Forbes' spirit of brotherhood in a common enterprise. This thing that I feel is simple undisguised indignation.

Two men passed him silently, wearing overalls, probably on their way to the second shift in one of the mills. Father

Scott watched them go by and cross the street, not talking —just going silently off to their jobs. Father Scott thought, I could have been anything else but a priest. My father wanted me to be a college professor. I could have done graduate work anywhere I wanted. I could have ended up repairing automobiles, or joining the army, or selling vacuum cleaners from door to door. I could have worked in a mill too, but I thought there was something else. Something big. He sighed.

The clink of coins against glass warned him and he looked up in time to see Mr. Shawn coming down the walk toward him. Father Scott stopped and waited until Mr. Shawn came up to him. It was impossible to see Mr. Shawn's face in the darkness, but he was sure there was a smile on it somewhere.

"Mr. Shawn," he said sternly, "I do not believe in coincidences."

"Neither do I," said Mr. Shawn. He had left his wig at home and now revealed streaked gray hair, cropped close, but the penny jar was still in his coat pocket.

"You have contrived to meet me here," said the Father.

"Yes," said Mr. Shawn, nodding his head. "I have been waiting on the corner for twenty minutes. They had a long meeting tonight."

Much to his surprise, Father Scott heard himself saying, "Come walk with me, Mr. Shawn."

"Thank you, sir," said Mr. Shawn. "I will."

They started up the walk together. Mr. Shawn is a great deal taller than I am, thought the Father irrelevantly.

"We are going to have a city-wide canvass," said Father Scott.

"Who suggested that, Myers or Forbes?"

Father Scott sighed. "I did. Out of nothing but sheer malice, Mr. Shawn, I myself made the suggestion."

Mr. Shawn began to laugh and went on laughing until he reached the far end of it. "That must have bothered everybody."

"It did," said the Father. They walked on and under their feet the dead leaves went to powder.

"It is a beautiful night," said Father Scott.

"The birds are almost gone," said Mr. Shawn. They walked on for a while in silence. Suddenly Father Scott stopped in the walk and looked at him.

"I will not apologize for the Church," he said abruptly. "There are bigger men than I to apologize for it."

Mr. Shawn smiled in the dark. "Did I ask for an apology?" he said. "Did I not rather ask for understanding?"

There was nothing to say to that, so the Father fell sheepishly into step again.

After a while Mr. Shawn said, "It will be winter soon."

One of the mill whistles on the edge of town hooted softly, and the working shifts changed accordingly; somewhere people were leaving machines and benches while other people—like the two men in overalls—were coming on. For a minute the whistle was an old hoot owl with a sore throat. "Who?" said the whistle. Everybody, thought Father Scott.

"We mentioned you in tonight's meeting," he said finally.

In the dark he could not see Mr. Shawn's face, but he saw the head turn and nod once or twice.

"They said you were Presbyterian. All of them wanted to make sure I would not be offended if the city-wide canvass took you away from me."

"And would you?" said Mr. Shawn.

Father Scott let out a long breath. "I would be a happy man," he said.

"I doubt it," said Mr. Shawn. "Once you begin questioning, there has to be some kind of answer."

Father Scott frowned at him. "I do not know if you believe in nothing, or if you believe in everything more profoundly than I do."

"You think about it," said Mr. Shawn.

A car drew up at the curb and Reverend Barker put his head at the window. "Can I give you a ride home, Father Scott?" he said. "And you, Mr. Shawn?"

"Not me," said the Father, "but thank you for the kindness."

"I am fond of walking in the leaves," added Mr. Shawn and Reverend Barker drove away.

Mr. Shawn said, "I think you are worth more than the others."

"Thank you," said Father Scott.

"It is a big world," said Mr. Shawn, "and a frightened one."

"Or it is a small world, depending on how you look at it," added the Father.

"You look at it big," said Mr. Shawn.

"It confuses me," said the Father.

"And that is why I like you," said Mr. Shawn. There seemed to be no answer to that. They were almost to the Father's front gate before Mr. Shawn spoke again.

"Winter is not far away," he said.

"You are saying something about the Church," said Father Scott, "but I do not follow you."

"Urgency," muttered Mr. Shawn. They were quiet again.

"It is almost Thanksgiving. And then it will be Christmas and Easter and all to do again. Time does fly," said the Father.

"The birds are almost gone," said Mr. Shawn. They were at the Father's house then, and he put his hand to the gate.

"Good night, Mr. Shawn."

"Good night, Father Scott."

Later, the Father decided he didn't understand a thing they had said to each other, and it had about it the quality of dreams, but he felt a lot better afterward.

He felt so much better that he commented on the whole thing to Mrs. Grimes the next morning. "St. Michael's is very small, Mrs. Grimes," said the Father.

"Oh no, sir, it's such a cozy little place," protested Mrs. Grimes, thinking of the small brick building and the ivy and the crucifixes.

He wagged his finger at her, feeling very pleased with himself.

"But look how big the world is, Mrs. Grimes," he crowed. "Look how big the world is! And getting bigger!"

"Yes, sir. . . ." said Mrs. Grimes, doubtfully.

I must raise that woman's salary, thought the Father.

The city-wide canvass got under way immediately after Thanksgiving was past. It was preceded by a great many speeches and prayer cells and community meetings; it had been hashed and rehashed at half a dozen Ladies' Auxiliary meetings, and finally, special squads of volunteer workers from all the churches in town met—at Park Elm Church—for last-minute instructions.

Reverend Forbes was responsible for the final send-off.

"There is one thing we must remember," said the Reverend from the rostrum, and everyone ceased to rattle their mimeographed instructions and turned their faces up—like shelves of empty dishes, thought the Father.

"There is in this group no division, no conflict, no selfish motive. We are the Christian representatives of an entire community, met to combine for the bettering of that community. As such, I beg you to remember that we are a team— we are one big team pulling together."

Father Scott was sitting in the back of the church with his own rather sparse delegation, nursing his misgivings about whether a Catholic parish should even be involved in this kind of thing.

"We are a team," Mr. Forbes was saying. "And we have only one Captain. We have also only one opposing team. There can be no question as to where the ultimate victory will lie."

The group, wearing an awed hush, filed out the auditorium. Rah, rah, thought Father Scott. Good old Coach Forbes.

He went out into the thin sunlight and saw the members of his parish go off on their rounds, looking rather doubtfully back over their shoulders at the Father.

He thought, I am growing bitter. I am becoming a malevolent influence.

Dr. Myers came down the front steps of the church smiling broadly. He wore a rose in his lapel.

"Inspiring meeting, wasn't it, Father?" said Dr. Myers.

"Very uplifting," muttered Father Scott.

"Can I give you a lift somewhere?"

The Father looked down at his list. "No, my people are all very close to St. Michael's. I'll just walk, thank you, Dr. Myers."

Dr. Myers climbed into his Buick and was gone in a great roar. The hydramatic church, thought Father Scott. Dr. Myers had been assigned the railroad-mill section. They'll fix him, he thought with some satisfaction. Absurdly he began to wish Mr. Shawn were there. They'll fix him, Mr. Shawn. His sense of pleasure was acute.

When he started toward St. Michael's he saw the bare maple trees lined up on each side of the street like bony old soldiers. They are guarding the edge of winter, thought Father Scott.

Mr. Shawn didn't appear any time that day or the next, and Father Scott—somewhat unwillingly—began to wonder about him. On the day the canvass opened, the Father found a poem in his mailbox which could have been from none other than Mr. Shawn himself. He read it several times that day and decided that it was actually a very poor poem. It was called "To Be Whispered during an Air Raid." Very melodramatic, thought the Father. He kept it propped on his desk and read it now and again.

To Be Whispered during an Air Raid

Let us believe in the other world
        a little while.
Let us put out a bowl of cream
Against the door at night and leave
A candle bleeding gold behind the sash.
Let us believe it now.
Let us believe in the little ones, who come

71

And drink, and tangle horses' manes
And ride on broomstraws when the sun is gone—
Believe in hidden crocks of gold and one old elf
Asleep above them.
Let us believe
     in
        something
          now.

Yes, thought Father Scott, it was actually a very poor poem. It had no rhythm. And a "candle bleeding gold." Really, Mr. Shawn! Because he felt for once he could begin by putting Mr. Shawn on the defensive, he waited for him to come, walking down the street with his pennies jingling and his pigtail dancing along behind him.

Besides, it was hardly like Mr. Shawn to remain in the background when such a thorough house cleaning as the City-wide Canvass was under way. Even the newspapers were full of it: editorials praising Dr. Myers and his "tireless workers" who "aimed only at the greater good"; and occasional photographs of volunteer ladies, armed with cards and lifetime fountain pens and holy faces.

"A new day has dawned here," said the *Clarion* on its editorial page. "A day when the Church will become again the center of our lives, and human decency and goodness will become actuality instead of potentiality."

I've read that someplace before, thought Father Scott.

Still, it was strange that Mr. Shawn was not abroad, with his gray pigtail quietly flaunting the workers and his jar of pennies tinkling behind them like little laughter. At first Father Scott marked his absence only vaguely; then he began to wonder about it and be curious, and finally an emotion he could only describe as akin to anxiety came over him.

On rereading the poem, Father Scott remembered their walk together in the night and the queer things they had said to each other. "Urgency," Mr. Shawn had muttered. ("Do you believe more profoundly than I?" the Father had asked him, and Mr. Shawn had chuckled. "You think about it.")

And the Father thought about it.

Mr. Shawn's absence left a hole in the Father's daily life, and he could not decide what to fill it with. After all, for at least the past year of Mr. Shawn's stay in the parish, Father Scott's every move had been witnessed and criticized. Never a talk had been delivered when Mr. Shawn was not in the back row, busily taking it down verbatim on a white pad to confront him with later. The two of them had remained strangers, and yet there was hardly a detail of the Father's life in which Mr. Shawn was not in some way involved.

Finally, half ashamed, Father Scott asked Mrs. Grimes about it. "Have you seen Mr. Shawn about anywhere lately?"

"No, I can't say as I have." She had been polishing the silver, and now she put it down thoughtfully on the table. "Come to think of it, Father, I don't remember having gone so long before and not seen him anywhere."

Father Scott tried to be light about it. "Perhaps he's hiding from the canvassers," he said smiling.

"They are doing a great work," said Mrs. Grimes.

Father Scott pulled his smile inside his mouth and hid it from her. "Yes, of course," said the Father.

"Perhaps he's ill," said Mrs. Grimes.

This only put into words what Father Scott had begun to suspect the night before. Mr. Shawn was desperately ill somewhere, and he would die without having told anyone about the wig and the pennies, and without having made any sort of peace with God. This made Mr. Shawn the direct spiritual duty of the Father.

"Do you suppose so?" he said now, hurriedly, to his housekeeper. "Yes, I'm sure that's it. Where does Mr. Shawn live? Does anyone know where Mr. Shawn lives?"

"I'm not sure, sir, but there's a rooming house right uptown—a dirty sort of place—and I'm told Mr. Shawn stays upstairs there. Though I've never seen him there myself."

That night, when he thought no one would see him and ask him where he was going (Nicodemus, he thought wryly), Father Scott went to the rooming house and found Mr. Shawn's room, but the door was locked—and though he tapped on the door and called the name aloud for a long time, there was never any answer.

The City-wide Canvass went on, but Father Scott's heart was not in it. For small St. Michael's, the canvass was virtually meaningless—its membership was small but earnest and not likely to be changed much by the campaign. There were not many Catholics in the town. And one by one, the workers from St. Michael's parish sensed the Father's disapproval of the canvass and suspected a general disapproval from the Greater Church, and they ceased to have a part in it. As for Father Scott, struck by a period of depression he did not understand, he began to spend much of his time reading in his study.

The first days he reread many of the books he had liked ten years before and was appalled to find what nonsense they were.

Once he said to Mrs. Grimes, "I am afraid to go into the streets in ordinary clothing, for fear I shall have to sign a pledge card of some sort."

"They are doing a great work," Mrs. Grimes had said.

"Of course," said the Father quickly.

One morning Dr. Myers called him for what he termed a "brotherly" chat about the progress of the campaign. Cain and Abel, thought the Father, frowning at the receiver.

"We have a card from a family down in the mill section who are interested in St. Michael's," crowed Dr. Myers. "Polish family, I think."

Perhaps I should build a bonfire, thought the Father grimly. But he was immediately ashamed and took down the names and made plans to call on the family. Here, he thought, are people who are perhaps in genuine need of the strength of the Church.

What is the strength of the Church? said Father Scott to Father Scott.

This infuriated him and he took two aspirins and strode back to the kitchen. "Mrs. Grimes!" he called. "Mrs. Grimes!"

She came out of the pantry and looked at him with big eyes. "Yes, Father?"

"Mrs. Grimes, do I look like Mr. Shawn to you?" said Father Scott.

It was all very confusing for Mrs. Grimes. "Oh no, sir," she said hurriedly. "Mr. Shawn has a pigtail."

"Thank you," said the Father. But he was not comforted.

The disappearance of Mr. Shawn and of his eternal questions seemed to leave somewhere a great gulf, and the absence of questioning was no longer enough to fill it as it had been before he came. Father Scott had a nagging sense that either he was to fill the void left by Mr. Shawn's going, or else to topple uselessly into it, and this angered him. It goes against a whole way of life, thought the Father.

He thought a great deal about Mr. Shawn and none of the thinking left him any easier in his mind. At first, after the disappearance of the queer old man, Father Scott had wondered from where he came and to what place he went, or if he had been, perhaps, some sort of dream.

But after a while, this curiosity faded, and it no longer seemed important to the Father. What mattered was Mr. Shawn himself and the things he had said, and these things returned in the night hours to plague the Father's sleep and to make him cross with Mrs. Grimes.

And back of all this, the canvass went on and the Father watched it with eyes he felt were no longer his own, watched thoughtfully the complacent workers with their smiles and their pencils and their small white pasteboard cards, 4 by 6, on which was encompassed (he thought rather angrily) everything that was meaningful in the universe.

Near the very end of the two-week canvass, when he was replenishing his aspirin supply at the drugstore, Father Scott came upon Reverend Forbes. There the Reverend stood by the drug counter, a *Reader's Digest* under one arm, inquiring after the merits of chlorophyll toothpaste, with his hair combed down with some pomade which smelled of tulips. He turned when the Father came in.

"Why, Father Scott, I haven't seen you lately."

The clerk, even without asking, got the new aspirins and handed them across the counter.

"I," said Father Scott, "have been sulking in my study."

Reverend Forbes let out a great healthy Methodist laugh. "Ah yes, well we all need to now and then, don't we? How do you think the campaign is going? They're broadcasting an appeal tonight for increased attendance Sunday. It's a great spiritual awakening."

Father Scott held out his new bottle of aspirins and it seemed to him that they changed in his hand to a mayonnaise jar of pennies. He looked at them with genuine surprise.

"An awakening from what to what?" said the Father. It was the only thing he could possibly have said. He rattled the aspirins and they made a brief metallic sound to his ears, and then they were aspirins again; but he was sure they were no longer exactly as they had been before.

Mr. Forbes coughed as if he had been eating a peach and had swallowed a worm by mistake.

"It's always wonderful to question values, isn't it, Father Scott?" smiled Reverend Forbes finally—that same smile that appeared automatically on his face in just the same area and quantity, and which he wore automatically on Sundays, with the same casual habit he also wore his trousers. "Always a healthy thing for the Church," he added.

Father Scott waited.

"The unexamined life and all that," said Reverend Forbes hastily.

Father Scott nodded his head and for a minute a long gray pigtail flapped against his shoulder; he shook his head curiously but there was nothing but his own hair then and

77

the moment had passed. That was when he understood about Mr. Shawn.

"Well, I'll be seeing you soon, Father. At the meeting on Thursday," said Reverend Forbes finally.

For the first time Father Scott smiled. "I'll come, Reverend Forbes, if I have the time. There's a great deal to be done quickly, you know." He felt again the way he had as a young priest performing his first altar rites, the same sense of dedication and importance hummed in him like electricity, and left in his limbs a delicious tingling sensation. "The sense of urgency," he added happily.

Reverend Forbes looked bewildered, but then he found the right button and the smile came on again. "Yes, of course. This campaign has broadened our horizons."

"It's almost wintertime," said the Father.

Reverend Forbes started for the door, frowning. "Yes," he said doubtfully. "Bit of a chill in the air. Days getting shorter."

Father Scott felt one high point of ecstasy. He stepped to the door before Reverend Forbes could get out of earshot.

"That's right," called Father Scott after him. "Work, for the night is coming!"

As the Ford automobile pulled off down familiar Main Street (with what seemed to the Father undue haste), he watched the smoke of the exhaust disappear with mingled feelings of humor and pity. Somewhere behind him, the Father thought he heard a gentle chuckle, but when he turned there was no one in sight. No one but himself.

Family Album

THE TIME I remember my Uncle Li most vividly was on a hot August afternoon, as he sat just inside the regular Assembly Building at our annual summer church conference. He was sitting solidly in an uncomfortable straight chair—the kind they use for religious meetings—talking to a missionary. The sun had only a moment before gone down behind the long building and some of the last of it had filtered past the dusty windows and fallen in narrow strips across the rows of benches inside. My Uncle Li and the missionary sat just within the entrance, where they could see the Youth Center and the Workers' Study Hall and a row of cedars, two plump balding men talking softly in the light of a downgoing afternoon. I can remember coming toward the building and noting that the top of Uncle Li's head seemed freshly greased, like a wet marble, and that he and the missionary wore suits and ties and buttoned shirts, even in the heat.

I was eight years old that summer and my Uncle Li had brought me to the conference on a real bus that we rode for three hours from home and up into the mountains to the church grounds. My Uncle Li was very proud of me because I was "representing our church" at the meeting; I had won the junior sunbeam contest for memory work, and only the Sunday before had stood on creaking new shoes and blurted rapidly to the congregation that "In the year that King Uzziah died" I had seen the "Lord high and lifted up and his trainfilledthetemple." It was this feat which had earned me a trip to the church camp on a real bus, and not even my teacher, Mrs. Willoughby, or my Uncle Li suspected that in those days I believed the Lord's train was a screaming locomotive which had run amuck in the tabernacle.

On that August afternoon I had been walking through the grounds, plucking the sticky rhododendron blossoms and the laurel and marveling at the iciness of the spring which fed Memorial Lake, and now—coming back toward the main buildings—I spotted Uncle Li and the missionary talking. When I came in front of the Assembly Building I could hear them speaking about the "needs of India," and how the ignorant natives there tried to wash off their sins in the Ganges River.

"There is a terrible need for young people in the mission field," Mr. Barnes was saying. Mr. Barnes had just come back from the mission field himself to show endless movies of his work with the natives and to end his lectures nightly with appeals for new laborers to go forth to the harvest.

"Young people," echoed Uncle Li. His voice was somewhat wistful and he fumbled in his pockets and lit his old pipe—the fat black one that Mother said was evil-smelling enough to nullify all his sermons. "The young," continued Uncle Li between initial puffs, "are busy with many things."

And since I felt Uncle Li was really talking about me because my name was Paul and I ought to grow up to be a Great-Man-for-God like Saul of Tarsus, I walked on by the building and left the two old men talking about the unsaved in India. I was kicking at tufts of grass as I walked away because I just didn't think I could be a Great-Man-for-God. (I didn't feel like it for one thing, even though I had tried everything that was supposed to work in making one hear the call; I always shut my eyes during prayers and I kept listening for the Holy Spirit, but nothing ever happened about it.)

That day remains to me unaccountably vivid—the flowers and the water, the sight and sound of the two old preachers talking, even the scuff of feet against grass when I went walking away. It is as if that scene were a final picture, a last page in an album of family portraits so that forever afterward on rainy afternoons when one thumbs the book, he stops over that snapshot of Uncle Li and the missionary with a flash of recognition, and then a search of the image for hidden meanings. The sharp finality of a memory carries with it a whole burden of significance so that one has to wonder, Why is it I remember this?

Beyond that vivid summer scene there is only a dim and indistinct epilogue—an illness that became serious overnight and some sterile, whitened room, and then his funeral at our house with crowds of uncomfortable people, old friends and former parishioners. I remember the people and the funeral. Everyone was trying desperately to say something concrete about the fruits of his life; they wanted to point even to a new church, to put into the cornerstone that he had inspired the building of it—to say anything or do anything that might have related his endless efforts to corresponding specific results. No one wanted to say that Uncle Li's life had touched nothing or that he had left the world much as he found it; people do not dare admit such things which may, not too far hence, be said of them. So they stood about miserably in our living room, trying to name some achievement, some special goal attained, seeking to justify not what Uncle Li was but what he did, as if that were, after all, the thing of real importance.

There wasn't really much you could say about what Uncle Li had done during his lifetime. He had married so-many and buried so-many, and from his pulpit in Grace Church he had made a certain number of prayers and delivered a weekly sermon and a prayer service. Yet he was a good man —everyone admitted that—and they stood unhappily around his bier trying to explain the function of goodness and desperately afraid they would go away without ever having found it and spoken it out.

My Uncle Li always looked like the good man he was, a quiet plump useful fellow who probably did bookkeeping or maybe was a small independent grocer. But he never looked at all like a preacher and one was always being reconvinced that he actually was; even on the day he and the missionary were talking he looked rather like a man who sold religious calendars, and having completed his business could not somehow escape gracefully from the other man.

He was always making up for the way he looked by dressing sternly and stiffly, and by holding his round head at an elevated angle. Mother always said he was the only person in our town that wore a cutaway coat.

"It's ridiculous," she would tell him when he came to see us. "You look like a tintype."

82

Then my Uncle Li would suck in his little bump of a stomach and draw himself up to his full five feet six inches and he would solidify his fat little face into a stern expression.

"Dignity," he would declare firmly. "The ministry demands a certain amount of dignity."

Uncle Li didn't have much natural dignity to start with. He was such a very round man, and his short arms and legs came out stiffly from his body like little sticks which had been poked into a ball of butter. And because every feature in his face was made of some combination of circles, every attempt to look solemn and dignified only made him appear faintly ridiculous, like a funnyman made up to seem a preacher.

I remember last of all what my mother said when she stopped at Uncle Li's coffin after the crowd of uncomfortable people had moved back to let the family through. In death his face had gotten almost thin; it was grave and still with angles I had never seen before, and I was glad Uncle Li could not see what had happened to his face now that he had no more use for it. When my mother looked at him and saw as I did the face he should have been born with, she said to me softly, "He was such a very earnest man." (They wrote on his gravestone, HE GAVE HIS LIFE IN SERVICE, but that had no meaning at all written like that, unqualified and unexplained; and I always liked best what my mother said. That was the way I remembered him from that long-ago August day, a picture of aging earnestness, his pipe smoke ascending and descending like Jacob's angels, speaking sadly of the lost across the sea.)

II

For Uncle Li, for all the Dennet family, there was first of all a place out of which everything else came. This is the way things must be: that there should be a special quality to places, a sacredness about The-House-Where-I-Was-Born that is lost on family and attending physician. These may be remembered as the agents and the inhabitants; but the other—this room, these walls—they constitute the First World, and there is something which seems to us later primeval about it, as if once we might understand all about where we originated then we would come nakedly upon our honest selves.

For the Dennets the place was Three Oaks, the family homestead in Chook County. They remembered it later as having no wholeness but as being a place where things were separate and isolated and had no relevance one to the other, as one always remembers a childhood thing. There was the rolling hill that went down greenly to the very front steps of the old house and just stopped short of going on inside. And toward the back yard, broad-trunked and gnarled of root, stood the mammoth oak trees that gave the place its name. Here they lived: my grandfather Nels, my grandmother Carrie, their children, Lionel, Alice, Isadora, and my mother Kate. I was to hear of Three Oaks for years afterwards: the brick underpinnings that had been laid by slaves in ante-bellum days, the carved staircase in the front hall, and the real glass tinklers that hung over the cherry dining table where candles could be lit for parties, and the upstairs window in panes of colored glass, so that the floor before it was always patched and vivid, like a bright stitched quilt.

In this house the four of them were children together, wiry dark-haired children in clumsy clothes not meant for running. Here they must have played the timeless games, on this staircase and before this stained-glass window, dug deep at the oak roots and rolled laughing down the green hillside after the way of children everywhere and in every generation. I cannot picture it so, and yet it must have been—in spite of Grandfather—at least until their mother died.

In the days of their childhood there still clung to Three Oaks the sense of a now departed grandeur, as mist clings to earth at dawn and will not be dispelled by people walking. There were still a few parties given, an occasional small dance; there remained two good riding horses which later perished in a stable fire (then too old to be aroused to danger); and there was yet a Negro cook and a so-called gardener who had slipped down to the level of hired man.

This was the place in those days, and after that the people who lived there, especially my grandfather, Nelson Kater Dennet, a man of six feet three or more with a gauntness in his face that made it seem stone-carven—the plane of nose and cheek, the jut of jaw, the hunch of eyebrow over sharp flint eyes—and with a straight-line back that held him firm until he died.

What he was really like, no one can guess.

The men with whom he traded in the county seat said merely that he was queer and quarrelsome, but he knew his land and his business. Every tenant family that came to Three Oaks regarded him with abject terror, as if he might at any moment turn and crush them grimly underfoot. The local preacher gave up calling at the house after Carrie Dennet died, because he said the old man had shouted fiercely at him and slapped his riding crop around and threatened to "dash his silly head against a fence post" if he didn't go off about his business. And as for his children, no one knows what fibers he sent down into their lives or what they really thought he was; yet each one reacted violently to his influence and at the same time seemed never quite free of it.

Perhaps Carrie Dennet was the missing link. Perhaps the two of them either loved or hated each other or knew some human relationship such as these. But no one knows; she died soon after Isadora, the youngest, was born; and all of them were too young to remember her except as a pair of small hands.

After Carrie died (of a fever, it is said, and no one knows *what* fever) Nels Dennet was left with Three Oaks, with his shy son and his three daughters, and with a rage that consumed him all his life until finally he died from it. No one ever knew at what his anger was directed. Perhaps he blamed the old Sherman march that had taken away past glory, or hated the tenant farmers and what they represented to him, or perhaps he was only bitterly enraged with some unknown and malicious god that had taken his wife and worn out the vitality of his farmland. (This was one of the favorite theories about him, for he seemed to have so violent and personal a hatred of the elements; when it rained or failed to rain contrary to his wish, he would stride through his fields examining grimly the cotton and tobacco and corn, and sometimes he would stop dead and stand among the rows shaking his riding crop furiously at the sky, as if he might flail it and make it conform to his needs.)

Whatever the cause, things that might have broken any other man—crop failures, physical exhaustion, and an unbelievable aloneness—these served merely as fuel to his unending anger, and when he died he passed into the other world darkly scowling, as if he expected to find it no better than the last.

The four Dennet children were alternately frightened and bewildered by their father. He left them largely to the care of the Negro cook (a slovenly old woman with a sense of injustice which she periodically visited on her wards) so that they were aware of him only dimly during the early years, as something which brooded inscrutably above them.

Yet there were moments when he would suddenly come among them with a great clatter and up-end the world.

My mother remembers the day he took her to the tenant house and showed her the Gil Sneed family as one might show off a particularly distasteful animal. There were eight living in the sagging little house, from the old grandmother down to the youngest, two months and dirty and forever crying. The old woman was out front when they came, sprawled on the porch floor; she had aged and maddened to the point of infantilism. While they stood in the yard she crawled about the porch on all fours and Kate could see along her chin where the spittle had drooled and dried and dirtied so that when she cackled at them the caked lips seemed literally to tear themselves apart.

"Remember, Kate," said my grandfather, "that this is you in your worst moment."

Kate hated him that day. He had a sense of basic affinity but it did not move him to pity, only to the profoundest contempt. He caught her glance of venom and almost smiled as if he had tolerantly expected some such foolishness of her. "Yesterday," he added softly, "must never be condoned simply because it was yesterday."

Nels Dennet hated everything that signified to him the slightest self-abasement, and this was multitude: condescension, compromise, religion, servitude and employment, modesty, disease, habit, anything in which a man was not aware of himself as lord and ruler of all. Mastery was what he sought, over all things, people, all of Nature, and all of himself.

My Uncle Li was his only son and to him, more than to the others, he would come with his sudden and strange attentions. He seemed eternally caught between the two desires, whether to dominate his son or to impart to him his own desire for dominance.

If he loved the boy it was with a wild fierceness. He would sometimes rouse Li in the night to do the very things of which he was most terrified, ride horses or take down the big guns and go out to shoot at homemade targets. Sometimes Li would recall those awful nights and coming sleepily down the staircase in the dark, staggering out under the moon with one of the heavy guns to shoot at a square of cloth tacked whitely on a tree. Sometimes he would take the boy off a sickbed and put him to work in the fields with the tenants, or he would come upon him at play and suddenly strike him without warning.

"You must not ask why these things are," he would say to Uncle Li with a glower. "To ask is a kind of submission. You must learn not to notice they are there."

That is exactly what Nels himself did with his youngest daughter, Isadora; because of her illness he did not permit himself to notice she was there. He had always hoped that Li would ignore her too.

"Isadora is a mistake of nature," he insisted to his son. "And since nature makes no provision for error, we are not meant to."

Isadora was youngest and frailest of the four, a girl with a very thin, pale face and two unexpected spots of color high on her cheekbones under gray eyes. She was not well from birth, being a premature child, and though she grew in body to girlhood, there was something curiously stunted about her mind so that she was alternately child and woman and never at home as either. She might have learned to speak as the rest of them if Carrie Dennet had lived to help her, but the cook did not care, and the other children were too young to recognize her need and meet it. So she spoke seldom, and then she put words together strangely as if it were a foreign tongue to her.

She was, from the first, terrified of her tall, dark father, and could not keep her hands from trembling whenever he looked at her, which was not often. For the most part Nels Dennet ignored her as scornfully as he would have ignored some sickness within his own body; to him she was a weak point in the structure of his family and he behaved toward her as if she were some slow infection which he might some day burn out of his flesh, but which for the present he chose to overlook.

Isadora's fear of her father ate away at her life the same way anger ate at his. In one way she was destroyed by the other side of the same force which festered in Nels Dennet, and her weakness was more closely akin to his strength than he would ever have admitted.

89

She was subject to long, unexplainable spells of crying. Sometimes they would hang on for a day and a night, and during that time her whole being seemed possessed and used by forces she could not control, and after the spell had passed she would sleep wearily as one dead. There was nothing that could be done for her during one of these attacks; she had no awareness of hunger or need, and only when she woke from that final exhausted slumber would she ask weakly for a little soup. After that, for a day or so she would droop about the house with a little withered face, and then she would mount to days when she was almost like her playmates before the thing came full cycle again, and there was another long bout of sadness.

My Uncle Li loved her more than any of them did, especially as he grew older and realized she would never be like his other sisters. His patience with her was endless and with help from Kate he taught her to speak a little and to knit. This was her solace; she turned out clumsy afghans and sometimes long tubes which she meant for socks, cooing delightedly to herself among her bits of colored wool.

There was the awful time, before she had come yet to her teens, when Isadora made a scarf—an awkward, shapeless thing it was—and left it shyly on her father's chair. It was the only gesture she ever made to him and when the others came in to dine and saw it there, they all went stiff with terror and did not dare to move, not even to get the thing out of sight.

When Nels Dennet came and sat at the table he only glanced at the knitted scarf and turning to his son said with a set face, "He who accepts gives most of all," and waited.

"Yes, sir," said Li, trying not to look at the miserable thing that Isadora had offered or at Isadora herself, yet not daring to look at his father in defiance.

"That cannot be permitted," added Nels.

That was the first rebellion, out of love for the younger sister who by now sat cringing in her chair. "I think it has to be permitted," said my Uncle Li.

"The strong man cannot afford to accept," said Nels, eyes growing steely as he took in his son, standing up now with his young jaw thrust forward. They were all waiting, my mother Kate, and watchful Alice, and Isadora, already whimpering with the vague knowledge of having committed sacrilege.

"Then he is afraid," said Uncle Li, "and he is not strong at all."

It was the end of the meal. His father rose, wordless, and called for the food to be taken away and took down his coat for one of the solitary walks he was habit to. He stared hard at Li once—all of them saw it—and something flickered briefly on his face; and then he slammed out of the house and did not come home till morning.

It was Grandfather Nels' striving for self-mastery that had led him originally to experiment with the possibilities of physical pain. He had become convinced that the human will and the human body were locked in a death enmity which had to end in the annihilation of one or the other, and because of this he was a strong advocate of the principle of self-inflicted pain.

It was to this personal pain he was in the habit of turning whenever he was disturbed, and after this first clash with Uncle Li over the knitted scarf, he took to long grim hours in the stable loft. No one ever saw his wounds, for it was part of his pride that they must remain hidden, but there would be a limp, or the barest perceptible flinch, or the slightest weakness in one arm by which the others knew.

Years afterward, my Uncle Li used to recall his father's hands, that they were of a dark color and seamed from old burns and cuts, and that in the center of each palm were deep puckered scars, as if someone had sharply gouged away the flesh. They were the crucified hands, my Uncle Li used to say, but on what cross they had hung he never told, or why, or if in the long run it achieved anything.

I remember that when I was fourteen and given to fanciful thinking, I would recall my grandfather as having been the "Perpetually Crucified Man." That was to have been the title of a long epic I would write, concerning how a potentially great man misdirected his greatness, and full of descriptions, such as that he had been nailed savagely onto his own personality, always dying and being resurrected to himself, until he was sick to death of his own destiny. I wrote a great deal of it down in those days: there was to have been a passage about each morning being Easter, and Black Friday coming on grimly each downsetting sun. I wonder now what my Uncle Li would have thought of all that his comment about the hands had called up in my mind, and whether or not he would have laughed. I do not know; he laughed so seldom, and then nervously, as if he might be overheard.

After Isadora, youngest and weakest, came my aunt Alice. And where Nels was moved to the infliction of physical pain, she turned almost blindly to its alleviation.

Alice had her own strength; it was the quality of unyieldingness. She never swerved in a course; she never altered or compromised or reconsidered. She never married, either; I can remember her visits to our home and how the starched white uniforms she wore had some terrible appropriateness about them. The crisp, the starched, the unyielding, and at base, the sterile—that was Alice, almost from her childhood.

Where Nels Dennet was concerned, Alice sought to overlook his very existence in the same manner he ignored Isadora. There existed between the two of them a watchful politeness, a temporary truce which seemed always on the verge of being broken. It was as if here were two people having concealed daggers, who by some mutual, unspoken pact were committed to do murder whenever the other's back was turned. And for years these two would carry their freshly sharpened knives in readiness, waiting for the opportunity that never came, and all that time neither of them daring to relax his guard for an instant.

It was Alice who announced calmly to her father that she intended to enter training as a nurse, and although at that time it was neither simple nor fashionable, he consented and paid for it. It seemed as if a refusal on his part would have constituted that momentary turn of the head, wherein her knife would have flashed and darted sweetly between his ribs. So when Alice told him her plans without pleading, Nels supplied the necessary funds without argument, and she accepted them with no thanks.

Thereafter, when Alice was home for her two nights a week, he would ask her—not showing any interest—"How is it?" and she would reply without enthusiasm, "It's all right."

And the two of them would eye each other warily, sheathing their blades.

Alice and her brother Lionel did not like each other very much. It was not active enough to amount to a real dislike; and yet each, finding the other incomprehensible, had the tendency to laugh off his accomplishments and to enlarge on his eccentricities.

Li used to talk about how conscious his sister was of infection, and to suggest that she, too, would go down on her knees in Heaven, but only to scrub the place with disinfectant.

And Alice was always finding something laughable about conscientous Uncle Li—"The Pot-Bellied Saint," she called him sometimes, and spoke of his congregation as the "ranks of the dear converted," which irritated him profoundly.

Uncle Li always grew very flustered in the pulpit when he looked out and spotted Alice sitting primly in the crowd; he had a way of clutching at his Bible as if it were literally a staff to hold him up, and immediately calling out the wrong hymn number. And whenever he made a point in his sermon, he would always peer out hopefully at her impassive face, and then purse his plump lips in exasperation and repeat himself, as if she would surely be convinced the second time.

But worst of all was the flippant way Alice, after she became a nurse, used to refer to the flames of Hell as the "Lord's Sterilizer."

"I guess he'll dip you in too, Li," she would say provokingly, "and all of your dear converted."

Uncle Li thought this was the profoundest sacrilege. He would turn helplessly to my mother (who was always thus prevented from being either indignant or amused) and declare that Alice was simply inviting destruction.

"You are absolutely demanding a visitation of wrath!" he would exclaim, growing a little pink from his agitation even though no fire fell from heaven. And Alice, unmoved, would watch him without expression.

Just after Uncle Li had completed his first year in seminary, he had high hopes about Alice. He came home with his head fairly swarming with high-minded principles which, he said, ought to motivate anyone engaged in the cure of human suffering. But when he tried to explain Original Sin to Alice, she said he had the whole thing mixed up with pathological bacteria, and that was her concern. And after that he abandoned her, with many a sigh, to her modern worldliness.

After Alice Dennet, and next to the youngest, there was my mother, Kate. In that family, she amounted to a mutation, for she emerged from Three Oaks a sympathetic but sensible woman, with flashes of insight and humor that were her mainstays throughout life. She seemed able to know them all intimately and with understanding, and yet with some degree of objectivity.

More than any of the rest of them she seemed, although without admiration, to understand her father. She regarded him with a patient tolerance which he considered an active form of disrespect, and now and then she would burst forth to criticize him, an audacity that usually left him openmouthed.

95

And as if these things were not enough for him to endure, Kate could not hide the fact that at heart she pitied him profoundly and this was the one thing he could not bear. He could be defeated only through such pity, and yet pity seemed so cruel that Kate seldom indulged in it.

She used to say later, "It would have been like knowing the one spot on his body where he could feel pain and then hitting him there, over and over again."

When my mother talked like that, I would feel that she had come closest of the four to loving Nels Dennet, although I think she would have denied this with her last breath. "Love," she said once with a wry smile, "would have been to him merely another weakness."

But sometimes when she spoke of him, however unfavorably, there would creep into her voice a tone of awe. She had a habit always of doodling and writing down comments on the people and places she knew, and once I found this sentence written after her father's name: "Even the pyramids are ugly, and yet because they are so big, we must constantly go to stare." That must have been how Nels seemed to her—hugely ugly, never understandable, too large to love and yet not small enough to hate.

I remember that in that fanciful fourteenth summer of mine, just before Three Oaks was finally to be sold, my mother drove me down to see it. All my life I had heard the exciting stories of parties once held there, of the beauty and grace of columns and staircases and the flash of sunlight through the colored glass; but that summer when we drove into the yard and parked the car under one of the great oak trees, there was only a bleak two-story house that leaned wistfully to the west. Even the grass around it had faded and grown pale, like the hair of tired old men; and up in the top of one of the oaks the faintest blight was beginning to shrivel and blanch the foliage.

I was smitten with a sharp and terrible disappointment and, turning almost angrily to my mother, exclaimed, "But it's old! It's just an old house!" and my mother repeated it quietly as if she were discovering something, "Just an old house."

We walked across the yard and the grass lay back under our feet and did not spring up again, and when we went cautiously up the front steps a dozen gray pigeons rose up from the porch roof and made sad noises at our coming.

Inside, too, Three Oaks was just an old house, sagging and leaning and very slowly toppling over. Mother kept saying, "Watch where you walk, Paul, it's rotten there," and nothing remained anywhere of angry old Nels Dennet. The spiderwebs and the quiet patient dust had gathered to muffle everything, so that we made no more noise than a pair of birds passing. My disappointment in the house was keen; even the renowned carved staircase had leaned off center so that I could not safely go up it, and at the top of the steps some small gray animal stopped, looked at me with blank bright eyes and was gone.

I wanted to walk across the hill that day to the family graveyard, and see for myself where Carrie Dennet and poor Isadora were buried, but mostly I wanted to see where they had laid my grandfather, feeling that there would be something different about this grave, and that perhaps out of his heart had grown up a thornbush holding small and bitter berries.

But Mother was in a hurry that day, and later my Uncle Li said it was a good thing we hadn't gone.

"It's all grown over now," he said, "and we've let it run down so badly. His grave's sunk in a lot, and water stands in it after a rain."

And because I was fourteen and fanciful, I believed my grandfather Nels would be bitterly angry about the water, and that underneath the soil his long yellow fingernails would tear savagely at the roots of toadstool plants which sprang up there in the dampness.

III

All of this was what went before. And then, the spring Uncle Li was seventeen years old, there came the "vision" which set his course for life.

Nobody in the Dennet family was ever very comfortable when Uncle Li spoke about his vision. I can remember his mentioning it at church and my mother peering suddenly at her feet as if she were somehow embarrassed for Li; or again when Aunt Alice, on one of her rare church visits, seemed on the verge of breaking into a snort. Everyone looked as if he or she had inadvertently come upon Uncle Li in his underwear and could not afterward meet his eyes for fear of giggling, or overapologizing, or something equally foolish. So none of them looked at Uncle Li or at each other, and though he pretended not to notice, whenever he went on to speak of the thunderous wrath of God and pounded his Bible vigorously, his fat little hand made a very unobtrusive sound, as if he were gently swatting flies.

It happened the April Li was seventeen.

It was a wet green morning; Nels had eaten early and gone out to berate the Sneed tenants for their perpetual inefficiency when Li came down, past the stained-glass window (I wonder if it seemed symbolic when he saw it that April morning) and down the carved staircase into the kitchen, where Kate and Isadora sat.

He said good morning to Isadora first, kindly, and then to Kate; and then he leaned over the table on his outspread hands and waited for a long moment. Isadora was bobbing her head and whispering "Coo law. Coo law," like a tiny bird, and Kate had barely glanced at Li until she saw with surprise his firm set face. It looked, she said, as if he had taken it with his hands before he came into the room and pushed it this way and that until it suited him, and was not his face at all.

"Li?" said Kate questioningly, and he shook his head to indicate that he was not ill, that he had not quarreled with his father.

"I've decided to enter the Christian ministry," he said very distinctly, as if there were long dashes between the words.

There was a moment, my mother remembers, that was absolutely empty, devoid of thought or reaction, in which Isadora tinkled her spoon against a glass and some bird outside let up a crusty squawk. Li's chin was thrust out a bit; he looked absurdly young, she thought irrelevantly, like a small boy planning to run away. Then his words seemed to register and she wondered why, and how, and what would happen when he told his father.

Li was watching her face hopefully. "Do you think I'm right, Kate?" He seemed anxious for her approval and leaned nearer across the table to hear her answer.

"I want to know if *you* think so," said Kate, and when he nodded so intensely she smiled at him. "Then I wish you the best in it, Li," she said, and for the first time some tension in him lessened, and he broke warmly into a smile.

His decision to become a preacher was probably not so sudden as it seemed that morning in the kitchen. Uncle Li had finished with his schooling the year before, and now that he was almost always at home he had time to look about him and to think about the future and what would become of them all. He spent much time alone in the big house and the rest of his hours went to Isadora, who—he saw—was becoming steadily weaker and growing farther into some separate world that none of them could reach. He had given whole days to talking with her, trying to understand the way she thought. (There was a weird logic about her sometimes, as if she lived in a world where it was axiomatic that two and two were nineteen and water fell upwards, and everything else was interrelated on this different scale.) And though she loved Li as she did none of the others, even when he came upon her without warning the suddenness of his appearance terrified her, so that she would run from him in panic with her long dark hair flying out behind her.

At first when he finished school, Li had planned to oversee the work at Three Oaks with his father, to step into it as an eldest son was supposed to do; but he had no talent for it and his heart was too kind. When he saw the state in which the Sneed tenants lived, he protested angrily to his father and insisted almost hysterically that human beings should have a warmer house and better food. And Nels, deeply contemptuous of such sympathy, had called him a "prying old woman," and forbidden him to interfere. But Uncle Li hated the sight of the thin, almost shrunken Sneed children, one of whom had a harelip, and when he had been near any of them he would hurry to the house trembling, while they snickered at his strangeness. So gradually he abandoned any pretense of helping his father about the farm and stayed about the house reading and trying to talk with Isadora.

The two of them could be found almost any afternoon in one of the dim parlors where the shadows lay thick as dust, Li reading aloud and Isadora nodding her dark head with enthusiasm. He read first from his own books and then those he could borrow from the school collection, Shakespeare and the poets, the *Odyssey,* Walter Scott, Dickens. Isadora listened with grave curiosity but she almost never smiled; and as she grew older her fits of crying settled into a long and nearly unbroken sadness and she abandoned all attempts at speech.

One thing alone could coax from her an expression of rapt pleasure—the weeping willow tree which grew in the back yard. She had loved it from the time she first learned its name, and she could be often found there, lying on her back in the grass and watching the clouds through limp, low-hanging branches. In the summertime, Li would take the books outside and read to her there, while she wound herself in a green curtain of willows, looking a very thin and pale Ophelia.

It was during one of these reading sessions that Li had begun to read the Psalms aloud, and after that the Sermon on the Mount, and then the whole Gospel of John. The words seemed to burn deep into him, and he began to turn new eyes on his father, glances which Nels found gentle and forgiving and altogether unbearable. Gradually, beginning about midwinter before the vision came, Li began to see the whole world as one gigantic moral lesson. He was forever considering the lily, and the sparrow falling, and the sower going forth to sow. It was a very tiresome period for the rest of them; Alice openly ridiculed his sudden piety and even Kate, though sympathetic, lost patience with Li's eternal sermons in stones.

But gradually this tendency had subsided, much to Alice's relief (it was probably biliousness all the time, she said) and things went back to normal until that spring morning he walked into the kitchen with his mind made up.

Years afterward, when Uncle Li was pastor of Grace Church in our town, he used to preach about his vision, while Mother sat in her pew examining her shoe toes and Alice frowned and flipped a hymnal.

"And one night," Li would begin impressively, "the Lord came to me in a dream and suffered me to hear the weeping and wailing and the gnashing of teeth from damned souls. And the Lord said unto me, 'Lionel Dennet, shall these things be?' Then I knew I must enter into His work."

If at that moment he could have been a tall man, some gaunt soul with deep-set, burning eyes, we might have heeded; he might have seemed to us a Wesley, an Edwards, a Sunday, speaking the directing and damning Word of God from Grace pulpit. But all of us knew it was plump, pink, balding Uncle Li, and everybody looked away from him quickly and glanced at watches.

I heard him speak often of his vision, and each time he spoke of it he gave a description of sound rather than sight.

At first, when I was a very little boy, I would inquire after the Holy Spirit—had it been a puff of smoke? Was it tall? Did a tongue of flame appear above his head? But always Uncle Li said merely that the Lord was a still small voice within, which disappointed me terribly.

Later, after I stopped being such a little boy and had heard all the family stories, I came to suspect that the weeping he heard might have been Isadora, and if there was the sound of tormented men who ground their teeth, it was probably no more than Nels Dennet, passing under Li's window on one of those midnight walks. I do not know if Li ever thought of this or not, but I suspect he did, for he was an honest man, and he never looked at Mother or Alice when he preached about his vision.

Still, I think the question he heard in his heart was real enough. "Lionel Dennet, shall these things be?" Is there only the one choice—to lash and strike at life and grow dark and brooding like Nels Dennet, or to be an Isadora, constantly lacerated by it, and forever weeping for countless, nameless things?

That spring morning after Li told my mother about his decision to preach, he left the house on one of the lonely walks he had only recently begun to take, and Kate stood at the kitchen door to watch him go, his short legs churning and his face turned upward now and then to catch the sun.

I asked her about it once on some slow Sunday afternoon after Uncle Li had preached on the call of the Holy Spirit; and I had wondered how it seemed to her when the Holy Spirit had been in her own house only the night before?

"I felt like crying that morning," she said to me then, remembering the lonely pudgy figure of her brother as he walked away from the house. "I said to Isadora, 'Poor Li. Poor Li.'" But Isadora did not understand and only whimpered a little at her voice, and so she turned away from watching him go and said no more.

In his sermon on the Holy Spirit that Sunday, Uncle Li had told about the solitary walk he took—his back turned to the house at Three Oaks as if by symbol—and the sun falling about him with a rush of light.

"There was a great wrestling in my soul," he had added solemnly, and I think that it was so.

He walked almost all that day, as if he had become oblivious to time and food and all such lesser things, across rolling Dennet pasture lands and over barbed-wire fences and turned fields, and through other pasture lands; he climbed up hills and took footpaths and crossed gutters where the land had washed redly away, like a wound; and dogs came out of people's houses to see him pass, but none of them barked, he said.

And what he thought about that day or how the world seemed to him then, one can only guess. It was during the first flush of springtime and honeysuckle ran riot and everywhere one looked greenness seemed to be exploding into sight, off trees and in clusters along streams and impatiently under passing feet; it must have seemed to Li prophecy and promise, all in one.

And after the sun had gone and the earth was cooling and he discovered the thickness of dusk coming, he made his way back to Three Oaks, abruptly tired and weak from hunger and for that moment, at least, very sure of everything. This day came finally, in retrospect, to sustain him; as he grew older he would look back to that day as the best single experience he could recall and he spoke of it wistfully, as something irretrievably lost.

When Uncle Li first came in sight across the far hill behind Three Oaks, Nels Dennet moved away from the kitchen door where he had been watching and sat down with his back to it, as if all the queer doings of his queer son were no concern of his; and when Li came in he had to clear his throat before his father turned. There was a long look between them that startled Uncle Li because there was not somehow sufficient antagonism in it; he felt foolish, the way a man feels when he has strained to lift a heavy weight and had it go flying lightly off. He said pettishly before his father could speak, "I've made up my mind," and Nels watched his face curiously.

"Kate told me," he said shortly.

Li swallowed. "I'll be wanting money for school this fall."

"I guess you will," said his father. He kept searching Li's face for something, as if suddenly it might spring up like a fire. Finally he grunted, "Why do you do this?" and Uncle Li grew red and flushed, and moved uncomfortably.

He said too loudly, "I had a vision."

Kate, who had been watching the two of them anxiously, saw then one of those rare moments when the iron went out of Nels Dennet and he looked suddenly like a tired and peevish old man. He said bitterly, "Is that all?" and a tremor ran up his neck and quivered under one eye. He turned from his son and walked around the table and sat on a chair as if suddenly he had realized that all his muscles were worn and frayed and could not hold him up any more.

It baffled Uncle Li. He looked at my mother blankly, and then at Isadora whose lip had begun to tremble; and he moved after his father making ineffectual motions with his hands, wanting to be firm about his decision and yet not knowing what else he might say in defense of it, or if it required his defending.

He stammered, "It came as a dream, Father, and there was weep . . ." but Nels only looked at him steadily until he fell silent and flushed faintly. In a few minutes he said stiffly, "I'll need money for school."

Isadora, bewildered, had begun quietly to cry and for an instant that was the only sound in the kitchen. Then Nels Dennet turned from his son to look at Kate, who was standing helplessly nearby, and said to her, "He is younger than I thought." And rising heavily he went upstairs and would eat no supper.

After that day, he tried to avoid as much as possible the necessity of speaking directly to Uncle Li. He would pass all his conversations through some third person without looking at his son, although the money for seminary appeared without argument, and although the details of Li's study appeared to interest him.

But whenever Uncle Li made the mistake of speaking directly to his father, Nels would stamp off furiously through the house and leave him there with his mouth open and the words in mid-air, or he would scream for Kate to come in and serve as intermediary.

Only a few times after that was he known to speak to his

son. My mother used to tell me about what he said to Uncle Li as he lay dying. Li was down on his knees by the bed when Nels Dennet lifted his gaunt head to stare at him and then put it down on the pillow again and called weakly for Kate.

"Kate, is he praying for me?" he whispered.

"Yes, I think so," said my mother.

His old gums grinned and he put out a withered hand and patted Uncle Li's head with it clumsily. "You would," he said, and after that he cackled soundlessly for a long time, sucking in his breath sharply between the bursts of laughter.

When I was in my fourteenth summer and remembered all that was said of the scarred hands of my grandfather and how I was going to write a tragic epic about him, I would think too of Uncle Li and where he would fit into the poem. I decided that if Grandfather Nels was to be the crucified man, then Uncle Li himself must be written in as the perpetual prodigal. But whenever his father saw him yet a long way off, he would not run and fall on his neck and kiss him; but would leave sulkily by the back door and walk alone with himself for a long time.

IV

The next years in the Dennet family are blurred; they were full of a crowd of isolated events and no one seems sure how meaningful any of these were. It seemed as if all four of them had reached the point of doing what they wished; they had come to the summit and found it only a step or so wide, so that involuntarily they seemed to be heading downhill again, not quite certain they had even passed the peak. Alice finished up her training and took up hospital residence and was a successful, but not exceptional, nurse. Li went away from Three Oaks to seminary in Richmond and here he did well but not remarkably, and learned as much as the average student learned, and rose from the table unsatisfied. Only Kate remained at Three Oaks with Isadora and her father, and even she had begun to be admittedly unhappy there. The Negro cook had died the year before, and now it was Kate who kept the old house, feeling she swept a floor which might fall in by morning.

For the house had begun, almost overnight, to sag, as if it were suddenly and thoroughly tired. Dirt sifted up out of the very foundations and settled everywhere and little piles of white dust marked the holes of greedy insects in the floors, and the roof weakened so that the ceilings began to streak after a heavy rain. It was as if the old house sensed that it was to be abandoned and had resigned itself and was making ready. For company there were only Nels and Isadora, so that the three of them sat at meals in heavy discomfort, longing to be gone but not knowing where.

Then, abruptly and without any warning, the long-time Three Oaks tenants, Gil Sneed and his family, left in the night in one of the Dennet wagons, after first setting fire to the main barn.

The first they knew of it was when there came faintly the smell of fire and ash, and Nels let out a bellow when he saw the flicker of orange light coming and going in his room. By the time he and Kate could get outside, the whole roof was blazing up like some huge torch in a gigantic hand; there was a moment when he seemed almost to smile at the enormity of Destruction before he moved to stop it. The barn was very old and the flames sucked up the dry straw and whipped around the whole structure almost as the two of them watched; there was barely time for them to get the stock outside before the top and sides were sucked in with a great whoosh and consumed. The two riding horses perished, making at the last a great screaming noise that was terrible to hear; and the next morning when the sun came up there was nothing out back but a black mound of smoldering ashes and wisps of floating smoke and the faintest acrid smell.

The whole incident seemed to daze Nels Dennet. It was not so much the loss of the barn but the mere knowledge that Gil Sneed should have possessed the audacity to deliberately set it afire; something of the sure structure of his world began to totter then. To him this was a revolt more momentous than the Southern secession, that the Sneed clan should have dared, should have presumed to revenge themselves upon him for anything; and for days afterwards he hung about the ruins poking at them doubtfully, as if he honestly could not believe what he saw.

After that, a steady procession of tenants came and went at Three Oaks, for now Nels had lost some of his cold contempt. He had never bothered himself with petty thievery before, but now he was suspicious of everything, as if he had acknowledged his fear of them, and behind his back they smiled and called him Old Dennet.

During these years Li was away at school and in the summers he took small country parishes and was seldom home. I have little idea what this time was like for him; he seldom mentioned seminary days and I have often wondered if they were happy or sad, if he was content with his choice and his preparation, if his decision was ever shaken. Even at Christmastime he would find some last-minute reason that kept him from coming to Three Oaks, as if—said Alice wryly—the Lord's birthday were too sacred a thing to celebrate in a profane country. When he wrote, he wrote largely to Kate with an occasional enclosure to be read to Isadora. I have seen some of these letters that Li sent from school and they are extraordinarily dull:

"I am well and pretty busy . . . not doing too well in Old Testament. . . . How is Isadora? Give her my fondest affections. . . . Was distressed to hear about the fire. Whatever could have possessed Gilbert Sneed. . . . A concert here Sunday. . . ."

But one thing fired him with enthusiasm. One can sense the difference in his letters before and after the passion came full force upon him. He fell in love with Milton.

For nearly a whole year, it seems, Uncle Li fairly walked under the Miltonic shadow, reading incessantly, talking to the point of acute boredom, and then rereading and talking again. He memorized great swatches of *Paradise Lost;* he read every available book, essay, and article on the life of the English poet; and I suspect he even experimented himself with writing the blank verse style. After he had become an established minister, he would quote long passages from his pulpit, the words rolling grandly and fondly off his tongue like old friends. I have heard him do the epic opening in tones at the same time wistful and thunderous, pausing tenderly over the part about asserting Eternal Providence and justifying the ways of God to men.

He wrote uncounted essays on Milton's work, some of which he later tried to publish in the *Sunday School Leader,* without success.

"Milton's *Paradise Lost,*" (the manuscript would begin grandly) "is a poetic explanation of how the principle of disorder entered into a harmonious universe."

"In Eden," began another, "Mankind fell; but God in His Infinite Patience leaned down to become Himself the Son of Man, who did not fall but rose, and drew all men to Him."

But other than the theological, there was another and perhaps a more valid reason for the responsive chord Milton's poem struck in my Uncle Li. It is not difficult to see. In an occasional letter to Kate in which Li expounds his views, it emerges only faintly and he never makes the logical connection between the opinion and his experience.

"Sometimes," Li wrote, "one wonders if Milton did not create his Devil of too epic a stature." (There was not much originality in this, but Li felt it was his own discovery even when he read it in the writings of a dozen critics.) "There is something admirable about him even when he is being most despicable." Then he adds hastily as if someone had prodded him in the back and reminded him of something important, "Of course, this is essential to the nature of sin, that it hold forth to man some form of attractiveness. And even when Milton gives to the Devil a magnificent courage, he is courageous only through his pride."

In all of his letters home Li wrote virtually nothing of his studies, his books, his special friends. He said little of how he spent any extra time. Most of his more thoughtful letters to Kate are like pointed little Essays-of-a-Seminary-Student

—dissertations (very dull) on the Holy Spirit, the problem of God Incarnate, the pastoral responsibility. It is amazing how little he spoke of his ambitions, of what he hoped to do, almost as if he were afraid once the words were out they would vanish in spurts of smoke and be lost to him forever.

When he did speak of these things it was comparatively, and on an almost hopeless scale: to be as great as Paul, as dedicated as Stephen, as enraptured of God as Saint Augustine.

He read widely and in many fields. He was particularly on the lookout for quotes to send along as an aid to Alice, in great bulky parcels which she left for the most part unread. She had become to him, even then, the personal manifestation of what he considered a genuine war—the scientific temper pitted forever against the religious. In his writings to her he relied heavily on God as revealed in the world's infinite complexity, an argument which seemed to him quite suitable and to Alice a little tiresome.

"I have had another sermon in today's post," she would sometimes scribble off angrily to Mother. "Li insists that I have no beliefs at all simply because I cannot pretend an intensity such as his. He sends me this time a volume by someone named Pascal who seems to me a weakling and a coward."

During all the time he was in school, Li mentioned only one other student by name. The letter followed one of his rare visits to Three Oaks, an uncomfortable occasion with Nels speaking to him only indirectly and Isadora twittering nervously to have them home, and all of them aware of strangeness. Li had struck them all then as having aged so much since the last time; he was becoming prematurely bald though yet in his twenties, and he seemed fatter and rounder than ever, a pot-bellied gnome of a man who was already middle-aged and a little tired. Alice had mentioned it to him, not unkindly it seems, but in her usual confident manner which assumed that anybody's health was her concern.

"You're growing wider," she had observed with her head cocked over. "Going to have to preach on tiptoes." And then, catching the look on his face and realizing she had hurt him, she apologized uncomfortably and everyone felt even more ill at ease.

It was after that visit that Li wrote home about Jamison Edwards, the man who later became a well-known minister and writer, and was made head of the District Convention. "Edwards," wrote Li wistfully, "is probably the best student to go forth from here in years. He preaches a fiery sermon and there is no more sincere man anywhere. Sometimes when he speaks in Chapel, you can hear nothing but your neighbor breathing and even the older preachers lean forward eagerly to hear what he has to say." Then he added as an afterthought, "Edwards is a very tall man and when he stands in a pulpit, the whole room seems to be full of him." Kate sent the letter along to Alice and she never mentioned his size again.

After his regular training was completed, Li stayed on at school an extra term, which puzzled them all. He did nothing special during this time, took only routine extra courses, made his customary marks. It was almost as if he were merely postponing the moment when he should be completely what he had set out to be, and there should be no turning back.

Yet the day came; he took a church of sixty members and a small Sunday school and set to work, as he put it, "in the Lord's vineyard." By accepted standards, his four years at Bethany Church were successful. His membership increased steadily; the women of the church organized; a large percentage of the members began to tithe.

Yet once he wrote as a cry of profound despair, "Kate, I have a feeling of complete uselessness here on Sunday mornings. Everyone waits expectantly in front of me, rows and rows of them. But just as I am ready to speak, I have the feeling they have opened to me one special room, a stiff and unused parlor, and have carefully barred the door and windows to prevent anything that is said here from leaking out into the rest of the house. Kate, does it matter? Does what I am telling them really, honestly matter?"

He never mentioned it again.

After Bethany there was another church, Shiloh First—a little larger, a bit more prosperous, a little farther into the suburbs. "You see?" my mother wrote him. "You are doing a fine job and you are progressing. It is a real promotion for you." But Uncle Li never wrote back about that.

At Three Oaks during Li's second pastorate, life seemed to move along spasmodically, like a worn-out machine that alternately stops and starts and cannot seem to get all the wheels to turning at the same time. Isadora plunged into strange hysterical outbursts one day, and then emerged into a state of suspension in which she looked about wildly and knew not even Kate. She would seek out the corners of the dimmest rooms in the old house and here she would squat, immobile, for hours, staring only at some fixed point in space. Nels would be in a rage one afternoon, and by the next day he was merely pettish and ill-tempered, and then he would fall into a long brooding silence, during which he would walk by the burned barn as if it still stood, sometimes putting out his hand to a wall which was not there. Or he would go to where he could see the house in which his new tenants lived, and from a distance he would make a great circle about it, eying the windows and doors with dark suspicion.

Alice came home more often now, although no one could imagine why, for she always had a miserable visit. Sometimes she seemed on the verge of making some overture to her father, but then she clamped her lips into a tight line and turned away.

Once to Kate she said bitterly, "He is getting old, Kate. Can't you see the way he is getting old?" And that day she left early and seemed to be deeply angry about something.

It was during the years in which Uncle Li was pastor at Shiloh that my mother and father met. He was a candidate at that time for the state legislature for reasons I have never understood (he was very young and knew nothing of politics and polled only 146 votes) and he met Kate while he was making a speech at the county seat. It was being given in front of the local courthouse; he was firmly haranguing a few uninterested loiterers and one curious little boy who thought he was the Governor, when Kate walked by with Alice and met his eyes. As luck would have it, he was distantly related to one of Li's schoolmates, and after much plotting and cautious planning, the two were finally introduced.

Alice didn't think much of John Tilley as a prospective mate for her sister. "He's the consumptive type," she assured Kate repeatedly, and even Uncle Li took time to write home to Three Oaks that politics was, at best, unsuitable for women. But Kate liked him, and even had the audacity to suggest to her father that he cast his vote for Mr. Tilley for the legislature.

"I don't believe in voting," said Nels shortly, "or in anything that makes men all of a kind."

After the Tilley political career came to such an unfavorable end, my father became resigned to a more sensible job with a mail-order company in Columbia, and he and my mother corresponded: neat formal letters at first for "My dear Miss Dennet," and then almost immediately to Kate and John, with no more nonsense about it. Each season he would mail to her a company catalog and they used it to write love messages in code—8346: page 8, col. 3, par. 4, word 6—silly things like that. And whenever he could afford the trip, John Tilley boarded the train in Columbia and made the long trip to call on her, very properly, and took her to the county horse races or the local agricultural fair.

They would have married right away but Isadora could not be left alone at Three Oaks with her father, and they had no money to speak of.

Nels asked her only once, "Are you going to marry this politician?"

"Yes, I am," said Kate firmly, and to that he only grunted without comment.

He had taken to a most peculiar habit during this time. In the middle of a meal he would suddenly abandon his food and stare away at nothing and with his eyes blank, the way a man will do when he is thinking deeply. Then, coming to himself again, he would look about him vaguely, as if he were not sure where he was or how he came to be there, and taking up his fork he would press the prongs into his wrist and take them away again, looking with faint surprise at the four white dots in the skin which pinkened and then faded pale again. This seemed to depress him deeply; he would brood listlessly over his food and glance again and again to his wrist and to his dinner fork.

On one such occasion he had abruptly put his silver down with a great clatter and turning to his youngest daughter had called her name, "Isadora!" in too loud a voice; it had so frightened her that she hid hysterically in the attic and would not come out for hours.

And again when Kate was writing her weekly letter to Li, he had come banging into the parlor and stood towering above her, breathing as if he had run all the way upstairs. "Tell him," said Nels, pointing to the letter with his limp riding crop (he carried it still, although there were no horses), and Kate wrote as he spoke, "tell him this—There is no sufficiency." Then he had turned on his heel and gone stiffly away. Whatever Li thought when he came across this message he did not say, and Kate also refrained from mentioning it, as though it were something shameful.

The year wore into a vivid fall, so that the whole world seemed to be burning. Even Isadora noticed it; she would come into the house from outside with armfuls of colored leaves and strew them brightly through the rooms, and because this pleased her so Kate waited until night to sweep them out again, knowing that by morning she would have forgotten.

Something hovering in the air that autumn seemed to make all of them quarrelsome. Uncle Li had sent to Alice some selections from Thomas à Kempis, and she—flying into a sudden rage—tore secretly from a library book the tale of the Wife of Bath and mailed it to him without comment. After that he had written Kate a bitter letter which came on the heels of a similar one from Alice so that Kate, who was only interested in getting married, lost patience with them both and said so.

Then suddenly Isadora died.

When the September rains began, she fell ill of some disease that alternately burned her and froze her, and within the week she was gone. Kate fought for her life desperately as if in penance, reproaching herself for a thousand omissions; but nothing seemed to help, and coming in one morning Kate found her already cold, as if life had gone out of her with a rush, not lingering for an instant. Her face in death wore a faintly puzzled look, as though nothing thus far had been understandable to her, least of all her own dying; and one small hand was open, waiting for something to be laid in it.

It dazed them all, even Nels, who kept bending down to peer at her curiously as if now he could look at her and wonder about her without its costing him anything. When Li and Alice arrived the two of them had dismissed the silly quarrel and were ashamed, feeling somehow it had contributed to Isadora's end, and longing for Kate to assure them *that* they could have done nothing had they been there.

It was a Thursday afternoon when Li read the final services over Isadora's grave in the family plot. It was a very silent day so that every word he spoke seemed excessively loud and when a small wind moved in the leaves it startled them all. Nobody cried, but rather stood numbly in a huddle while Mr. Neely, the tenant, lifted the dirt over the side. His red face and his harsh panting struck them all as obscene, and they turned away quickly from the sight of him leveling off the place and went across the hill toward home. Only when they had come all the way to Three Oaks did Kate notice again the red and orange in the trees and catch her breath sharply, remembering.

Afterwards Nels Dennet took to walking to the plot late of an evening; and when the willow sapling Kate had set began to put forth new leaves he watched it daily, as if it evoked within him some bitter terror.

It was a long winter—the coldest to hit that section in twenty years, they said, and it took its toll of the countryside, blanching the grass everywhere and stripping the trees with grim efficiency until even the three great oaks stood hugely naked in the yard. The wind and the constant leaden skies made everything seem drawn away and unfriendly, and by now the house was falling into such disrepair that cold sifted in between the cracks and remained throughout the winter.

Kate was utterly miserable that winter, so soon after Isadora's passing; and Alice, sensing that she was lonely and depressed, made frequent visits even though she hated to come and nearly always went away upset.

Finally even Nels Dennet took notice of the way Kate was moping about the house and told her sharply to get married and be done with it and leave him to his thoughts.

"What will you do with none of us here?" protested Kate, but his face was such a fierce denial of any dependence that she did not push the matter further.

"It suits me here," said Nels shortly, and the very next morning went into town and hired John and Sarah Low-carp to keep the house and do his cooking. "Now you have no excuse," he said to Kate shortly, "and if these two tire me, I can withhold the wage."

So on May third of that year, Kate became Mrs. John Tilley. Li read the services for the wedding, looking pink and hot like a figure candle in a wax scene, melting from the inside, and a little flustered because Kate had refused to ask her father to give her away. It seemed to him an indecent denial of a relationship which Kate said firmly had never existed. "He wouldn't like it," she said, and when Li attempted to broach the subject himself Nels fixed him with an insulted stare and walked away before he could finish.

Kate always said Li read a beautiful wedding, with that sense of holiness peculiar to one who has never been in love and will not ever be. They held the ceremony at a small church nearby and only the family came—Nels, who had of his own accord unearthed a black silk jacket from some-where, and Alice, resplendent in a new frock and looking as if she might have wept if she had not been Alice—and the regular pastor, who had never seen Mr. Dennet within the church walls before and was terribly nervous, as if the man might suddenly take it into his head to break up the furniture.

I do not know what life was like for Grandfather Nels in those first years after Kate was gone. Alice came to visit him at first, but the strain between them was too great, and after a while she contented herself with an occasional letter and almost never went to Three Oaks.

After a rare trip home, her letters were always long and rambling, filled with sprawling but somehow jerky sentences: "Father is, I suppose, as well as he ever was. Although I cannot believe it is good for him to be alone in that old house. He hates his housekeepers; he insists they are thieves and gluttons and bloodsuckers."

And another one: "He is growing old since you left, Kate, although he would never confess that it was so. Once while I was there, he fell while going up the staircase. I was at the foot of the steps, Kate, but I had to just stand there and watch him while he got to his feet again. He turned around and looked at me once, and it was as if he hated me because I saw him fall."

Everything in Columbia, where my mother and father lived, was different from anything Kate had ever known before. There was no silence in this new house, and all her life my mother feared it; she clattered about the rooms noisily, like African bushmen driving off evil spirits. There was a great calling of names in the house, from upstairs and downstairs; and people always seemed to be standing in the front door yelling last-minute directions to someone going out, or screaming delighted greetings to the visitor dismounting at the curb.

Later when Edison made the gramophone, my mother played it incessantly and with great contentment, as if she had fallen on some mechanized libation that left her free for other things.

After his time was up with the congregation at Shiloh Church, Uncle Li came to the Grace pulpit in Columbia, and he was forever in and out of the Tilley home as if he, too, savored the din of life being lived.

There were probably no two men less comfortable with each other than my father and Uncle Li. The two of them made a great jolly effort, especially when Kate was in the room, and always met and parted with much back-banging and shaking of hands, as if this visible touch were the only contact they could manage.

When they were left alone together, they became utterly miserable at once, and would eye each other guiltily, signaling, "It is all my fault, but what shall I say to you?"

The World Outside was their salvation. It seemed almost as if the Great War had been occasioned to help them out of their difficulty and they seized upon it with delighted cluckings. The front room was always resounding with current affairs after that. It was because of Albania and keeping Serbia from the sea, they said; and who could believe the whole world could become involved in a Hapsburg dying (howbeit involuntarily) in Sarajevo? The Schlieffen plan, the Battle of the Marne, Jutland, Churchill and his folly with the Dardanelles—these they mouthed eagerly, like small boys who know the code but can think of no messages to send with it.

It was providential that the Bolsheviks rose in Russia and the United States went into the war just as they were running short of subject matter. And after that there were Wilson's Fourteen Points to toy with, and the whole idea of the League of Nations.

"But if we remove barriers in international trade, it is this country that will be the loser," vowed my father.

And Uncle Li really did not know about this, but he always abandoned trade and turned with enthusiasm to the idea of the League. He took to preaching weekly sermons on beating swords into ploughshares, and on the word of Christ to go into all the world and to every creature. The League was not very popular in Grace Church (which, incidentally, numbered not one sinner or near sinner in the total enrollment), but no one was really disturbed by Uncle Li's suggestions. It was actually a prime function of the Church, they said, to promote in words what was at base impractical. Not that it destroyed the validity of the idea, they hastened to add. But what kind of crazy world would we have, for instance, they asked tolerantly, if everyone really went around abiding by the Sermon on the Mount? And so they went on dropping the customary amounts into the plate at service, saying what a fine sermon it had been, and leaving it all behind them in the vestibule, like rubbers that had the heel out anyway.

Uncle Li was frantic. "Sovereignty," he stormed after reading a newspaper editorial (looking somewhat amusing, for he was not of the proper size for storming), "I give up my sovereignty every day, to city and state and country and God. Why cannot a nation spare a little sovereignty?"

My Aunt Alice was there for that week end and she was

not of Li's persuasion. "Trouble with you," she observed dryly, "is that you've got the League mixed up with the Kingdom of Heaven."

Uncle Li stopped in his pacing and looked at her with an unhappy intensity. "Well, it might be!" he cried. "Don't you see it might be? I don't know. But I know they thought Jesus was just a carpenter!"

This comparison haunted him for years, the feeling that perhaps the whole world had again observed merely some impractical carpentering, and had crucified it almost with nonchalance. He was disappointed about Versailles ("It is either too weak or too strong," he worried, "and nothing will come of it"), but when the United States refused to ratify it at all, he grew completely disheartened.

He came over one night to talk with my father about the guarantee treaty.

"I told you the Senate wouldn't have it," said my father. "How do we dare promise to come in on any future Franco-German war?"

My Uncle Li was very sad that night. "This belongs in a sermon," he said slowly, "but let me show you what I mean. Suppose next door there is a man with gangrene in his legs and I am a skilled doctor. I go over and amputate the sickness off and I do a fine job of the operation. But after that I leave him legless, still lying on the table, and I come home and say he must look after himself now; it is no concern of mine."

"Like most of the examples of preachers," said my father somewhat testily, "that cannot be applied on a large scale."

"It has to be," said my Uncle Li firmly, his face beginning to redden.

And if Kate had not come in at that very moment, they would probably have gotten into a violent quarrel. As it was, the two of them never mastered the art of conversation again, not even about the morning news events. The world changed; they were both equally opposed to the Bolsheviks and the New Deal without concrete reasons and they found no pleasure in perpetual agreement, as each suspected the other of hypocrisy. So they grew farther apart again until it must be said at last that they did not know each other at all and never could have.

I was born in the summer of 1921, that dreadful summer —said my Uncle Li—when the country got hold of all the advantages of Versailles without any of its responsibilities. My birth was a big event in the Dennet family and the letters flew back and forth: How much had I weighed? Did I have the Dennet nose? At what time of day was I born? They were all absurdly full of hope, as though I were not just an ordinary baby but by wishing to be born at all had proved myself already quite unique.

Alice's letter of congratulation was later lost, and with it went much invaluable information on the rearing and discipline of small children, but Mother kept Li's note and often smiled over it later, but with tenderness.

"How happy I am to hear that the young man is to be named Paul," he wrote. "It is a big name for such a small fellow, but I am sure he will find his own ways of living up to it."

I believe Uncle Li had hopes that there would be someday for me my own vision and that it would take me farther and higher than Grace Church in Columbia. He sent a white

Bible to my christening, with my own name embossed in curly gold letters across the cover—John Paul Tilley—and with a list of Scripture references written out in his neat round hand across the flyleaf. These referred to verses which were supposed to supply divine nearness at all the landmarks of life, in moments of great happiness or sadness or need. I remember that for a long time the awareness of this holy list was a special talisman to me, an unused refuge that would care for any situation when called upon, until one afternoon I looked them all up, one after the other, in hurt and astonishment.

I remember some of them still:

Do all things without murmerings and disputings.
The fear of the Lord is the beginning of wisdom.
My help cometh from the Lord which made Heaven and
earth.

I must have been about seven then; I remember running into the living room almost blinded by tears of rage and interrupting Uncle Li and my parents, pushing the Bible out to him and wailing angrily, "But there's nothing there! There's nothing there!"

I remember too the stricken look on Li's face and the way he leaned backwards as if he had been pushed, and later sitting on the arm of his chair, I remember his voice while he talked to me very seriously—Was it sadly? I do not remember that—about something or other.

There was also written in the front of my white Bible a personal inscription from my Uncle Li which I was always to come across guiltily: "For Paul—may you desire earnestly the spiritual stature of your namesake."

I was two years old when Grandfather Nels died. He saw me only once, and that was before I was even old enough to walk. I am told that he would not take me and hold me baby-fashion, but that he only took one arm between thumb and forefinger as if he were measuring the size of it and that he said, "So here you are," thoughtfully, to himself.

After that, my mother says, he paid me no more attention until the visit to Three Oaks was over, and then only to lift a hand and peer at it curiously, as if he doubted human hands began so small.

"He stood in the doorway tall and straight when we left," Kate always remembered. "I could see him until the whole house went out of sight, and if I had not noticed it before I went down the front steps, I would never have guessed that he supported his weight by leaning against the sill."

His illness was sudden and sharp, as if something merciful were due to happen to him at last. Word came suddenly from the Lowcarps, who kept his house, that Nels had fallen in the field and was ill; and there was only time for the one scene I have described before he was dead.

They say that even the undertaker winced when he saw the frown on the dead man's face (Death ought to wipe a man's face clean of the years so that it becomes anonymous and no one minds burying it) and grumbled only that he would do the best he could.

But the end product of all his work turned out to be a rather enigmatic and fearsome grin on the corpse's face, so that no one at the final services felt wholly comfortable; and all went home feeling vaguely that something sacred had been mocked, without knowing more than that.

Uncle Li was there; he wept but once and no one really knew why or for whom, but it was a desperate weeping and would not be comforted.

Alice came and went again silently, as if she were not sure yet what she felt, and later there was a frenzied note from her to Kate, blaming herself for the day when Nels had fallen on the stairs and she had been there to see it. "On that day," she wrote, "he hated me simply for having eyes."

My mother did not cry. She says that throughout the funeral she was ashamed and embarrassed that they should do this thing, make a public show of him now that he was beyond stopping it all. I think she half expected he might rise up from his cushions in terrible rage, and, shaking off the blossoms, stamp out through the assembly without so much as a nod.

They buried him in the family plot. Li would not read these rites; he stood away from the grave without word or expression and seemed to draw up tight into himself so that when they left the plot and walked across the hill he seemed three inches shorter, as though some great hand had fallen upon him and flattened him out a little. It was Kate who insisted that the grave should be dug over to one side and apart from Isadora's, where no shadow of the willow tree might fall across it; and she was never able to say why she felt this must be done.

In that fanciful fourteenth summer when I was going to write it all down, it seemed to me I had come upon the perfect climax to it all, and I remember asking her if the willow tree had lived after that.

She looked at me strangely. "That's funny, your thinking of that, Paul. Oh yes, it lived and grew and finally shaded everything. Whatever made you ask?"

I remember I was terribly disappointed.

Serpents and Doves

MISS PAULA knew how much the Old Man depended on her. He could do nothing for himself any more except go to the bathroom, and this his body managed only under protest; so that one could hear him puffing and panting down the hall and dragging his feet as if they were a dead weight to him.

"You can answer your own calls of nature," Miss Paula had insisted to the Old Man. "I'm no nurse. It would be different if I was a nurse."

And so the Old Man would lie in agony on his bed, holding back the need to relieve himself for as long as he could, until finally with a moan of defeat he would be off on his laborious journey to the bathroom, sometimes dribbling a bit in the hall.

"He's just like a year-old child," Miss Paula would say, shaking her broad head grimly. "Just like a child."

The Old Man, who lived next door to Miss Paula on the third floor, had moved into the Turner Rooming House several years ago. This was before arthritis had caught him firmly by the limbs and wrenched them all angrily from place. He was only limping a little then—a sparse old man who was retired from a job he never talked about into a bewildering emptiness. In the first days, he used to come around to all the other tenants asking if he might repair something for them, and they had kindly given him their least complex appliances and kitchen gadgets. He had been happy with these small tasks for days on end, prolonging each job as if it were the vital one that separated him from the realization of uselessness.

They soon discovered that the Old Man could whittle too. He showed a skill with his knife that could only have come from many hours of patient practice, which led Miss Paula to believe he had enjoyed an inactive youth and was now being punished for idleness. For a time after he moved into the rooming house, the children of the neighborhood collected wooden thread spools from their mothers, and if the wood was soft enough the Old Man would turn each into a painstaking replica of the child's face. All of it would be there—the wide eyes and the awed mouth and the straight, sweet hair of little girls.

But all of these things were before his fingers drew in and puckered up like twigs on a dying tree, until screw drivers and whittling knives fell uselessly out of his hands to where he could not reach them; and he would stare down at the fallen tools, wearing an old sad face.

The Old Man (Mr. Jonathan Sykes, it said on his pension check) was a native of the South, where he had worked as a foreman for a chaingang. This he hid within himself and told to no one, for when he thought of it even now a tide of shame rose in him and he longed to have the years back again. He could remember days and days under the summer sun, cradling his shotgun across brown arms (strong then and straight) and watching the men work, quietly, without the talk that is the salvation of ordinary laborers. He had worn a pistol then too, tucked in a wide black belt, and in those younger days he had possessed a big voice that commanded respect among his charges. (It had left him since; he felt as if some old and trusted dog had slunk off in the night and deserted him.) With the passage of years his face had changed, too. All the sharp tanned features had faded and blurred like stones worn down by weather or running streams, until now when the Old Man put up his fingers it was just another tired face, sick and nondescript. Sometimes he would wake in the dark to touch his face and would be terrified that it was no longer his own; there was something anonymous about it now, as if in growing old he had passed beyond identity.

Before the Old Man grew sick, he would talk at great length to the neighborhood boys and girls while he made their faces in wood; he would tell them fondly about the South—about how the flowering wisteria hung purple around back porches, and the way hot weather made the roads look wet ahead of a traveler, and how in the swampy regions the Spanish moss dripped off the trees like the dead hair of beautiful women. He would talk about summertime and red slabs of watermelons burst open in the furrows, and about cotton fields that stretched whitely for flat miles under the sunshine. Then he would grow deeply homesick and tell them about the Southern mountains—the deep blue Appalachians with their singing longleaf pine trees, and the way daylight came and went in the Blue Ridge. According to the Old Man, there was nothing else like the dawns and dusks of the Southern mountain country, where the shadows appeared from nowhere and seemed suddenly so deep you could swim in them.

The Old Man told the children all this about the South, but he never told them he had guarded prisoners for a living. He never mentioned the miles of highway he had seen come up and go down, or the heavy shotgun and the pistol that was stuck down in his belt. They would have found this exciting, whereas they grew sometimes a little restless under his talk of hills and sun and swampland. But that was all the Old Man would talk about. He never told them about the other.

Miss Paula always said if he loved the South so much, he ought to go back to it and leave the care of him to rightful relatives. Miss Paula said she had enough to do without always running whenever the Old Man lifted his little finger. Miss Paula said, however, that she had always been a Christian woman who put herself out for other people.

None of them knew exactly why the Old Man had ever left his beloved Southland to come here. One day he had appeared before the Turner Rooming House (a renovated old brownstone) and had talked to Callie Turner about indefinite lodging. And so he had moved in on the third floor, for Callie made her living by rooming and boarding, and every month when his pension came he paid for the room and his food, regular as clockwork, Callie said.

In his first days at the rooming house with the repairing and wood carving and storytelling, the Old Man was happy. He walked each day to the Y.M.C.A. park playground, and sat in some sheltered spot to watch the birds. But in the wintertime these walks had served only to make him sad;

he would come home slowly as if the leaden skies and the bent bare trees were his own personal tragedy, and he would remark to Callie Turner, "No birds today," as if this had inspired in him the most profound sort of grief.

Yet he would be childishly delighted whenever the scrawny winter sparrows were there; their very presence struck him as miraculous, and on those days he would come in reddened and brisk and smiling, and seeming younger than he was.

"Hardy little fellows, those sparrows," he would exclaim proudly, and save his roll from dinner to crumble on the windowsill.

It may have been that these walks, sometimes in rain or bitter cold or through the tanginess of falling snow, hastened and intensified his illness; certainly it hit him sharply in the fall and when the next April came he was almost constantly in bed, a little drawn-up twig of a man who could not see the birds winging back now from the Southland.

That was when Miss Paula began to take care of him.

Although the Old Man was a newcomer to Callie Turner's boarding house, Miss Paula had been there for no one knew how long. One had a feeling that she had been built into the house when the workmen were constructing it, and had never bothered to go out again.

There was a darkness about Miss Paula. It was hard to describe the thing that made one apprehensive about her, but it was something about the eyes. They were a tired brown that just stopped short of going into hazel, but somehow no light stirred in them so that one had the impression dull marbles were set, rather inexpertly, into her ample skull.

She was a big woman—a stocky, compressed woman on tree-stump legs—with streaked black hair and the shadow of a mustache on her upper lip. She dressed always the same, a polka-dot crepe in winter and a dotted swiss for hot weather, blue and white, and changeless.

And although no one at Callie Turner's knew much about the Old Man except that he was a Southerner and retired, it was impossible to be unaware of Miss Paula's origins.

"I don't believe in being too silent," Miss Paula always said, snapping her broad face forward aggressively. "It's the sign of a bad conscience."

Miss Paula had, evidently, a very excellent conscience, for she talked of her past glibly. She was a widow; her husband had mined coal in West Virginia and ushered at the Baptist Church on alternate Sundays, until one day several tons of earth and rock fell in upon him and put an end to that. The mining company had paid a handsome insurance for his demise, however, and Miss Paula would never have to turn a hand the rest of her life. That's what she always said, for the rest of her life she wouldn't have to turn a hand. Not that this made up for losing him, she always added, almost as an afterthought.

There had been one son, Ernest, but no one knew what had finally become of him, not even Miss Paula. He had always been a dutiful boy, had originally planned to marry and settle in West Virginia and open a hardware store, as soon as his mother would lend him the necessary money out of his father's insurance. But the years dragged by and there was always some perfectly logical reason why the hardware store must wait. So finally when Ernest was thirty-eight, and the girl had long since married someone else and

136

there were three other hardware stores prospering in town, he had walked quietly out of the house one night and simply not come back. Miss Paula said it all went to show how ungrateful one's own flesh and blood could be.

"Right then I saw he'd never wanted anything but money," said Miss Paula. "It was a good thing I knew it when I did. I might of give him the money for his business without ever finding it out." Here she would nod her head sharply, so that something snapped faintly in her fleshy neck.

Once a year Miss Paula received a Christmas card from the ungrateful Ernest, not bearing a return address and having various postmarks—San Francisco, Cleveland, Chicago. This had led her to believe that Ernest (A Boy Who Would Desert His Mother Would Do Anything) was now touring the country, selling obscene literature. Miss Paula had prevailed upon Callie Turner to end the supper blessings always with "And forgive Ernest." But whether this had any effect no one could say. Anyway, it was doubtful whether anyone at the supper table really put his heart into it.

The only reason Miss Paula was chosen to care for the Old Man after he grew steadily more helpless was a geographical one; her room was next to his and she was always at home. At first the Old Man had merely asked her to run a few errands for him—bring in a newspaper or carry up his meals and for these services he paid her out of his monthly check. But eventually Miss Paula was doing almost everything for him, and finally he just turned the check over to her, so that she paid Callie Turner and the laundryman and deducted her own fee.

The Old Man was a little afraid of Miss Paula. It was

nothing she did or said, but it lay in a look that crossed her broad face sometimes when she watched him, a look that was neither kindness nor contempt, but a sort of studied indifference. It gave him the same feeling as when he woke in the darkness and found his own face had grown strange to him; he would watch Miss Paula cautiously, doubting that he was an individual any more and almost doubting his own existence. That was the way Miss Paula was—she reduced one to a nonentity by a single glance and one was never completely sure again that it made any difference if he were alive or dead.

Yet in spite of himself, the Old Man would talk to Miss Paula. As he grew weaker he had a compulsion to talk, as if this were but another symptom of the encroaching disease which was upon him. At first his talk was aimless—it dealt with the beauty of home and the childhood memories which seemed so vivid now; but gradually the Old Man became aware that he was not so much talking about these things as he was avoiding talk about something else. After that it was an agonizing battle for him—to talk above and below and around the one thing he wanted desperately to tell someone. Someone, yes (he thought), but not Miss Paula.

Now and again it struck the Old Man that Miss Paula took a pleasure in his illness, and this filled him with terrible dread. There was something about the way she tended his wants (slowly, as if she were prolonging something) that gave him the feeling she savored his helplessness and that it filled to brimming some dark chasm within her. He would watch her when she brought his food, watch the deliberation of her movements and the way a slight smile flicked her mouth when she saw his hunger and impatience.

Then that, too, became a silent battle for the Old Man; he would fight off the impulse to reveal to her the slightest need because it made him naked before her in a way he did not understand.

Sometimes he could fight off the need to talk to Miss Paula or to make some request of her by leaving her firmly rooted in the present while he went back to a set of old memories she could not possibly know about. He would burrow underneath the years like a mole and come up unexpectedly into some bright blue day when he was sixteen and in the prime of youth. It was startling to come upon himself that way; it was so much like spying on a stranger that he grew ashamed to even remember that other person in those other days.

That was how he knew he was truly old, because he had no real desire to become again what he had been. It was as though youth were a fever in which he had once known exciting deliriums, but now he was cured and could not recall it with desire.

The other memory—the bad one—came to him differently, like a live thing, like a cat worrying a mouse; and pawed him this way and that without ever quite permitting him to be shut of it. Then he would talk to Miss Paula again, almost coming out with the whole thing.

"Self-pity is a privilege," the Old Man would say, and he said it over and over as if it were an epigram he had learned tediously at school and only recalled in later, older years, when the words came back to him with a pungency he could taste on his tongue.

"A privilege," and he would be off into a deep spell of musing across which, sooner or later, the Little Nigger moved and the shot was fired. That would end it; he would start up as from an agony of dreams and begin feverishly to enumerate to Miss Paula the vices and virtues of the climate, painting over that other scene with hurried clumsy splashes.

It might have long since passed out of him like waste from an experience already digested if the Little Nigger himself had been different—if he had been bold or arrogant or even sullen. But the Little Nigger was a slow, soft-spoken man, a little man who had shrunk up into his clothes and left sleeves and trousers dangling absurdly, a man whose life had been evenly divided between the pleasures of food and sleep and music before he did murder.

(Here the Old Man would pass a dazed hand across his brow. Was there ever a less likely murderer than the Little Nigger, who at rare rest periods would laze fingers across the guitar strings and hum softly to himself, or would nod to the Old Man as they started out in the prison truck, deferentially, like an employee?)

Yet it had happened. One day the Little Nigger had been resting in the shade in his back yard after chopping a few sticks of stove wood, when the wife had come to the back screen and begun her customary railing at him. The wife believed that the absence of work was the guarantee of the presence of evil and why she had ever married the Little Nigger eleven years before no one could ever say.

However it was, that particular day was the day of last straws and worms turning, for the Little Nigger had clambered to his feet and gone to the door saying over and over again mildly, "Here now, here now," and when this had no effect he had abruptly brought the ax down through the rusted old screen where it divided her head neatly, halfway to the shoulder. (The wife had, in her industriousness, sharpened it to a razor edge only the morning before.)

There she had lain, blood coursing over the two halves of her face and washing redly into the wide and unbelieving eyes. And the Little Nigger had looked at her for a few minutes, somewhat surprised himself, and had finally shuffled into town with the bloody ax in one hand and presented himself to the sheriff.

(He had thought of the possibility of running away, of course, but it seemed a tiresome thing to undertake in July, and the Little Nigger had a fear of being hunted by bloodhounds, like a rabbit or a renegade dog.)

And having considered these things he put the ax (it dripped a little onto his back) across one sparse shoulder and walked down the road toward town, not forgetting to pick up his guitar from the porch as something to while the waiting past.

That was how the Little Nigger had come to be in prison and to work under the Old Man and to become, eventually, almost a friend of his.

Everybody liked the Little Nigger, his songs and his easy-going ways and the smile he had (half apologetic) and his kindness. For he *was* kind, and in those days the Old Man (who was not old then) was bothered by this inconsistency in human beings. It seemed that for whatever God there was to maintain any sort of orderliness in the universe, a man ought to be all good or all bad, and a deed be classed as one or the other, without these half-and-halfs like the Little Nigger was.

Still, the Little Nigger, who on the one hand could cleave his wife's skull without a qualm and on the other could be considered, and rightly, a kind man, was liked by them all, including the Old Man himself.

Once the Old Man saw what he thought was a parody of the Little Nigger's crime. It happened one hot afternoon when they had stopped work briefly to hand a water jug around, and a fly was buzzing about an open sore on the Little Nigger's hand. Abruptly he brought both hands together, ignoring the impact against his wound, and a squash of fly had toppled out upon the road.

One of the other men said smiling, "I never knowed you to kill a fly before."

And the Little Nigger, ducking his head and grinning, had answered softly, "It has to bother me considerable."

That's how it was, thought the Old Man, listening. That's how he came to do it.

The Little Nigger was a teller of jokes, and because laughter was often more vital and precious to those men than food, he became a kind of king. They were never very funny, those jokes; it was a gentle, skinny kind of humor like the Little Nigger himself.

"Mistah Sykes, you hear about the man went crazy working in the apple business?"

"No, what was that?"

"Seems he was supposed to pick out the big apples from the little apples. Went plumb crazy." (Here the Little Nigger would purse his lips and look very clever and pleased with himself, and turn his eyeballs up until one felt he must be examining his own forehead.

"Seems he couldn't face making all them decisions," he

would finish happily. Then they would laugh, all of them—the jailor and the jailed.

Such moments as these were the few times the Old Man did not feel ashamed before the men. Sometimes when he stood by in the sun and watched the bending backs and the glistening faces, he would be struck by a terrible sense of wrong, as if he ought wordlessly to stand his gun against some tree and step into line beside them. Times like these he would be convinced no man had a right to hold a gun over another man; in some inescapable way the guard became then a part of the prisoner and of whatever ugliness he had done. Standing worriedly in the sunglare then, the Old Man would feel himself thief and murderer by his very participation, and he would handle the shotgun nervously, as if it might go off at him out of sheer caprice.

But the Old Man didn't know exactly what else should be done with them; he had a very real feeling that the thief and the murderer should not be welcome in the house where he had stolen or killed; and that the man who ignored the rights of others renounced the right to be accepted among them.

Yet this did not help the wrongness; when he saw that punishment was given as if to an animal or child, the Old Man could not help but wonder if in this men were not being encouraged to be no more than animals or children. So that sometimes it seemed to him he was a sort of cog in a great machine which kept all of mankind to a level, and he was a cog with conscience.

Yes, the Old Man was not old in those days, and he was a worrier and an asker of questions. He hated his job, of

143

course—he went to it no more happily than the men under his care, but he went solely because he feared the presence of power in the hands of another man than himself. So his job was at once for him a participation in the wrongdoing of all men, and an expiation for his part in it. It was very complicated.

Once (the Old Man remembered), they had been working on a quiet stretch of road when a long string of cars had approached; it seemed to hit them as a man that this was not ordinary traffic but some country funeral, and they stopped work in a body to watch it come and pass on the narrow right-of-way: the long black one first, and the stone-faced relatives, and then the flower cars and the last, almost indifferent ones, eager to be done with the service and home again. In that way death had passed silently among them, taking no one this time; but giving an object lesson of his power, and the silent men had watched until the last dust settled on the road ahead.

Something in the Old Man had been nearly wrenched loose that day the funeral passed; it was the one time he was ever to see a whole group of men in quiet acceptance of a common destiny. It was as if he had witnessed something in miniature, a mere replica of the vaster cortege wending its way through the world as a grim reminder to all of them. He had felt very old that day and the gun was heavy, and there was something he shared with the prisoners that had slashed them in an instant to equality.

He thought of telling that to Miss Paula, but then he thought better of it.

She thinks I am only a wearisome old man, he mused, and it pleased him that she did not know his thoughts, or who and what he was; and he felt himself temporarily invulnerable against her smallness.

It was springtime when the Old Man's arthritis grew unbearable and it lessened only slightly during the hot season. Summer was over almost in a flick of sun, and the Old Man was never sure what had gone with it all until he sensed it was seeping away, first noticeable in the mornings and evenings; and it seemed to him that his limbs wrenched themselves and shriveled up for winter.

About the time summer's edge lapped over into fall, there descended upon the city a great dampness, which seeped in everywhere and made the flesh clammy and caused a faint sad smell to rise from blankets and woolen garments. It was, thought the Old Man, an intolerable season. One was both too hot and too cold at the same time, and there was a great deal of putting on and taking off of jackets, and fretful grumblings.

Miss Paula sat in the Old Man's room each afternoon of these oppressive first fall days, knitting placidly in drab-gray wool that gave off a musty smell.

"What are you making?" the Old Man asked once without interest.

She inclined her head patronizingly. "It's for the soldier boys," she said, holding up a hoodlike affair that slipped over all the head like a giant sock, with a slit cut out for eyes. The Old Man did not like it, picturing a whole platoon of boys in line with drab-gray turtle's heads. "It's a bad thing, the war," said Miss Paula, leaning back in her chair and cupping hands over a copious stomach.

"Of course it is," said the Old Man almost angrily.

Miss Paula's humanitarianism always struck him as bordering on obscenity, though he could not say why.

"Cold some of them places, too," said Miss Paula, beginning to click the long cruel needles again. "Boys always losing hands and feet from frostbite." She looked very comfortable and superior, as though she might have abated winter by flipping some secret switch, but rather thought it served them right for leaving their gloves at home.

The Old Man said thoughtfully, "Miss Paula, you indulge yourself," and when she looked at him questioningly (but without real curiosity, he thought) he added, "You take a terrible luxury." He felt very pleased with himself, despite the sure knowledge that Miss Paula would repeat all this as further evidence of his mental decline. It seemed to the Old Man that he had come upon the great secret about Miss Paula, that she fed like carrion on other people's pain, indulging her appetite almost daintily, like a connoisseur. He started at this. I must not antagonize her, he thought. I must be careful. I am in her hands.

In that fall season, it seemed to the Old Man that there was hardly a true passage of days, only the wetness against his window was alternately light and dark, and sometimes the wind was trapped between houses where it cried softly. He took a strange pleasure in all of this ugliness, the perverse pleasure of age, he supposed, that dwelt with kinship on all declining things, even the tired year.

Sometimes as he lay abed (he could see nothing from his bed but four small squares of sky, made wavery by the rain) the Old Man grew sick for home, remembering how vivid those hillsides would be in September and how the quick sharp showers there passed off into sunlight, leaving the color still showing through a wet shine. Of these things he talked sometimes to Miss Paula: how with the passing of August a slow blue haze settled on everything, and the early morning air came down a man's throat like a knife, and how almost overnight the trees blazed into color, as if all of them had waited for strange prearranged signals.

Once, breaking off in the midst of his ramblings, the Old Man had said shortly, "If I speak of these things to you, it is only because I must," peering at Miss Paula from under lowered brows. She had shrugged it off without even a curious glance (she'd always been too easygoing, she reflected), but the Old Man wished he had not spoken. It would be better to give her nothing, he thought, to hold oneself inviolate.

And although he tried this too, he found Miss Paula to be a woman of deep cunning. He would believe her absorbed in her endless knitting and purling and binding off, and then she would catch him unawares with a question, "What were you looking so thoughtful about just now?"

Then the Old Man would begin feverishly to pull his privacy about him like a tattered garment. "Nothing really," he would sputter hastily. "Absolutely unimportant. Nothing at all." And it seemed to him her eyes glittered, as if she scented prey.

Even within himself, the Old Man repeated these same unconvincing denials. "Nothing really. Absolutely unimportant." Sometimes this process was very nearly consummated, and he would grow sure of it and be close to swaggering. Why have I wasted so much thought on one incident? he would rage at himself. Of what importance was the one life, taken as it was not in malice but in error?

At such times he would recall the Little Nigger with bitterness. "You who were less than nothing have robbed me," he would accuse him angrily. "I owe you nothing."

But underneath his bravado he would recall the Little Nigger and the jokes and the tipping of the hat in the mornings, and he knew his own lying. It seemed to him then that his deed was more evil than the earlier ax-killing of the nagging wife; a man who willed harm had at least the solace of intent, he thought. Then he would be plunged into deeper anger at himself because this associated solace with slumbering conscience. I am an old man, he would reflect bitterly, and I have developed self-deception to an art.

It would often strike the Old Man as the most vicious of ironies that he had once stood guard over the Punished, that he had himself been fully absolved of guilt, and that while the prisoners could feel at least a tangible propitiation, in himself the punishment went on without abatement, and was like a hunger that would not be fed.

Some men, thought the Old Man, have a capacity for punishment and into some it cannot penetrate at all. Miss Paula for instance; one might shut her into prison for a thousand years, and she would never be punished because it was not in the realm of her experience. And for days after he thought of this the Old Man hated Miss Paula bitterly, so great was his envy.

Then he thought suddenly of Jesus of Nazareth and it seemed to him that for an instant he brushed against something quite vast, and he drew back, not sure what he had discovered. But after that he could look on Miss Paula without any envy, and he knew with finality that he and she were in opposite camps, each merely spying on a city that was alien and strange—and hence, terrible.

Perhaps it was the eternal dampness or only that he was old and lay abed so much, but sometime during the long autumn there began a long slow cough; it would start somewhere deep in the Old Man's body and rake out, tugging at breath and strength and throat, and leaving him all used up and gone out of himself. At first the intervals were long between, but they shortened until the coughs overlapped and seemed to be one continuous thing and the Old Man's temperature began to rise.

"I'm sick," said the Old Man huskily to Miss Paula, noting how rapid his breathing was so that his chest seemed to be full of small birds.

Miss Paula looked at him (he thought) without compassion, and with a superb irrelevance he reflected that everyone was in debt except Miss Paula, who owed nobody anything.

"It's just a cold," said Miss Paula. "It'll go away when the rain does."

After this he avoided any mention of his illness for days, not wanting to give himself over to her. But finally his misery was too great to care, and he said with what he hoped was sternness, "I must have a physician."

She very nearly shrugged, and yet she went to call for one, as though this were not important enough to argue about. Later the sick man wondered that he had used the old-fashioned term "physician"; there was something about it that precluded a cure; it seemed to him a form of acceptance.

It was pneumonia, said Doctor Lacken, a sparse young man with a voice as weary as his limp mustache. "Congestion of the lungs," he added, not ever really looking at the Old Man, but fixing his eyes on some undetermined spot in the chin, as if he saw some cancer there but did not want to make an issue of it. He carried in one hand a bag which had once been tan, but now assumed some indeterminate shade made up of splotches of medicine and dirt and salve. Into this he reached for some capsules to lower the fever and a bottle for the cough and put into the Old Man's arm a shot of something that burned a little.

"Keep him quiet," he said to Miss Paula, closing the bag with a click and rising to his feet. "Liquids and juices."

A rage rose in the Old Man that he was being so much ignored, and he asked irritably, "Am I going to die then?"

"Don't think of that," said the doctor, attending to the buttons on his overcoat. "I'll be back tomorrow."

It was in this fashion the Old Man knew he would not recover from the pneumonia, by the way he was so impersonally touched and medicated and talked about. To be sick, he thought with anger, is to be already nearly dead, as if one were suspended somewhere off above the poor tired body waiting for the last connecting thread to go. And he hated the Doctor and Miss Paula because they were not troubled by this knowledge, and neither was fighting to draw him back.

During the next days after the doctor's visit, the Old Man tried to get everything in order for dying, as if he were laying the coppers against his own eyes and then folding the blue-veined hands, just so, across the chest.

Something must be done about the Little Nigger, he

thought, and tried to determine what propitiation he could make on this bed and in this room. I should have done it before, he thought angrily. And he took a sharp hatred for clocks and would have none in his room, because of all the times they had gone around before and how few they would go around for him hence. In those days he despised his ineffectuality.

But there were other days, almost blessed now, when a great weariness put him to sleep and he was spared from thinking. Sometimes he dreamed, usually of vast mechanisms which seemed to be roaring in his ears, and once he relived painfully the day he did a small boy's theft (only a few marbles taken) with remorse grown sharper in perspective, and he thought later, This is what it means, to account for all of it.

He was terrified that at the last he would lose his senses, and he began as discipline a very frustrating mental game. He would see how much he could remember of his sixth year, or his twentieth, or his thirty-third, and the vagueness of it all depressed him terribly. Where has it all gone? he wondered, and he threshed in the covers as if to stir up stagnant memories.

The dream came to him on the first day of November, just before twilight. It wasn't a dream really; it was simply a re-examination in which everything stood out vividly, sun and shade and faces and the undulating heat waves coming off the asphalt. He started when he came across himself (That man? That was me?) leaning against a tree watching, the face neither kind nor cruel but holding a great neutrality, as is the way of judges and hangmen and guards. The prisoners were working ahead of him silently (some men sing as they work but not these; they only sing going and coming, he thought) and sometimes one of them would call to him (for he was a lenient man):

"Stop for a drink of water?"

"Stone in my shoe."

"Leg bad again."

He never questioned any of the excuses they gave him for moving off and sitting down a bit. Let them have the pride of lying to me, he thought.

Then the Little Nigger stepped out without calling, moved over, walked toward the underbrush; it happened so quickly—he had been in line and then suddenly he was moving away. The Old Man stood taller and called to him (had it been loud enough?) and then cried halt a time or two, and then the gun went off.

That was always the way it seemed to him later, that the gun had abruptly gone off in his arms, without reason. The sound of it made him jump with sickening fear and all the time he watched the Little Nigger, watched him turn around, half-startled, as if a hand had fallen on his shoulder, and then begin to go down (so slowly; it took an eternity for him to fall) and then crumple utterly, so that a heap of clothing lay darkly in the grass—no more—only the limp sleeves and flaccid trouser-legs of the suddenly dead.

After that there was the Silence.

Nothing stirred for miles on either side, the men stood motionless, and up above his head not one leaf touched any other leaf for a long moment before he began to run. "Carson," he called hoarsely (it was the only time he ever called the Little Nigger by name, as if he had saved it for a time when it might be needed) but nothing answered; he was the only thing in the whole world that was moving and each step against the earth was an eternity between, until a year or so later he stood above the crumpled bit of clothing in the grass and said the name again, softly this time, the way one speaks to a sleeper he does not want to startle.

Somewhere the gears meshed and the universe came groggily back into motion; he heard the wind begin and saw dimly a bird go by, and heard the others coming, staring, forming an awed cluster about him, not saying anything. Later he wondered that no one ran for freedom, that no one took the gun from where it had dropped from nerveless fingers; but that all of them stood there, so that from where he knelt he saw thin legs and dusty hands hanging down helplessly, and was aware of men breathing.

It was said later that the Little Nigger had only been going aside to piss in the brush, and that he chose the place not from modesty but because he had heard there a mocking bird; and unlikely as it seemed, the Old Man knew with finality that it was true. He made his report; officials agreed he had been given sufficient justification for the deed, but nothing helped. He could do the work no longer and he became a so-called guard in the prison and would not carry arms.

There existed among the other prisoners a firm sympathy for him; they were careful never to mention the Little Nigger in his presence and tried by every means to show that they thought him harmless and kind. But he was never convinced.

Also he never again trusted the inanimate, remembering that the gun had leaped in his grasp like a live thing. He had a feeling afterwards that all objects were imbued with a nearly tangible urge to fulfill their function, and he mistrusted tools and gadgets and was watchful, and only repaired them as a means of self-defense.

All of this was in the dream the Old Man had on the first of November, even the eternal prison grayness and the color and sound and grass of that very day, and the exact weight and feel and texture of the gun he had been holding. The Old Man stirred and moaned helplessly in his sleep; and Miss Paula leaned forward to watch him curiously for awhile, but when he spoke nothing she tired of it, and went out to buy a newspaper.

It was sometime later that he woke to discover the young man sitting on the foot of his bed, regarding him with a quizzical expression.

"Well, you've been long enough about it," said the stranger. "Sleep well?"

"No," returned the Old Man shortly, still shaken from the dream and trying to remember if this was a doctor or a visitor and whether or not he had been there before the nap. He asked finally, "Who are you anyway?"

The young man directed eyes skyward. "Lord," he said wearily. "Here we go again. It's always the same. I don't know why I don't throw the whole thing over. The same old thing every time."

By now the Old Man was completely awake and completely baffled; the echoes of the gunshot slipped away and he put the dream aside for this new thing. "I don't know you," he said frowning. "No, I'm sure I don't know you."

"Lord," said the strange young man. Then he turned to the Old Man and shook his head. "Look again. You sure?"

The Old Man examined him critically. He found there was something familiar about his visitor, something in the eyes and the way the eyebrows turned, something in the flick of his mouth and the cut of his chin and the way he sat. He closed his eyes tightly and then opened them again and looked and tried to remember.

"It's funny," said the Old Man slowly, "but it seems to me I ought to know you. It seems I ought to know you from some place else."

"Here we go," said the visitor, looking up again. "Same old thing."

Something clicked sharply into place; it was as if his eyes came into a sudden focus so that details he had missed before were etched sharply and suddenly into place and the suddenness of knowledge made him reel. The Old Man cried, "Why, you look like . . . why, you look like me!"

The visitor stood up from the bed, smiling amiably; and walked back and forth for the Old Man to see him, posing and gesturing like a professional model. "Same carriage, same gait," he remarked glibly and without interest. "Similar bone structure, facial expression. Slight discrepancy in age because it wouldn't do for me to be affected by the processes of disintegration. Otherwise a ringer, wouldn't you say so?"

The Old Man was stunned. It was a stupefying experience, to say the least, to discover a twin hovering at one's sickbed. It was as if life could not wait for him to be through with it, but while he slept had stolen his face and voice and manner and stamped them into other flesh for mockery. The Old Man closed his eyes again, expecting the apparition to go away, but when he looked another time it was still there, walking about his bedroom and smiling at him. The Old Man glanced apprehensively at the mirror, half-expecting it had shattered when his image tore loose from the glass, and the stranger—seeing his gesture—laughed loudly and slapped his knee. He seemed an uncommonly humorous man.

"No, not from there," he said pleasantly. Then he added, "You're now supposed to believe I am a dream." (The Old Man started visibly, for he had just been recalling that other dream, how real it had been, everything coming in sequence and all the details right.) "And then I let you touch me," the Stranger went on, "and make some joke about Doubting Thomas which is really monstrously funny when you think about it, and after awhile we get around to it. We quit playing around after a little while."

The Old Man felt the chilliness of fear stealing through him; it began at the base of his neck and sifted through his whole body as silently as smoke, and when it was over he was quite cold. "Who are you then?" he managed to say.

The eyes again went upward in resignation. "Lord," sighed the stranger. Then he sat down on the bed again and leaned forward like someone preparing to confide. "I always have to say it, don't I? Everybody waits for me to tell my name and then we have to go through the business of not believing it and all over the matter of whether or not I'm just another dream. What a tiresome business. You still want to know who I am?"

The Old Man watched him silently.

"Very well," said the stranger in some irritation. "If we have to do it that way. I'm the Devil." (The Old Man jerked his head at this and his visitor leaned forward and patted him solicitously on the chest, smiling to reassure him.) "Yes, I really am the Devil. Now can we dispense with all this other business?"

Dimly the Old Man was beginning to understand and some of the first coldness ebbed away; he felt his blood begin to flow again, slowly at first, then with momentum. He had no intention of doubting his visitor's word as to identity; it remained only to discover what he was doing there and why he was disguised as the Old Man himself. "I'm dead, then?"

The Devil shook his head. "No, not yet," he answered calmly. He consulted his watch. "We've a little time yet. I suspect you'd like to talk a little. They usually want to tell me things." He flipped out a deck of cards hopefully. "Or we could pass the time in any sociable game, though I'm not a gambling man. Something light and pleasant?"

"What kind of things?" asked the Old Man with interest, going back to the former question. He felt a surge of well-being and alertness; as a matter of fact he felt better than he had for days.

Looking disappointed, the Devil replaced the deck in his suit. "Reasons," he said. "I get mostly unsolicited reasons and excuses; everybody wants to tell me why everything wasn't more successful than it was."

"I don't see why people talk about things like that to you."

The Devil shook his head. "You wouldn't think so, would you? They seem to think I'm a court of last appeal. Then too, most of them have the misconception that I've come for them, and they set to work to talk me out of it."

"And haven't you come for them?"

He shook his head. "Not at all. This is the only time, for instance, that you and I will ever meet. It's a tiresome business really; sometimes I've grown quite fond of this or that one, and it's sad to have everything done with." He frowned briefly at this and then shrugged and resumed his perpetual half-smile.

Involuntarily the Old Man smiled too. "I had not thought," he said, "that fondness would be one of your stronger traits."

The Devil looked at him thoughtfully before he asked, "It's still not come home to you, has it? The whole significance of my face."

The Old Man thought a minute. Then he said, "You mean there's more than just looking like me . . ." (a nod of encouragement) . . . "You are like me in other ways?"

He nodded again. "Actually we two are inseparable," he said. "In this particular guise, I have no existence apart from you." And to prove his point he related the events of the day Jonathan Sikes was born, and what had happened on a winter's day in the third grade. "I have a perfect memory where mortal lives are concerned," he explained somewhat vainly, "because time is all of a piece to me."

The Old Man leaned back against the pillow and closed his eyes. "It's nothing like I thought," he mused, half to himself. The Devil made no answer to this and the silence in the room seemed to have an audible ebb and flow, like a mammoth sea, until he lifted tired lids again. He knew then that he was weaker than before and his sense of well-being was an illusion which came and went. "Tell me then," he asked curiously, "what is there after this?"

The Devil shrugged his shoulders without much interest

in the subject. "Nothing, I suppose. No one ever emerges again that I have seen. It just seems to all come to a stop and then there isn't anything."

The Old Man leaned forward, visibly excited now, and feeling as though he might take the Devil by the shoulders and shake him viciously. "But you," he said, his voice straining with hope, "you must know. You are supposed to know these things."

The Devil frowned. "How shall I describe it to you?" Then he seemed to hit upon something. "Let's see: I have not really been outside the realm of life. I move in it just as you do." Then, seeing the Old Man's surprise, he squinted thoughtfully and went on. "You might say human lives are like stepping stones. I go from one to the other, but there is never a moment when I am off and outside the plane of life and can look down on it from something not temporal." Finishing this thought he seemed to be relieved at being done with it, and took out a pouch of colored stones and began to play with them aimlessly. "Worthless of course," he remarked in an aside to the Old Man, "but pretty things, wouldn't you say?"

The Old Man was incredulous. "But if you are so bound up with us, then you are mortal too!"

For a minute the Devil seemed shocked and startled; the stones wavered in his fingers and seemed about to fall. He moved to protest and then nodded ruefully, putting them away. "A little impertinent of you to say so, though," he observed. "You seem to live until you wear out your own body, so I suppose I shall only live until I wear out the total flesh of man. Seems reasonable." He frowned. "I've always thought, however," he added, "that my own meditations

159

on immortality must mean I was capable . . ." He broke off, and the Old Man could not help but smile.

"That was one of our arguments too," said the Old Man.

There was another silence in which the Devil paced about the room, his face indicating that he felt himself cheated of something. The Old Man hardly noticed him, he was so deep in thought, rising only to the surface now and then to marvel at his own detachment.

"Heaven and Hell," he mused half to himself. "All over, and I never noticed."

"You notice it now, don't you?" snapped the Devil. He seemed all of a sudden in a bad humor.

"Oh, hush now," the Old Man chided. "You've been told nothing worse than what you've said to all of us. Be a man about it." (At this the Devil fixed him with a bitter stare, and the Old Man sought for some more apt phrasing.) "Inevitability," added the Old Man weakly.

"It's just that it goes against all tradition," said the Devil irritably. The Old Man started to bring up the tradition of Heaven and Hell but never succeeded in doing more than getting his mouth set for speech. "It flaunts all of history." Suddenly the Devil's face brightened. "I wonder if it's flaunt or flout. I had an old crank of a grammarian once and he was always getting worked up about things like that. Used to write letters to the London *Times* about editorial errors." He turned conversationally to the Old Man, who marveled at how quickly he could dismiss consternation. "I never quite got over that grammarian," he added. "Fellow was correcting my word usage right to the last. Never could remember the differences though."

"In some things you seem to have a short memory," observed the Old Man.

"What? Oh. Yes, I suppose that's one of my qualities, isn't it? It's not possible to have conscience unless you have a good personal memory."

The Old Man thought about that without saying anything and during this time the Devil took a slim cigar, a cheroot really, out of a pocket and bit the end off, daintily, like a weasel.

"You're not really a fallen angel then?" asked the Old Man after a bit.

The Devil frowned. "I suppose not," he said. "At least I don't remember anything of the kind." He shrugged his shoulders slightly and watching him the Old Man suddenly felt tired and a shadow lingered in front of both his eyes for an instant and gradually dispersed. He rubbed a hand across them. "I feel a little strange," said the Old Man.

Immediately the Devil snatched out his watch (ebony and silver it was, and on a heavy silver chain) and consulted it thoughtfully. "One might say," he began pleasantly, "that I am tiring you to death." And then— catching the wince—he added, "Just a joke, you understand. I really hate to lose you, you know. It means starting all over again for me."

The Old Man shook his head in bewilderment. "I don't understand you really," he said.

The Devil nodded briskly. "Trouble is, you expected a red suit and gleeful malice. Some good in the worst of us," he quipped glibly. "I really doubt that anything can be all of one or the other, with conditions constantly chang-

161

ing." (He puffed hard on the cheroot, gave off a whirl of smoke.) "Take God, for instance," said the Devil. "Personally I've always suspected he had a runny nose."

The Old Man was genuinely shocked. "But that's blasphemous!"

The Devil dismissed his charge grandly. "All in character, all in character," he said, waving the cigar. Then he leaned forward confidentially. "Tell me," he said, "what do you think of all this roadgang business now?"

The Old Man started but regained his calm quickly, being now more accustomed to surprises. He thought a minute; then, "It seems to me I've wasted a lot of worry on it," he said.

"True, true," nodded the Devil, smiling. "I've always said so." He took out the deck of cards again, raised his eyebrows in invitation.

The Old Man was looking at him angrily. "What should I have done?" he demanded. "Taken the man's life unjustly and then dismissed it?"

The Devil broke into a smile. "I swear, you are an odd man! I've not been asked a question like that since I was in France in 1918. Think of asking the Devil about moral responsibility!" He gave off a peal of laughter as if the joke were too much for him.

"I'm glad you're amused," said the Old Man testily.

The Devil sobered at once. "Here now, I didn't mean to offend you. Only think of the contradiction." (He shook his head again, smiling.) "Now what was your question? Oh yes, should you have simply forgotten it. Well, what do you think, now that it's nearly over?"

The Old Man was suddenly suffused with bitterness. "We

ought to be told," he said sharply. "We ought to be told one life is all we have."

The Devil frowned. "So reproach is only tied to eventual punishment. That's what I've always maintained, that man had no real conscience, only a fear." He looked quite smug. "Besides, maybe there is another world for someone, saints and things. I wouldn't know about that. Saints aren't in my line." He took out a music box and became instantly absorbed in the tinkling tune.

"Even so, I'd rather have that lie than the old one," grumbled the Old Man.

"What?" The Devil tried to remember what they had been talking about and then nodded. "Feel cheated, don't you?" he grinned.

"Cheated? Yes." (The Old Man set his jaw.) "Yes I do. I do feel cheated."

"But by whom?" asked the Devil maliciously.

"By me! By me, you old . . ." (Here he paused, unable to think of an epithet that seemed appropriate for insulting his tormenter.)

The Devil was delighted. "I do think you're on the verge of calling me names!" (He looked like an excited little boy.) "What now? Cast aspersions on my fatherhood? Compare me to human excrement?"

The Old Man halted and watched him narrowly for a long moment, and then there came to him a great illumination. He said slowly, half to himself, "I think I have just come upon something very important." He knit his brows, reminding himself that every good lie was composed of at least a little truth, and sought to penetrate to that truth and catch hold of it. The smile faded slightly from the face of the Devil and a worried expression gradually replaced it. "I think," said the Old Man, feeling his way, "that I know at last your secret. I think you are always coming to tell us that what is important is really trivial, that first you make us fool away our lives and at the last you convince us they were never important. And you're always laughing and being very good-natured about it, to convince us that it really didn't matter. I think you are always banging us on the back, and telling us to cheer up—we have a roof over our heads and three square meals a day, and these are sufficient for us. And then we wake up old and tired one morning, and you come along—still smiling—to give us the bad news. 'I'm sorry,' you tell us in a friendly voice, 'it turns out there isn't any more. You've just used it all up and it turns out there isn't any more where that came from.'" (It was a long speech, but the Old Man did not feel tired. While he talked, the Devil's face had gotten darker and darker and now he looked very angry, but with a small anger, as if he might stamp his foot or kick a chair or throw his hat out the window if only he had a hat.)

"And I think," said the Devil sharply, "that you are a very unpleasant old man." He walked the length of the room and back again, clasping and unclasping his hands behind him. "We might have enjoyed a nice half hour together without you throwing in all these useless details. I'm not considered bad company, you know. We might at least have passed the time pleasantly."

The Old Man, watching him, had begun to smile. "I've won, haven't I?" he said softly.

"And besides," went on the Devil without noticing (posturing, waving a hand indignantly), "there ought to be a certain healthy respect for a man in my position." It seemed to the Old Man that the Devil's face was changing and the resemblance was not quite so strong.

"I didn't mean to kill the man," said the Old Man, "and I shouldn't have let it paralyze me from any atonement or accomplishment. But it's not unimportant. And being alive was never unimportant."

The Devil was beginning to look indistinct, dim about the edges, as if he were dissolving from the inside. "Time's up anyway," he cried maliciously. "At least I told you right. There isn't any more. There isn't anything else for you, Old Man."

"So what?" said the Old Man. Strangely enough he seemed to be standing on his feet although there was no pain, and he saw that the Devil was a small man really, without much substance to him. "And if there *was* anything," said the Old Man in a firm voice, "you wouldn't know about it. You wouldn't have noticed."

The Devil seemed to be turning into a wizened little man with a wrinkled raisin face. His voice had grown shriller and turned into a whine. "And even if there is," he cried, "you wouldn't like it. It's all hard work and there isn't any golden city, just working and learning and going back again."

The Old Man took a step forward on straight young legs. "Get out of my house!" he said. And the Devil went.

They came early in the long black car to carry the Old Man away, and the other roomers stood in nightclothes just outside their doors and watched the stretcher go up light and come down heavy. The blanket's edge had slipped;

165

they had an unexpected view of the dead face, eyes kindly closed, looking as though the Old Man was having a not unpleasant dream. There was a look on that face: What was it? Peace? Or triumph? Miss Paula started when it passed her and took a step or so, as if she might walk alongside and watch it all the way downstairs. But she did not; she turned and went inside her room and closed the door and put her back against it stiffly, like an old woman. She was suddenly and sharply frightened.

Downstairs the front door banged.

The Gentle Insurrection

THIS IS the last time, she thought, looking down into the crumbling old well. This is the last time I will do this as long as I live. No matter how old I get to be, I will not do this any more.

And when she thought about it and about what tomorrow would be like, she smiled.

The handle flew around and the rope flung itself off and down and away; and in the darkness the old bucket made a splatting sound when it hit the water. She let it settle before she began to wind the rope back up. For one minute she pulled on one end of the rope and the whole world pulled on the other; and then the bucket began to come slowly out of the well. The rope curled back up again and the old bucket came into sight and she lifted it off onto the shelf.

I've beat you again, she said to the world that was at the bottom of the well. This was your last chance and I have beat you again.

"Lettie, you fell in?"

"No," she said.

"Well, goddamn it, bring me some water then!"

Mama said, "Don't swear."

Lettie poured some of the water into a blue lard can and

carried it into the house. She put it down on the kitchen table.

"Here's your goddamn water," she said.

"Don't swear, Lettie," Mama said.

"Well, make him leave me alone, then."

Mama said, "Theo, how come you don't leave your sister alone? How come you don't, Theo?"

But Theo was swallowing a great dipperful of water and did not answer. The water ran out the corners of his wide mouth and cut little rivers down the dirt on his chin.

"Theo's crazy," Lettie said.

But even when she said it, it didn't matter any more. She said it almost tenderly, looking at big Theo dribbling the water down his chin and over the kitchen floor. She put her hand down on his pale hair and leaned up against the kitchen chair.

"You're crazy, ain't you, Theo?"

Theo jerked his head away and banged the tin dipper into the blue lard can. Lettie went on smiling at the way Theo was always hitting at things and put her hand back down at her side. Go ahead, Theo, crazy, crazy Theo. There won't be any more times after this one, she thought. Because no matter how old you get to be, this is the last time.

She said fondly, "Poor crazy Theo," and he hit the table with his hand and moved the tired old chair away.

Mama was shelling beans. They were hard little white beans, and they made noises against the pan like rain in the middle of the night when you come awake to hear bits of it hitting the roof and wonder if the field will be muddy tomorrow.

Mama said, "What's the matter with you, Lettie? How come you say things like that to your brother?" Her skinny fingers cut the bean pods in one motion and she never looked at her hands while she talked. "How come you and Theo got to be making racket all the time at each other?"

Lettie sat down in another chair, took a lapful of beans and began to shell them.

" 'Cause me and Theo don't like each other," she said, slitting a bean pod carefully, counting the small white seeds. There were seven, like the days of the week. She grinned at her brother. "We don't like each other a damn bit, do we, Theo?"

Theo drank another dipperful of water and then went to the screen door and spat it out into the yard without answering her. A few skinny chickens ran out from under the house to see what Theo had spit into the yard and he emptied the lard can at them and laughed when they scattered, screaming.

Lettie watched him, not saying anything. Mama watched him too. Mama and Lettie spent most of their time watching Theo, frightened that he might get sick and not be able to work, or that he might insult Mr. Chambers and cost them everything.

Theo came back and sat down at the table and watched the fingers of the two women.

He said, "I don't like beans."

Nobody said anything to him.

He said louder, "Beans ain't much to feed a man."

Mama gave him a tired uninterested glance. "When you know a way to get better, you can complain louder," she said. "If you'd get us a little bit ahead, maybe we could eat better. Maybe we could buy apples, or Lettie and me could put up pickles in the summertime."

Lettie stared into the pan where the white beans were falling like noisy pieces of a rainstorm. Let them fuss about the beans and about getting ahead like they always did. After tonight she wouldn't have to hear it. She wouldn't have to hear Mama's high whining voice and Theo's big and angry voice pushing at each other. And she wouldn't have to eat any more beans.

"I work hard as I can," Theo muttered. "Mama, I work harder than a man ought to have to work." He kicked at a table leg, frowning. "Hell, we don't get it anyway. That man, *he* gets it. Hell, he gets it all."

"Don't swear, Theo," said Mama.

"That man, *he*," was Mr. Chambers and he owned the land and the worn-out little house. Lettie had seen him several times; he would come around at planting and harvest time and he and Theo would talk about the cotton. In the spring and fall when Mr. Chambers came around to talk to them, Theo was very civil. He would stand in the field with a battered old hat in his hand, and he would call him "Mr. Chambers" and not "That man, *he.*"

Lettie said, "Why don't you tell him about it, Theo? Why don't you tell Mr. Chambers we don't make no profit? And about how you work harder than a man ought to and he don't give us enough?" She grinned at her brother again. "Poor crazy Theo."

Theo pushed his big red hand through his pale hair and glared at her. "Shut up, will you, Lettie? You just shut up now."

Mama put her beans into Lettie's lap and got up to put a stick of stovewood on the fire. Mama was little and twisted, like a stunted birch tree, and her shoulders came up sharply and cramped her gray head down between them.

Mama said, "Now there you go, Theo. How come you don't ever talk nice to your sister? Mr. Chambers is a nice man. Maybe if you said it pleasant to him, he'd give us a bigger piece of the cotton money. Maybe he'd give us enough money to set out some vegetables, Theo. Why don't you ask him pleasant?" When she put the wood into the stove, a few sparks scattered upward, and she poked inside with the handle.

Theo pushed his hand through his hair again, restlessly. "He wouldn't. That man, *he* wouldn't do it." He looked down at the floor and Lettie could see the streaks of dust and sweat on the back of his red neck. "That man, he hates us," Theo finished glumly.

Mama sat back down and filled her lap with beans. "Now that's not right, Theo. You know that's not right. He's just too busy to come by and see how we're getting on. When your Pa was alive . . ."

Lettie didn't want to hear it again, even if it was for the last time. She looked at Mama and she felt tight all over, as if strings were pulling at every part of her. She said hurriedly, "Why don't you say it out about Pa? He's not dead. You don't know that he's dead." She got up and went to the window where a torn piece of screen hung open and the heat and flies came in. "He just left, that's all." She put out her hand to push the screen together but she knew it wouldn't stay. No matter what you did to that house, nothing ever changed. Nothing stayed fixed and the heat and flies just kept coming in. "Papa's not dead; he just left and you know it. You don't like to say it out because he just up and went away and you're still here working. But it's the truth, and you might as well say it out to Theo and me." She said it all very fast without looking up from the window.

Mama began to shell beans very fast and a new wrinkle appeared in her cheek as if it had been slashed there with a knife. Mama's fingers flew over the beans and they tumbled into the pan—they thumped and plunked and rattled about, but Mama didn't say anything.

Theo got up from the tired old kitchen chair and looked down at Lettie. Theo was very tall. "How come you had to say that?" he asked her, his eyebrows hunched forward. "How come you had to say that to Mama?" And Lettie didn't know why she had said it and she was ashamed.

She put her hand out and rested it softly on Mama's arm, a thin arm that ended in skinny twisted bits of fingers. "I'm sorry, Mama," she whispered. "I'm sorry I said it about Papa."

But Mama went on shelling beans very fast and she did not say anything.

Theo put his big hand down on Mama's shoulder. "She's sorry, Mama," he said awkwardly. "She didn't mean to say it about Papa and make you mad. Lettie said she was sorry."

But Mama's shoulders hunched forward a little farther and cramped her head and neck between them, and the beans kept falling quickly into the pan. Theo looked at Lettie across Mama's head and shuffled his feet uncomfortably.

"Guess I'll go feed the mules," he said.

He looked down at Mama and then said it a little louder. "I said I think I'll go feed them mules."

The beans made rainy noises when they hit the pot, very fast.

Lettie took her hand off Mama's twisted little arm and put her apronful of beans up on the kitchen table. "I'll come too," she said. "I'll see if the hens are laying in the barn again. Maybe we've got some eggs we don't know about." She stood up, looked at Theo, then looked down at Mama again. "I said, I think I'll go down to the barn with Theo."

"All right," said Mama. They went out the door.

In the barn, Theo put a few ears of hard corn into the long trough and unhappily examined a long sore on Bob's back.

"How you reckon that damn mule hurt his back that way?" he said to Lettie, but she didn't pay him any attention. She sat down on a bale of hay and swung her feet back and forth against it. She took a big smell of everything, so she would be able to remember it, and be glad she had left it all behind.

"I don't know, Theo," she said absently, "How should I know about an old mule?" She swung her feet back and forth and smelled the hay and the mules and the wet old wood.

Theo turned away from the mule. "How come you had to say that about Papa?" he said. He came over and sat down beside her on the bale of hay. "What did you say it for, Lettie?"

Lettie pursed her lips and lifted her shoulders. "I just got sick of hearing it, that's all. What good does it do if we pretend he died?" She swung her feet against the hay and they made quick sharp clunks, like the sound of Mama's beans falling into the pan. "Everybody knows Papa's been gone for years. Ever since we had to quit high school and come home." She looked up at Theo. "Sometimes I think everybody knows it but Mama. I think she keeps saying how dead he is and she's nearly forgotten he just up and left us and we had to quit school and come home. I think she believes it, Theo."

Theo stood up and frowned at her. "Well, let her believe it then. It makes her feel better."

Lettie leaned back against another bale of hay and looked up into the rafters of the barn. Cobwebs hung in great strips from the corners, and the rotting posts were covered with mud daubers' nests like small red sores.

Lettie said, "I wonder what became of Papa. I wonder where he went." She almost smiled at Theo. After all, this was the last time.

Theo climbed down into the stall and looked at the long sore on the mule's back again. "I don't know," he said. "I guess he really *is* dead."

Lettie stood up abruptly from the haybale and stared at him. "Don't you say that, Theo Barnes!" she cried angrily. "Just don't say that." She kicked in the hay then, feeling like Theo when he banged the table or threw water at the chickens. She said louder, "He is *not* dead—he went somewhere and did something that he liked, and he is *not* dead. And don't you say he is!" And then she began to cry with little hiccoughing sobs that made her throat burn.

174

Theo looked at her, bewildered. "What's the matter with you?" he said.

She kicked furiously at the hay again. "Nothing, Theo Barnes. Nothing, crazy crazy Theo! Just you keep quiet, that's all."

She swallowed the little sobs and the burning in her throat, and ran out of the barn towards the house. Theo did not come with her. He stayed to look at the sore on Bob's back.

There wasn't anything to do after supper. There never was. The eggs would be gathered and the old cow milked and put away, and after supper everything got quiet. Lettie and Mama would wash the dishes in the striped pan, and then they would go sit on the porch with Theo, watching him. Theo was usually too tired to talk. He would sit on the porch and not say anything, and Mama and Lettie would find a chair and sit down beside him. And after a while the sun would go all the way down.

Lettie sat down, almost smiling this time. This is the last time, she thought, and when she thought about it she could forget everything else, and she felt like kissing Mama on top of her gray hair or putting her arms around Theo's big red neck.

Mama said, "You gonna wash tonight?" and Theo said he was. She went back into the house to put the kettle on the stove.

Theo looked at Lettie for a long time before he said anything. Then he said, "When's he coming?" and Lettie stiffened in her chair and didn't move or breathe for a long

175

minute. An irritable bird coughed in the oak tree, but everything else was quiet.

Then she said, "Who told you?"

Theo looked over his shoulder to make sure Mama was in the kitchen.

"He did."

The irritable old bird began to fly about in the oak tree, looking for someplace that suited it.

Lettie thought she was going to cry again but she swallowed hard and the burning in her throat slipped down out of sight. "How come he told you?" she asked him. She moved in the chair then, and it screamed against the porch floor. She said, "How come he had to go and tell you about it?" The oak tree rustled and moved again and she turned to it angrily. "Fly away, old bird!" she cried desperately, "Just fly on out of here!" and the bird went away.

Theo didn't say anything. Lettie could hear the thumping of the handle turning on the old well to let the bucket down. Mama was filling up the kettle for Theo to wash. The handle would be flying round and round while the rope flung itself off and down the well till the world took hold of the bucket at the other end.

Lettie said, "What did Mama say about it?" and Theo looked at her then. He got up and walked to the edge of the porch and stood looking out at the oak tree. The bird was gone, but Theo kept watching the oak tree and he did not look at her.

"I didn't tell Mama," he said.

Lettie's arms and legs felt suddenly like wet old rags and she let loose a long breath. She said, "What are you going to do about it?" but she knew already that he wasn't going to try to stop her.

Theo put his big hand around one of the porch posts and squeezed it, hard. His big red hand closed around the post and he choked the life out of it while he stood watching the oak tree.

He said carefully, "I'm kind of tired. I reckon I'm just too goddamn tired to do anything about it."

Lettie sat there smiling. Theo wasn't going to do anything. When the sun went all the way down and the threshers passed on the road, he would come whistle for her, down in the woods like an old hoot owl and she would go and not be afraid, because Theo wasn't going to do anything.

She said, still smiling, "Thanks, Theo. Thanks, crazy crazy Theo." But he did not look at her.

Theo's fingers choked the porch post again, as if he wanted to pull it out and bring the roof down on the two of them. He said angrily, "Don't thank me, Lettie. God-damn it, don't you thank me. Go on and leave with him and the other threshers and don't come back, but don't you sit here on this porch thanking me." He turned and looked at her then, and his look was level and it was angry. "I'm just too goddamn tired to be thanked," he said.

Mama came out then and they didn't say any more. Theo sat back down and Lettie looked off into the oak tree. The bird had flown away; every leaf in the old tree was quiet and sleepy and the sky was getting gray between them. Once she looked up at big crazy Theo, but he had fallen asleep in his chair. Poor crazy Theo, he *was* tired. It was hard for him to be forever growing things on land that was not his own, getting tired and sleepy, with nothing to do in the evenings but sit on the porch and feel how tired he was.

Mama woke him up after a while.

"You said you was gonna wash," she said, and he got up.

"Yeah," he said. "I'm dirty. But you never get it all off." And he went inside the house.

Lettie sat out on the porch with Mama for the last time. A restless wind came up to the oak tree and stirred the leaves curiously, but it wasn't the same as the bird.

Lettie said, "Mama, I'm awful sorry for what I said about Papa."

Mama said, "That's all right, Lettie. You was just tired. I guess we all get tired." She hollered through the door, "You got enough water?" and Theo said he had enough water.

Mama said, "Theo works too hard. This place is too much for one man to work when it ain't his own land," and Lettie said "Yes."

"We used to talk about how we'd buy a place of our own when we got a little bit ahead," Mama said. "We was always going to get away from this place. But that was before Papa di—that was before he went away. I guess maybe we'll get away and have a place of our own yet."

She smiled at Lettie and touched her timidly on the arm with a row of gnarled little fingers. "We'll have one yet, Lettie. You and Theo will have some place to settle, and I'll be here to see it."

Lettie took her arm away. "Yes," she said. "We'll have a

place, you and me and Theo." And the wind moved in the oak tree again, looking for birds.

Theo came back out on the porch. He stood there, clean and damp, but with a brownness that would not wash away. He said, "I think I'll turn in. I'm tired. And there'll be a lot to do tomorrow." He did not look at Lettie.

She got up from her chair. "You work too hard, Theo," she said, and it was a question and an invitation when she said it. "You ought not to work so hard. You ought to do the easy things."

Mama was happy again, now that she and Lettie and Theo were not quarreling at each other. "You get a good night's sleep, Theo," she said smiling. "After this season we'll make us enough cotton to get ahead. We'll buy us a place of our own and we won't work hard any more."

Theo looked down at her and his cheek moved back and forth for a minute before he said, "That's right, Mama."

He went into the house, walking slowly, as if his feet were heavy to lift up and set down. Mama and Lettie sat there awhile, watching the sun go all the way down before they went into the house, too.

Mama said, "You want to sleep down here where it's cool?" but Lettie said she'd sleep up in the loft. She wanted to sleep up in the loft on the last night.

When Lettie climbed the ladder, she was smiling. This was the last time she'd go up that ladder into the loft, to lie awake and think about going somewhere like Pa had done.

Mama said, "You sleep good, Lettie."

And Lettie said, "You sleep good, Mama."

She climbed up the ladder into the loft, still smiling. The

bedsprings creaked once downstairs when Mama crawled into bed. In the far corner of the loft, Theo had already begun to snore.

Outside, down in the woods, there came a little whistle like an old hoot owl. It hooted once; then there was a long silence. After that, it hooted over and over again, insistently. The night came on blackly, and the moon scrambled up the sky until it shone into the loft, and after a long time the hoot owl quit making noises down in the woods.

Lettie lay in her bed, an old pillow tight over her head and her hands pushed fiercely into her eyes. She cried for a long time after the hoot owl went away. She went on crying softly and hopelessly, even when the sky began to grow gray and the light appeared faintly in strips along the floor. She was still crying when the sun rose, but she knew it was for the last time.

The Sword

THE DAYS fell out of the sick man's life sluggishly, like dead coals slipping finally onto the hearth from an old fire. Every evening when he blew the lamp and raised the shade, Bert would stand in the dark thinking, This is the last one. Tomorrow he will be gone.

But the next morning, when Bert started awake in the leather chair and strained his ears for silence, he could still hear the tired in-and-out of breathing and his arms and legs would loosen in the chair as he listened to it.

Bert was almost never out of the sick man's room, until the smell of it seemed right to him and he could look at the flowers on the wall and not know if they were blue or green.

His mother would enter and leave the room all day long, standing with one hand curled around the bed rail and looking down at the sick man, her face set into awkward squares like blocks heaped up by some clumsy child.

"Is he any better, Bert?"

"No, I think he is about the same. Maybe a little weaker."

Then she would whisper it under her breath as if it hurt her mouth to make the words. "A little weaker . . ."

At first Bert had put out his hand to her, but she had not

seemed to notice, and after a while he stood at the window when his mother came in and stared at the leaves that tossed and shifted on the grass when the wind went by. She wanted to be left alone, he supposed. She had been left to herself for a long time now.

Always she would say hopefully, "Lester? How are you today, Lester?" But there was the suck and push of the old man's breathing and nothing else, and she would go away, watching her feet.

He had been sick for three weeks when Bert first came home, and he was still able to talk a little and smile and look around him.

He had been smiling when Bert came into the room that first day and put his coat on the leather chair and walked over to the bed.

"Hello, Father," Bert said.

The old man said slowly, "It's Bert, isn't it? Have you come home awhile, Bert?"

And he said, "Yes, Father. I've come home a little while."

But there were two more weeks gone now since that day and the old man still lay in bed—no longer smiling—and breathing in and out while Bert watched him.

This morning the doctor had come early, so that Bert was out of his chair before the sun was well into the room.

"Morning, Bert."

"Hello, Dr. Herman. You're early today."

"This is going to be a busy one. Did he rest last night?"

"Yes sir, he sleeps almost all the time now."

Only once during the examination had the sick man opened his eyes and then he had looked at the doctor without interest and closed them again.

182

"How is he, Dr. Herman?"

The doctor made a shrugging motion. "Holding his own. We're just waiting, I'm afraid."

Later, putting his things away, he had added, "I'm glad you've come home, Bert. Your father was always talking about you. He was very proud."

Was he? thought Bert.

Bert stood by the window and watched the doctor go down the walk, his black bag banging against his knee every other step. We're just waiting, the doctor had said. Once he stopped in the walk to tie his shoe and the wind rose in the oak tree—almost bare now—and came to flap the doctor's coat, impatiently.

After the doctor was out of sight, his mother came and stood by the bed and put her head against the post, as if she were tired of holding it up.

"Does the doctor think he is any better, Bert?" she said.

Bert said, "No, he seems about the same."

She sat down in the leather chair stiffly, leaning her head back, and he saw the hairs springing up from her braid like grass after feet go by.

She said to herself, "At first I thought he would get well. Even after the first week or so I thought he would get well."

"We both thought so," said Bert.

She said, "I wish he knew things. He'd be so glad you were home again. These last years all he could talk about before Christmas was that you would be home awhile. He looked forward to it so."

He looked forward to it, Bert thought. Always forward. What was I expected to do? The sick man moved and coughed and Bert went closer to the bed to see if he was all right. Nothing else was said, and after awhile his mother got up from the chair and went out to the kitchen.

No one else came in the rest of the morning, although Jubah put her head at the door once and smiled at him and Bert sat alone in the room and watched his father's face. He wondered how in five years features he had once known well could fold in upon themselves until the face was strange to him, with its pinched nose and sharp chin, and the cheeks that looked as if they had been pressed deep inside the mouth.

Sometimes Bert would try to remember how his father had looked a long time ago—when he had driven him to school on winter mornings, or across a hundred dinner tables, or on those few special times when he had gone hunting with his father and three other men. But all Bert could remember of those times was the bigness of the other hunters, and the early morning smell of woods and rain, and once his father stopping to put a hand against a poplar tree and smile.

His father had been a very poor hunter; he almost never made a successful shot. But he had been proud when Bert learned to shoot well. And when Bert began bringing home almost all the game, he could remember his father coming into the kitchen at dusk and calling, "Ruth? Come see what your son did!" And the rabbits would be spread on the table for his mother to exclaim about, while his father stood quietly at the sink, washing his hands.

After Bert became such a good shot his father complimented and praised him but gradually they went hunting less and less until one Christmas he had given his gun to Bert. "I was never much with guns," he said then. And after that, the two of them never went hunting again, and the gun was finally stacked away in some closet.

The only time Bert could remember his father's face clearly was that time he had come home from the army and they had sat up after the others were in bed—his father oddly expectant, with waiting eyebrows and a half-formed smile, and his own feelings of awkwardness and discomfort, until the two of them had fallen into separate silences and finally gone to bed. He remembered how his father had looked then.

At noon Mother brought the tray and they whispered at the sick man until he lifted his eyelids and looked at them, waiting, expecting nothing and yet seeming to expect anything.

Mother said, "It's lunchtime, Lester. Hot soup." And the sick man made a noise in his throat that might have meant yes or no, and might have meant nothing at all. She fed him slowly and all the time he never looked at the soup or the spoon or her hand holding it; he lay there watching her mouth with that funny look on his face.

Bert watched them for awhile, but he could not keep his hands still; they kept plunging into his pockets or picking at each other until he went to the window and made them into fists and leaned them against the glass. Sometimes the wind would catch a leaf and drive it against the glass where it paused and then tumbled off. Bert thought, My father is going to die, but he did not believe it. He believed the wind and the leaves and the window-glass; but he did not believe that about his father.

When the sick man had eaten, Mother came over to the window and touched Bert's arm; it startled him for a minute and he snapped his head over one shoulder and stared at her; then the muscles that had grown tight around his eyes and forehead let themselves go and he smiled.

She said, "He will sleep some more, Bert. Why don't you come sit out front with me?"

"All right," said Bert.

She whispered, "We'll leave the door open."

He took the tray from her and carried it out into the kitchen where he put it down on the table. His mother called, "Can you bring me a glass of water?" and he filled a glass at the sink and carried it into the front room to her.

She had put her feet up into a big chair and rested an arm against her eyes, and fine hairs were standing up out of her braid all over her head. Bert put the glass into her other hand, and she rubbed at her forehead with the arm and thanked him. He sat down opposite her.

She said, "I wish you'd let me stay with him, Bert. You've hardly been out of that room since you came home."

Bert shook his head. He had to stay with his father now. He had to do that much.

For a time neither of them spoke and he looked thoughtfully around the room. Here he had sat with his father when he came home from the army—his father had been in the big chair smiling, and Bert had sat just where he was now, moving his feet back and forth against the rug and looking now and then at his father thinking, What does he want of me?

His mother said, "At first I thought he would get well, Bert. I thought he would get well at first." For a minute Bert wanted to say, Did you like him? Did you really like my father? Do you know something I don't? But he didn't

186

say anything; he just watched the movement in her face. He thought she was going to shed her first tears then, but she took her feet off the chair and moved around and shifted until the desire for tears went away. She looked suddenly like a brave little girl: a fat girl with chubby features and hair that would not stay in place. Bert wondered what she would do after the sick man died and if it would mean any real change in her life. Sometimes he thought he knew his mother very well and yet this thing he did not know. Does it mean a lot to her? Is there something in me that does not understand him? She'll just have me then, he thought, and he didn't feel quite so helpless for a minute. She's got to prepare herself.

Aloud he said, "Father is very weak now and his age is against him."

She said, "I know now he's not ever going to be well again. I know it and I don't know it all at the same time and that's a queer feeling, Bert, both at the same time."

When she said that, Bert felt his whole body tighten. His mother was right; that's the way it was for him too, maybe for everybody. Nobody believed it. The one thing that was glaring and obvious and unmistakable in the universe and nobody really believed it. Bert wondered if his father believed it now, waiting every day in bed to see if it were true.

He said, "Dr. Herman will be back tomorrow." He said it rapidly as if he had just thought of it, but it was because he couldn't think of anything else to tell her. "We're to call him if we need him for anything."

His mother said, "Yes," and drank the water very fast so that it must have hurt her throat to swallow so hard. Bert took the glass back into the kitchen.

He stacked the dishes off the tray into the sink and began to pour water on them from the kettle and then to wash them with a soapy rag. He thought, it seems to me now that if it were new again, I would be different than I was; but he didn't know exactly what he meant by that. Jubah came in from the back porch; she stopped in the doorway and stood there straight as a knife handle and watched him.

"What you doing, Mister Bert?" she said.

He said, "Dishes."

She came on into the kitchen and wiped her hands on a paper towel and threw it away.

"I'll do them," she said. "How's Mr. Lester?"

Bert watched her brown hands go down into the water and slush it up into soapsuds.

He said, "No different, Jubah. He just lies there but there isn't any change."

Jubah shook her head back and forth and made a tut-tut sound with her tongue. "Sometimes it comes up slow," she said.

When he went back into the front room, his mother looked as if she had been crying, but it was hard to tell. She had not cried before. That night he had come in from the station, she had stood in the hall holding one hand with another, looking something like a queen, he thought. She'd said, "I'm sorry to call you from your business, Bert. But it seemed best . . ."

He'd dropped his bag at the door and come to put his arm around her. "How is he?"

Just for a minute, she'd put her head down on his shoulder and rested it there and then she'd caught his arm in tight fingers and made a little smile. "He'll be glad you're here," she'd said.

Now, coming into the front room, he thought perhaps she had been crying, but he could not be sure. He sat down in the chair again and looked at her, trying to decide about it.

His mother said rapidly, "Do you know what Jubah said this morning? I was just walking through the kitchen and Jubah said—Death comes up slow like an old cat but after she waits a long time she jumps and it's all gone then—I was just walking by her and she looked up from the stove and said that, Bert, and I thought I would fall down right there to hear her say it."

Bert said, "Jubah talks too much," but he turned it over in his mind and looked at it in front and behind and on both sides. Death comes up slow like an old cat but after she waits a long time she jumps and it's all gone then.

He tried to remember what it had been like in the army, but he couldn't remember what he had thought about death then. He and Charlie used to talk about it sometimes, but always in terms of somebody else—the fellow in the next bunk, or the ship that left yesterday, or the list in the paper.

Charlie always said, "I don't believe nothing can hurt you till your time comes." He used to say it over and over, confidently, and Bert had listened just as confidently, because both of them knew their time hadn't come.

And it didn't seem to, because they got through all right and Charlie went home to his filling station in Maine and he'd never heard from him.

There'd been another boy, confident as they were, who

said that ever since he was a kid he'd known he was going to die during a storm. Every time they had any kind of storm, he'd walk the floor smoking on a cigar, and jumping at the sound of thunder. They'd laughed at him.

"It's whenever your time comes," Charlie always told him.

But as it turned out Bert and Charlie had come home all right, and the other boy (funny that he couldn't remember his name) had died in Africa, they said, and there wasn't even a cloud in the sky.

But that didn't prove anything about what Charlie had said. It didn't prove anything except what his mother had said, that nobody really believed in it. Bert felt tired.

He frowned. "Sometimes," he began, "sometimes, Mother, I wish I could . . ." but he stopped there and didn't know what he wished. It had something to do with the old hunting trips and with his father and with Jubah, but he didn't know what it was. He put his head into his hands and smashed the palms into his eyes. He thought, I have known people and been known by people. That proves something, doesn't it?

His mother was looking at him. She said, "Your father loved you so, Bert." He kept his palms tight against his eyes where the pressure made him see sparks and gray wheels spinning and something like a Roman candle. He wondered, Was that it? Was that all it was all these years? And that made him tired too.

Bert said, "I'll see if he's awake now."

He tiptoed into the room and looked down at the sick man, who was awake—lying there with that look on his face. Bert looked down at him, at his faded eyes on each side of the pinched nose and the mouth, bent in now as if the corners had been tugged from the inside. Slow, he thought, slow like a big cat, and for a minute he hated Jubah for telling his mother about the cat.

The old man closed his eyes and Bert felt suddenly that two doors had been shut against him and he no longer had anything to do with his father. He came back into the front room and sat down, then he got up and took a magazine and sat again. He thought, I'm trying, damn it. I've always been trying.

Big letters crawling crookedly on the magazine said CHILDBIRTH, IT CAN BE PAINLESS. OUR GROWING TRAFFIC DEATHS. RUSSIA AND THE ATOM. He leafed through it, not reading anything.

Sometimes since his father had been sick, Bert had tried to remember some vivid detail, some special time, some conversation that had happened when he was a boy that was important. That's where a psychologist began, with the little boy, and he could say, "It is here that it began to go wrong, when you were three, or seven, or nine." But Bert could never find anything.

He remembered the time he came home from the army only because it was so much like everything else that it seemed important in itself.

His father and mother had met him at the train-station; she had hugged him and Father had shaken his hand and stood there smiling, looking at him curiously and—yes, he was sure of it, warmly—until he stammered, "Well, let's go home now." So they had piled into the Ford and gone home, making a lot of noise on the road about souvenirs and about old friends, and about what-he-was-going-to-do-now.

And that night, when Mother and Aunt Mary had gone to bed, and Jubah had called good night from the back-door and thanked him again for the silk shawl, Bert and his father had sat in this same front room; his father in the big chair, looking expectant, with his eyebrows up and an underdeveloped smile fooling with his mouth. Bert felt then the same way he did when he and his father came in from hunting and put the rabbits down on the kitchen table.

But his father hadn't seemed uncomfortable at all; he just sat across from him smiling, and Bert moved his feet back and forth against the rug thinking, What is it you want of me?

Finally he said, "You know, Father, I brought souvenirs to the others, but I didn't know what to bring you. I didn't know what you would like."

And his father had gone on smiling, looking at him out of a quiet face, his faded eyes making a question and yet not a curious question.

And Bert had said nervously, "So I just thought I'd give you the money, Sir, and let you get something you liked and wanted for yourself," holding out the envelope in a hand that was carved from wood or clay, but was not his hand.

His father had said slowly, "That was nice of you, Bert. Thank you very much," and had taken the envelope and turned it over and over in his hands, not opening it, just turning it over in his fingers.

After that the two of them had sat for a little longer until they fell into separate silences and went to bed.

Sometimes now, when Bert sat in the leather chair and watched his father breathe in and out, he would remember that night and try to think what else he should have done. The pistol? But his father had never been much with guns. Silk shawls or bits of jade? And what would his father have done with a Japanese sword or a rising-sun flag?

When his mother spoke now it frightened him because he had forgotten she was in the room.

She said, "What are you reading, Bert?" and he jumped and his eyes caught at the words in the magazine like fingers.

He said, "Childbirth. Painless Childbirth," and she almost smiled.

She said thoughtfully, "I remember the day you were born," but she didn't say any more. Bert tried to picture his father on that day. Had he been proud? Had he said perhaps, softly and to himself, "My son?"

Jubah called them to supper and Bert ate it automatically, watching Jubah's sharp hipbones shift when she moved about the kitchen. Jubah was very thin. She was almost as old as his father and she had been with them a long time. That was a funny thing, Jubah's loyalty to Mr. Lester. They were often laughing as if old and yellowed secrets were between them. I should have known Jubah better, Bert thought now, watching her go about the kitchen. Perhaps she would have told me.

Jubah said, "I'll stay over tonight, Mister Bert," and he didn't argue with her.

His mother said, "Your bed's fixed, Jubah," and she thanked her.

Later, when Bert blew out the lamp and raised the shade in

the sick man's room he thought how tired he was, and he went to sleep quickly in the chair.

When he woke again, it was almost day and he heard the old man choking and wheezing on the bed and he knew this was the last day. He called his mother and they lit the lamp and stood by the bed while Jubah telephoned the doctor.

His mother didn't say anything or bend down to touch the sick man; she just stood there listening to him cough and the tears ran out her eyes and down her cheeks and fell off.

Now that it had come, Bert found his hands were trembling and the lamplight jiggled and splashed against the flowered wall every time his father made a noise with his throat, but even when he squeezed his eyes together they were dry.

Suddenly his father said, "Ruth," and she sat down on the side of the bed and took both his hands in hers and his eyelids flew up and he looked at her, until Bert felt he could not bear that look.

Bert put the lamp on the table and bent over the old man, feeling the hiccoughing begin in his throat and the tightness clamp across his chest. He put a hand against the old man's shoulder and said suddenly, "I should have given you the sword," and his voice was too loud.

The sick man's eyes flashed to him once, flicked his face and went away and he gargled a sound in his throat. His mother frowned at Bert and shook her head sharply.

"Hush," she said sternly. "Hush, he does not know anything," and the old man raised his head off the pillow stiffly and put it down again and was dead.

194

Bert backed out the door when Jubah came in; his mother had put her head down on the bed and begun to cry with a great sucking sound, and Bert went heavily into the front room and fell into the big chair, saying aloud over and over, "He is dead. He is already dead. He is dead."

He put his forehead down against his arm, but he could not even cry.

Miss Parker Possessed

M ISS PARKER—Age: 40, Occupation: Librarian—
was possessed by a devil every bit as venomous as
any of those recorded in the pages of the New Testament,
and seemingly much less likely to be sidetracked into a herd
of innocent swine.

The whole thing was all the more frightening because it
seemed suddenly to have descended and settled on her from
nowhere, and laid claim to everything she had always considered most stable. She now spent most of her waking
hours trying to shake loose from the fearsome thing that
held her, and every failure was more thorough and complete
than the last; so that she had taken to slipping back in the
shadows and leaning her head against a row of books in
sheer exhaustion.

"Oh dear," she would remark to the silent shelves around
her, "I really am quite mad."

It was somehow comforting to have it out and admitted
like that, in the same manner that one felt better for having
thrown up a disagreeable breakfast. If there were now
some mental toilet chain to tug, the whole terrible experience might go chugging and churning down the porcelain

and out of her life forever; how glorious that would be! Miss Parker closed her eyes at the luxury of the thought and then the counter bell jingled and she sighed and went out front to check a rental.

"Morning, Miss Parker."

"Good morning, Mrs. Head."

(She choked back a giggle at the name and at her recent thoughts about a mental toilet bowl and peered through her glasses in great concentration until she felt mistress of herself again. This was part of The Thing. It had not always been this way.)

"Oh yes, eight cents, Mrs. Head."

(And then sharply through the glasses again to hold back the twitching that pulled on fatal strings just at the edge of her lips, until the book and the nickel and three pennies lay securely on the desk and the front door had closed behind the patron—Miss Parker always spoke of them as patrons.) But by that time she had developed a case of hiccups. Hiccups, too, were unlike her; she had always put them into the same class as the Public Belch, and of late she had grown quite subject to them, and only a glass of water that was downed while she held her nose between thumb and forefinger seemed to help. She went wearily down the hall to the water fountain.

Since the unprecedented change in herself, Miss Parker felt perpetually tired, as if she had waked up one morning to find this Thing hung round her neck like a dead albatross, and had by now worn herself out with carrying it around. She kicked almost automatically at the old water fountain, which coughed up sporadic spurts into her paper cup, grumbling somewhere deep inside. It was lukewarm water and had a rusty taste; but at least it would suffice for hiccups.

Miss Parker climbed mentally out of her own head and watched herself drinking the water. The weariness and discouragement were like an outline that drew her into some drab old photograph; she surveyed herself for a moment as impartially as a stranger, reading it like a paragraph:

> The tired Miss Parker went wearily down the hall for a cup of water. For a heavy cup of water. She drank the stale liquid listlessly, letting her hand fall back to her side from the weight of its own fatigue . . .

Miss Parker sighed. That's the way it was now, day in and day out, this terrible consuming exhaustion that came from fighting down and holding back and warding off. The time would come, she thought, when her guard would relax but for an instant, and the whole thing would sweep over her like a flood. I shall go berserk, I suppose, thought Miss Parker in resignation, and do all sorts of horrible things. I shall rob the bank, and as for Mr. Harvey—she shuddered and clipped the thought off as neatly as if it had been a string and threw the other end away. She would not even permit herself to think of Mr. Harvey. That was the worst of all, the scandalous thoughts she had about Lewis Harvey.

While she was still suspended outside herself like that, Miss Parker took a good look at the woman drinking the cup of water—tall, thin, long spread feet in the sturdy shoes, tedious brown hair that was tucked (there was no other word for it) above and behind each ear and ended in a stubby shortness at the back of the neck, gray dress, navy blue sweater, eyes that were rather like chocolate drops muddied from exposure to the sun, and rimless glasses. Nothing unusual about her, you would say, passing her on the street or stepping back to let her on the trolley. Certainly you would never suspect that after forty placid years there had erupted within her a wild springtime of thinking . . . .

Miss Parker sighed and crumpled the cup, and then lowered herself by a trapdoor securely into her own head again. She put her chin forward like a duck and contracted her throat but no sound came; at least the hiccups were gone for a little while. Now there was one more day to get through without anyone's noticing the albatross.

Back at her desk (it was depressingly neat, she thought abruptly, the ink cap on tightly and the blotter bare, and all the pencil erasers turned the same way) Miss Parker thought about these strange new emotions. She thought she must be what was called a schizophrenic, a divided personality. On the surface she remained her usual self—tidy Miss Parker, quiet, respectable librarian Agnes Parker; but underneath there moved some startling stranger, a much younger woman who was given to poking fun at things and wearing scarlet lipstick and thinking the unexpected, and looking at Lewis Harvey as if . . . as if . . .

Miss Parker shuddered. She refused to believe this alien creature had lived within her all this time. No, it was a disease of some sort; it had introduced this altogether foreign element like a . . . like an unwanted virus!

However it had come about, Miss Parker had become a somewhat subdued case of Dr. Jekyll and Mr. Hyde. Yes, it was better to face it openly like that and admit everything. Suddenly and with no warning, some part of her had split off and taken up an existence of its own, and now was about to plague her real self to death—just as the drug had released from Jekyll a demon he had never dreamed was there. Perhaps if Jekyll had been a librarian instead of a medical man, his aberrations, too, might have been somewhat more restrained. There was something, thought Miss Parker ruefully, something about a small town library that was more conducive to napping than to doing in some old gentleman in the reference room. Even that thought was a shade unlike her and pointed out the terrible infiltrations this Second Self was making into her whole way of life; she shook her head to clear it and glanced around the room where she had worked for so many years. That at least lent her some sense of stability, and stability was Miss Parker's source of strength.

Miss Parker had been city librarian for eighteen years. It was said of her that she could "lay her hand on any book in three minutes," and without such modern aids as the card catalog, either. (The card catalog sat over in one corner as if it were rather ashamed to be there at all, and was occasionally shuffled through by students from Mac Gray High School whenever Miss Parker was too busy to help them.) Keeping it up to date was simplified by the fact that not many new books were ever received into the Carville Public Library. It was one of the boasts of local readers that most of the circulating material was composed of literature that had "stood the test of time," by which they meant Scott, and Dickens, and romantic brown leather volumes of the English poets. As a result, most of the younger Carville citizens took their reading matter from between lurid paper covers at the local Hawkins Drug Store—covers on which buxom damsels were forever bent back in haystacks, fighting rather unenthusiastically for their respective virtues—and in full color.

If any Carville citizen wanted to donate a volume to the library, he must first make application on a mimeographed sheet, be checked and double checked and approved by Miss Parker, and finally receive from the office of the Council-men (who supervised the library's general management) a formal request to place the book at the disposal of Carville readers.

Miss Parker sighed again, glanced at her watch. It was not such a bad life, she supposed, the day-to-day library routines and the two rooms she had from Mrs. Jamison and the lunches uptown and the bi-monthly Ladies' Book Club.

Miss Parker started when she remembered the Book Club, because that had been one of the first times she felt her self-control slipping. Miss Parker actually enjoyed her work with the Book Club. She was sure of that. Certainly she had never doubted it before. She was, as a matter of fact, indispensable to it; and she had never by word or deed implied that she found it dull or tedious or stuffy.

The Ladies' Bi-Monthly Book Club (organized 1938) met each Thursday evening at the home of one of its members; and alternated between the English teachers at Mac Gray High School and Miss Parker herself for its informative lectures on great literary men. She had not missed a meeting for years. Indeed, she could still remember that impressive candlelight ceremony when the president, Ida Rickerts, had presented her with the special satin book-mark, after a speech which paid sincere tribute to her loyalty and devotion.

But lately, after this terrible neurosis (Miss Parker was

vague about psychological terms) had come upon her, the Book Club had begun to seem unbearable beyond description and she had caught herself on the verge of doing absolutely monstrous things at its meetings.

There had been, in particular, the last meeting in her own apartment, at which Miss Whitley (Grade A certificate, Flora MacDonald, '22) had discussed naturalism in English poetry. Even now Miss Parker was vague as to how naturalism had been defined, but she knew it was in some way synonymous with "To a Mountain Daisy," and she retained an impression that William Wordsworth had figured largely in the examples given. Then there had been also Robert Burns, with his plowshare overturning the homes of dazed rodents; she could remember Miss Whitley dwelling at some length on Robert Burns.

"Of course, Mr. Burns" (here Miss Whitley had simpered, all one hundred and seventy-four pounds of her) "had something of a way with the ladies."

And everyone in the club had tittered discreetly, not pursuing the matter farther than that, but just permitting themselves delicate amusement at Miss Whitley's sophisticated boldness. Everyone, that is, except Miss Parker, who—to her still undimmed amazement—had given forth a raucous heehaw that was more obscene than any Anglo-Saxon fence scrawl, and had felt (with horror) the muscular tic that had drawn her left eye down into a lewd wink.

It had all been dreadfully shocking. Miss Parker clucked her tongue now at the unpleasant memory, seeing again the delicate amusement frozen in mid-air, and the long white faces turning toward her as cautiously as sleeping tabbies who discover a mouse has passed among them unawares.

Later, as the guests were leaving (eyes sweeping towards each other like hungry little brooms that would gather up everything of interest) she had protested vaguely an illness, and received many sympathetic glances; yet the evil had not been wholly undone, she knew. They had left her apartment only to hurry home and to buzz on party lines as to whatever was happening to gentle Agnes Parker, who had never before committed an indelicate act in all her forty years.

"Well, anyway, they're gone, the whole nasty lot of them," Miss Parker had declared aloud to herself when she closed the door, and somehow she had giggled in relief, like a child let out of school.

"Mr. Burns," she had announced mockingly to the long antique mirror that had belonged to Mrs. Jamison's great-aunt (who was—depressingly enough—a Yankee) "Mr. Burns had quite a way with the ladies." And she pursed her lips just demurely enough and curtsied at her own reflection. After that she had some dim recollection of draping herself in Mrs. Jamison's best fringed bedspread and indulging in some dance that relied heavily on the hop and skip, and of finally having gone to bed with all her clothes on.

As if the Book Club incident were not sufficiently bad, there was always this propensity of the Second Personality to do the totally unexpected thing at the most unlikely time. This frightened Miss Parker more than anything about it, for she felt sooner or later it would pass completely out of her control and set about wrecking everything. There had been an evening not long ago when It had attempted to destroy her altogether. She had been walking home to Mrs. Jamison's after a long day, and was crossing the small bridge on lower Center where water moved silently through a matting of honeysuckle many feet below; and suddenly it had come to The Thing to throw Miss Parker over the rail and into the dark vines. She had stopped quite dead and stared down into the thickness (it had seemed to her for an instant to be a pit of writhing snakes and she thought of the medieval therapy for madness and grew quite faint) and all the time something in her was chuckling because of the consternation that would be rampant in Carville next morning when little Miss Parker was found, quite glassy-eyed, in the Center Street sewage stream.

Then too (here she closed her eyes at the awful memory) there had been the Committee of Councilmen Supervising Library Management, and there was Miss Parker rising to make her usual recommendations on purchase or donation of new books to the library. All was quite regular and normal; everything had proceeded in the same manner as at hundreds of other such meetings. She had been standing there (in the same position and at the same chair as at all the other meetings) when she had known abruptly that as soon as she opened her mouth, a great squawk would come rushing out from somewhere and demand a competent text-book on sex for the library shelves; the realization had caused Miss Parker to clutch the table faintly, not even knowing all the horrors involved but sensing the tremendous and terrible complications that would surely follow such a suggestion . . . .

"Sex," she croaked between clenched teeth (or it was

205

wrung from her as a moan), and Chairman Brown leaped to his feet and cried, "She says she's sick!" to no one in particular and fetched her a drink of water.

She had been so upset by the whole thing that she had left her neatly written report in the hands of the committee secretary and accepted weakly Mr. Harvey's offer of an immediate ride home. Just for a minute the scene rose in her head again—she and Mr. Harvey going down the courthouse steps and climbing into his Plymouth automobile, and then she slammed the door on thinking of any more of it. There was no need to go into that part of it. That was the worst thing of all.

But in spite of her resolution, Miss Parker caught herself dwelling on the incident. Mr. Harvey had, she recalled, been kindness itself the evening he drove her home from the meeting; he had insisted on cupping one hand beneath her elbow and standing at the front door until Mrs. Jamison came to receive her in like a great mother hen. (The house *did,* as a matter of fact, smell faintly of wet feathers; Miss Parker marveled that she had never placed it before.) And the next day as she was taking her lunch hour—a scrupulous sixty minutes and no more—Mr. Harvey had come all the way across Broad Street with his hat in his hand to ask after her.

Mr. Harvey, she mused almost involuntarily, had been wifeless now for eleven years, which was certainly a discreet waiting period, even for Carville. (Something that was startlingly like a small Chinese bell went off in the region of Miss Parker's spine whenever she permitted herself to think of Mr. Harvey. Sometimes she caught a mental vision of Mr. Harvey in repose, the straight features relaxed and softened by sleep. It was all a very proper vision, of course; she pictured him beneath very thick coverlets still wearing his starched shirt and with every hair in place. Still, she had to admit, it was a strange day indeed when Agnes Parker would permit even the fringes of her never very active imagination to linger in a male bedroom.)

Mr. Harvey (she went back to the original musing) had been with the Merchants and Industrial Bank for years even before his marriage. He had started in as an errand boy or sweeper or something, and now he was head teller and wore impeccable starched shirts under deep-gray suiting. Miss Parker always made her weekly deposit at his window, where she could not help but admire the tailored pink and white of his nails, and the way his fingers shuffled almost contemptuously through the stacks of bills.

That was another time when Miss Parker could feel the terrible Other Self boiling dangerously near the surface. She knew as surely as if she had already been spectator to the scene what was due to happen:

. . . Suddenly the small librarian would take a step backward and stand spraddle-legged before Mr. Harvey's window with a smoking (though unfired; Miss Parker was terrified of guns) revolver in one hand.

"O.K., Harvey old boy" (that dreadful nasal voice), "let's have the boodle."

And Mr. Harvey, transformed in a twinkling into a quailing bewildered creature whose impeccable shirt collar was fairly wilting from fear, would begin stuffing the green stacks of cash into an ordinary paper bag for her; and off she would go with the sack under one arm, stopping perhaps to express her general contempt by spitting soundly into the sand-filled brass basin which stood conveniently near the entrance. . . .

If Mr. Harvey could detect this dangerous mental preview while he accepted her weekly deposit and stamped things pleasantly into her bankbook, he gave no sign; and lately she had taken to snatching the book from him quickly and hurrying away before the dreadful notion should become reality. Once out on the street again, Miss Parker would clutch the bankbook against the throbbing in her chest and cross quickly to Hawkins' for a soft drink. She felt safe in one of these booths; no criminal, however vile and depraved, could rise from a soda and saunter forth to rob a bank. She was sure of that.

And after the first swallow or two of the tangy liquid (it always put her just on the verge of sneezing) Miss Parker would come to herself enough to tuck the deposit book into her handbag and click it shut firmly, as if she had just imprisoned a dragon therein.

Certainly Mr. Harvey had suspected nothing of this when he drove her home from the Committee of Councilmen after her seizure. She still felt like a scoundrel at deceiving him about her true nature. Should she have spoken out with real candor?

"Mr. Harvey, I am seriously thinking of robbing your bank."

"Really, my dear? Whatever for?"

Here Miss Parker's imagination ran out of fuel and sputtered to a stop, for she could honestly think of no sensible reason. Besides, Mr. Harvey would never *never* have called her "my dear," not even in so studied a British manner.

Indeed, Mr. Harvey—like the good citizen he was—would probably have turned his Plymouth off Broad Street and delivered her soundlessly over to the police. Think how confusing this would have been to Sheriff White, who never in his fourteen years of service had been called upon to cope with anything more alarming than a lost child or a mild traffic violator—to have suddenly dumped upon his doorstep a potential bank robber, and a mad one at that. Miss Parker permitted herself to smile at the thought; then her face settled into lines of sadness.

. . . The courtroom fell abruptly silent as the lovely woman rose to say what must be said. She faced them all, the people who had known her, and squared her shoulders.

"Not guilty, Your Honor. Not guilty by reason of insanity," she half-whispered.

The silence was broken by the rising wail of a hysterical woman. Agnes Parker turned again and looked out at the courtroom.

"That will do, Mrs. Jamison," she said quietly . . . .

Just then someone came into the library and cleared a throat; Miss Parker started visibly and looked up from her desk. In a moment she had lost herself gratefully in the intricacy of number and date and rubber stamp pad, and the whole disagreeable notion passed out of her mind and was forgotten.

Agnes Parker had always lived in Carville. She was born there in 1913 to a rather sickly woman who looked upon her as some sort of terrible payment life demanded; if you lived a life, you must replenish it with still another. Once the actual ordeal of birth was over, Cassie Parker considered her account settled once and for all and seldom noticed her daughter except with an air of faint reproach; and went to her reward two years later, a little smug over her superb timing.

Miss Parker lived with her father during her childhood and girlhood. One might have thought she was the daughter of a "tyrannical Presbyterian minister," but it was rather the other face of the coin; for Adam Parker had indeed planned to enter the ministry, but a combination of scholastic and financial limitations forced him to drop the idea early in his preministerial work, and to become a barber instead.

This left him with a confirmed suspicion of preachers as a class—the sons of the idle rich, they were, with more book learning than good sense, and as the years passed he finally abandoned the church altogether and became its bitterest enemy. He said that the church was actually anti-Christ in the world, and that many less perceptive men and women were being deceived by Satan's slyness into mistaking it for the kingdom.

He was especially firm about this idea on Saturday nights after he had been by the only Carville saloon, which managed to survive the annual sermons preached against it by all local denominations. Then he would storm drunkenly through the house, shouting that the church was really the Whore of Babylon, a usage that left Miss Parker's mind naturally vague on certain definitions of terms.

Father and daughter lived well enough on his earnings, however, and although Miss Parker was forbidden to attend the church affairs which made up so large a part of Carville social life, nobody really blamed her because of it. After all, a child's first duty was to his parent, even so misguided a parent as Adam Parker, and no one doubted that the heart of his shy plain daughter was really "in the right place" in spite of him. It might have been suspected of terrible deviation had she been handsome or even gay, but there was something about her solemnity and her plain features that convinced everyone of her righteous nature.

Agnes Parker went through school without noticeable brilliance or stupidity, and developed her sole consuming interest during Grade Nine, when she became a helper in the Mac Gray High School Library. There she immersed herself in respectful silence among all the world's literary masterpieces; she read the classic novels with awe and with very limited understanding; and she experienced her first sense of individual importance whenever she was called upon to get information for her fellow students from the library shelves. She was like a hostess in an immaculate home, quick to sense and meet the slightest of her guests' desires.

The inevitable occurred, and—just as inevitably—passed away as quickly as it had come, leaving little mark upon her. The library became to Agnes Parker for almost an entire spring semester the church she had been forced to renounce, and she walked along between the shelves with the awe of a pietist in a cathedral. She permitted most of literature to remain a mystery to her, for that preserved the religious sense, and she was untroubled by her bafflement at Shakespeare, for instance, sensing that this was right and proper and the way things ought to be. She permitted herself to be lost and swallowed up in her literary interests, but it was a blind loss without effort or volition, so that it faded almost as abruptly as it had come and eventually she forgot all about it.

Later, when she became full-fledged library assistant, she experienced the brief disillusionment of the priest, touching now with his own hands the bread and wine, and unable to reconcile the material with the miracle. Agnes Parker was never able to reconcile the two, and so she put the miracle out of her life as calmly as one might snuff a no longer needed candle, and her library work became merely a job to her.

In the spring of her senior year, Adam Parker died. It happened while he was clipping the sparse tufts of Reverend Kaiser's hair and beard, with ill-concealed indignation at the degrading position he was in. He had turned, muttering, to reach for something, when he was mercifully stricken by a heart attack, and slumped down soundlessly behind the barber chair. They say that as he fell he cast up his hand as one warding off a blow, and the razor wavered and bit out a piece of flesh from his cheek almost viciously, as if it had long been waiting for a chance to get the upper hand of him.

After her father died, Miss Parker wondered for the first time if she had loved him, and was for a time disturbed because she did not know. It bothered her that two people could live together for so long without wondering, and then be unable to know for a certainty even when it was over.

There was some local discussion over whether or not Adam Parker should be placed in hallowed ground, but affection for his daughter moved them all. The Reverends Lassiter and Kaiser conducted a rather awkward funeral service, which leaned heavily on the quoting of scripture, and they laid him—almost with relief—behind the Lyndale Presbyterian Church. For several years afterward, Miss Parker tried to beautify her father's grave, but nothing—not even a geranium—would grow. (It was said by the caretaker that this was due to the thick oak shade in the cemetery, and finally gravel was scattered over the plot, from which in summertime a faint white powder rose irritably and did not settle at all until late in the rainy days.)

Miss Parker stayed on at the high school library after her father's death, first selling the brownstone house and taking rooms with Mrs. Jamison; and when the Carville Councilmen erected the public building, she was the logical choice to manage it. The day she first took up her new duties in the new Carville Public Library and found the shelves still shining and her own front desk gleaming (shipped directly from Michigan, the local paper said) it seemed to Miss Parker that there was something she almost remembered—a glow of pleasure she could almost touch again. Then it was gone, and did not come to her again, and she ceased to wonder if she had loved her father and set herself to the business of operating the library efficiently.

Somewhere there ought to have been a beau for Miss Parker, even some dull fellow in a worn serge who played backgammon with her on Tuesday nights or walked her home after piano recitals. But there never was—none of her high school companions, or the library patrons, and neither of the unmarried but doddering councilmen—none of these ever vied for her attentions, until she lost the notion that she had any to bestow.

Once, when she was only twenty-eight and had not wholly passed into immunity, there was a young high school *history teacher who fell into the habit of preparing his class lectures at the library. Mr. Bunkle was rumored to be somewhat gay for the general moral standards at Mac Gray High School; and once he and Miss Parker had collided in the reference room (due to a quite understandable lighting problem) and she felt for one wild instant that he was going to clasp her in an impetuous kiss.*

That split second of waiting had all the vividness of crisis and catastrophe, so that Agnes Parker swam back into her past and saw a little girl with a school slate, and forward into her future to where it faded and became a nebulous mass and then smoke, and then nothing at all. It was as if she had for that instant a God's-Eye view—she saw herself whole from cradle to grave, and it was like a meaningless flicker in a night she did not understand, so that her face contorted painfully; and the young man drew back and made a fumbling apology.

Neither of these experiences ever came to her again—the young man or that merciless once-over view. Mr. Bunkle never came near her again and always seemed a little embarrassed to meet her eyes or even to be in the library at all; and when spring came, the school did not renew his contract. He went away from Carville and within a month Agnes Parker could not have called his name or remembered his face, and by now she had forgotten his very existence.

There had been no other man for Miss Parker, and there had not been even the novel read in secret, or the crush on a stage star; there had been only the library and the Book Club, and night after night between the cool starched sheets at Mrs. Jamison's.

MISS PARKER POSSESSED

As a matter of fact, there had been nothing much of anything until this queer possession that wracked her and shook her and stalked through her life tearing up the important things, like an inexperienced gardener pulling up the cultivated flowers and swearing they were weeds.

It was after Miss Parker became aware of this demon which she called her schizophrenia that she began to cast lustful eyes at Mr. Harvey.

Certainly she would never have described them thus. It was only that at these regular Committee meetings she would see him there, almost at the other end of the table, and the close-cropped hairs at the base of her neck would begin to tingle, like phone wires singing in a wind. He was always bent thoughtfully over a paper or a memorandum of some sort; and Miss Parker would be seized with a spasm of coughing until finally he looked up and she met his eyes apologetically. After that she would feel quite strengthened for awhile, as though something tangible had spilled from his glance into hers, and she would get into the business of approving book donations with the greatest of composure.

And still that Other One bothered her, always just under the surface, never exactly saying the terrible things out but leaving them just under the top skim of her mind, where their shapes and bulges made identity unmistakeable.

There would be, for instance, Mr. Harvey's left hand. Just down the inside of his index finger there ran a long protruding scar, where the lips of puckered flesh stood up on each side, and Miss Parker would know quite suddenly just what it was like to have that hand upon her, and to feel that wedge of skin moving ever so softly against her own; until

215

sometimes she would grow quite faint with horror at her thoughts.

And there were also Mr. Harvey's front teeth, much too long for handsomeness, which gave him a solemn rabbit's face; those were the biting teeth, and looking at him thus she could feel the goose bumps prickle inside her thighs, and she would take one hand and twist it angrily with the other as if she were killing some vicious animal.

She had taken to dreaming of him too—there was one dream in which she was bound in tape as tightly as a dug-up mummy, and she was spinning and spinning wildly while the long white shreds unwound, with Mr. Harvey holding smiling onto the other end.

Or the two of them would be small children again, plump and pink and naked as cherubs, playing with butterflies in a garden of scarlet flowers that went to jelly underneath their feet.

Or sometimes she would be robbing the Merchants and Industrial Bank, and Mr. Harvey would come whimpering from his teller's cage and swear unfailing devotion, and then he would turn into a great white horse and she would ride him out of town and into a robber's cave.

On the night Mr. Harvey had driven her home from the Councilmen's meeting after that terrible exhibition, and put one hand gently beneath her elbow to aid her up Mrs. Jamison's front stairs, she had felt recurrently faint; the sensation washed over her in waves, so that when she was safely inside her own room she had closed the door weakly and put her back against it, feeling the clamminess that began in her palms and ended somewhere just above the wrist.

Then, as suddenly as the terrible possession had come upon her, bisecting her into two such foreign creatures and striking at the roots of everything that was sane and sensible in her life, it went away again. There was perhaps a sharp sickening moment when it wrenched out of her like part of flesh and marrow; but after that there was no feeling at all—not even of relief—and all the pieces dropped obediently into the old pattern.

It all happened at the next committee meeting, and once it was gone, Miss Parker could never really remember having experienced it at all.

It was an evening in late March when the Councilmen met again, and she had walked uptown from Mrs. Jamison's to the courthouse where the meetings were always held. There had been a long rain that afternoon, sharpening the air and strengthening the illusion that even beneath the concrete walkways of Main Street a thousand slumbering seeds were on the verge of erupting upward. She could almost picture them the next morning—great tall oaks sprung up overnight with slabs of sidewalk still clinging crazily to the topmost branches, and the Committee on City Improvement standing in bunched consternation on the courthouse lawn, unable to comprehend such vandalism. Miss Parker smiled, for The Thing was not yet gone; and she could still envision with amusement such sights. She forced the smile down quickly, however; there must be no repetition tonight of that last terrible meeting; this time she must remain utterly in control of herself.

The day at the library had been long and dull; now, even in the sweet wet air, Miss Parker found herself overly conscious of her own tiredness. It was as if her backbone had grown limp as string, leaving her ribs to flop uselessly on each side whenever she drew breath.

The committee meeting at least would be short; she had only two requests—a book on flower gardening and one containing detailed directions for tree surgery—both of which seemed to her reasonable and respectable offers. After that part was over, she would ask to be excused, for the library fiscal year began in April, and the group would be discussing her salary. She knew beforehand that they would not vary it by so much as a single penny either way, but still, her presence might prove embarrassing while this decision was being reached.

Mr. Harvey was just going up the courthouse steps ahead of her as she approached; he stopped and waited for her to catch up with him. Some bird that had gotten imprisoned under her breastbone fluttered its wings and made a little whimper; Miss Parker swallowed hard.

"Good evening, Miss Parker."

"How are you, Mr. Harvey?"

Involuntarily she giggled; she was able only by a serious mental effort to transform at least part of the explosive sound into a cough, although the force of it made her feel like a TB inmate.

"I hope you're feeling better these days, Miss Parker," said Mr. Harvey kindly. He was holding back the door and she went through with her head high, enjoying for an instant the sensation that a long skirt swept regally behind her. Then she came back to the practicality of his question.

"Oh, yes." She nodded her head gravely. "Digestive. Merely digestive."

"I understand," said Mr. Harvey in tones of real sympathy. He was so kind. Miss Parker shivered deliciously; how gentle he would be with a woman—coaxing without seeming to coax—until all her reserve toppled and . . . she caught herself and yanked furiously at one hand with the other, as if moving the lever that would shut such thoughts away. But the bird in her chest moved gently, and the wings brushed against her with a whisper.

Then the two of them were going up the narrow steps that led to the third floor, and Miss Parker felt his eyes on her hips; she could honestly feel the warm spots where they rested, and her terrible Other Self reached down and twitched them a little more than was necessary in any normal walk. By the time they came to the top of the stairs, her face was afire with shame.

She excused herself with what she hoped was composure and slipped into the Ladies' Room to tidy her hair before the meeting opened. She had always found something depressing about this particular Ladies' Room; it was more like a tomb than a toilet, with its high tiled walls faded to an acid yellow, and the dim bulb way off in the ceiling somewhere.

Miss Parker moved to the window and began to comb at her stubby hair, glancing out to the street three stories below; it was drying now in patches from the rain and looked like the speckled haunch of some large animal. Miss Parker was almost singing—he *was* concerned about her health (the imaginary bird turned as if it were floating in a small wind) and if she could only submerge that Other Self, perhaps he would see her as she really was, perhaps he would—she could not dwell on the thought. She dismissed it as superstitiously as the child who feels that by counting too much on Saturday's picnic will be merely delivering it over to some malevolent spirit who will send it to smash out of sheer caprice.

When Miss Parker went down the hall again, she felt that everything was under control; she paused to drink briefly from the hall fountain and bending there, she heard Mr. Harvey speaking to Mr. Brown inside the Councilmen's office. She listened to the buzz of his voice pleasantly without distinguishing the words and then Mr. Brown answered in his comparatively gruff tones.

"Poor soul," said Mr. Brown.

"And she's not as young as she once was, Clarence. You remember that incident at last month's meeting."

"That's true," said Clarence Brown. "But she's been with the library so long."

Miss Parker felt as if she were choking, but she went on drawing in water from the fountain involuntarily, as if it were beyond her power to release the handle, and as if from some vantage point she was standing off and looking at her transparent self while every limb filled up and drowned and died from the water.

"She has some serious digestive ailment," Mr. Harvey was saying. (Mr. Harvey of the gentle smile and the hand beneath her elbow; her fingers tightened at the fountain.) "It seems to me an assistant for this next year, and then an out-and-out pension would be the only kind thing."

"I believe you're right," said Mr. Brown, and then added something that Miss Parker could not make out. "I had no idea the old girl was going downhill so fast," he finished. "Bad time of life and all that, of course."

"I was noticing the jerky quality in her walk while we were coming up the stairs," said Mr. Harvey. "Rheumatism, I shouldn't doubt."

Miss Parker could bear no more. She turned and stumbled away from the fountain, conscious of her fullness and the sense of water settling heavily into her chest where nothing fluttered any longer. Once she was down the hall and safely inside the Ladies' Room again, she sank onto the cold radiator and stared down first at her feet and then at her hands, a little startled to find they were all intact, a little surprised that everything had not crumbled and fallen off into the hallway.

She felt dazed and choked; watching her hands she had the feeling that her whole body had suddenly gone empty and that if she pushed with a finger anywhere it would go crackling through the thin shell of skin and cloth that covered the nothing. She lifted her feet onto the radiator and lowered her head wearily against her knees. I ought to feel something, she thought. I really ought to feel something.

She was more shocked than anything else when she felt the wetness creeping through her skirt and discovered that she was crying—the slow, wrung-out tears that seemed to have come from somewhere away off, and to have passed through her without mattering much. She dried her eyes automatically as if they belonged to someone else, and folded her handkerchief along the original square and put it away again.

It came to her that after awhile one learned to feel absolutely nothing about anything, and that was because one had gained a perspective—one knew the ache would finally be gone, and so one simply bypassed the experience of feeling it in the first place. Since the rain would soon dry off anyway, one could walk through it and have no sensation of drops hitting the skin. It's all in having a perspective, thought Miss Parker firmly. She climbed off the radiator and looked down at the street from the narrow window. Under the street lights, the concrete was almost completely dry, except for the lines where tires had tracked it from one puddle to another.

Miss Parker was the last one to arrive at the meeting, and all the Councilmen looked up from the table in surprise, knowing her punctual habits.

"You're well, I hope?" said Chairman Brown jovially, and she nodded her head and smiled.

"Quite well, thank you," said Miss Parker. It was true, she realized. She probed mentally for the Second Self that was always seated within her like a shadow and it evaded her. Perhaps it was gone.

"She's looking better, don't you think?" smiled Mr. Harvey. Her hand shook once when she arranged her papers but it steadied quickly, and she did not look up.

When she was called upon to present the two books for consideration, she did so in her usual efficient manner, explaining crisply why she thought these volumes would be an asset to the Carville Public Library. She did not look at Mr. Harvey for a long time, and when she did it was with a sense of secret apprehension.

But nothing happened. There sat a balding bank teller with protruding teeth and a somewhat unpleasant scar along one finger. She noticed for the first time the mole beneath his ear and the four or five limp hairs that grew from the top of it. He met her eyes but there was nothing in his glance and she let out a long breath.

She really felt quite limp from the rush of her relief. It was all over, then, and Agnes Parker was safe.

Child So Fair

HE LOOKED like a little rotted thing when she came to the door and held him out in front of her.

"Can we come in?" she said.

I said, "I reckon so," and went back in the kitchen and stirred one of the pots, even if I'd stirred it just before I heard her at the door.

She looked bad; all skin and bones she was, and the little thing she was carrying didn't look no better.

"That your boy?" I said.

She nodded her head and when she smiled her face didn't look quite so peaked. "Yessum, that's him. That's Abner."

I put the spoon down and looked at her with a hardness. "That ain't no name for a boy," I said. "You've made an evil choosing when you called the boy Abner."

Thea looked scared. "It's what Will wanted," she said.

I hate to hear anybody whine on about anything. "It was Abner and David," I said to her. "It was Abner done him evil."

She was looking down at the baby with her mouth all open and I got tired of seeing it. "Where's Will anyhow?" I said.

Right then she started to cry, laying her hands against her face and getting them wet between the fingers.

"Gone again, Mama. Will's done gone off again."

I stirred in the pot around and around. I don't hold much with that way of acting, since Thea knew what he was like when she married him.

"No need to cry," I told her. "It's not the first and it won't be the last. No need to waste crying on it."

She quit crying then and blew her nose on the baby's wrapping. "I know it, Mama," she said. She just sounded a little wearied.

'You don't look so good, Thea," I said. "You been sick after the baby?"

She nodded her head. "He's just suckling out my strength," she said. "And Will fusses and rares. All the time he does."

"He gone with that Maple Street woman this time?"

"I don't know. I guess so."

I went over and took the baby from her and looked down at him, although I don't see so good any more. He was a mighty puny thing, but he didn't make any noise. That was one thing I had to say for his advantage—he didn't make any noise. I handed him back.

"How you been, Mama?" said Thea. She didn't hardly look at the baby, like it wasn't really hers.

I said, "I'm not so fair. I see everything funny. I see everything like it was through water."

"You been to the village?"

"I been. They said it was cataracts."

"That's too bad," said Thea.

"I guess so," I said. I went into the back room and left her alone with the cooking pots so she would know she could eat if she wanted to.

When I went back she looked a little better and her face was greasy. I said, "I fixed your bed down."

"Thank you, Mama," said Thea.

"You reckon Will's gonna come back?"

"One of these days," she said.

I'd been living and aging in the house by myself for many a year when Thea come home again. All the young ones went away to houses of their own, or down to the village where the new sawmill was and the money came.

My man built the house when he took me to wife, and every piece of it lays steady because his hand put it in careful. There used to be a place you could look out the back window and see between two hills for far and far, but that was before my seeing left me.

There's no grass will grow in the yard, but that's because of the great pine trees and the way needles mat up the ground every season. Sometimes I fall to smiling over all those pine needles outside in the yard. They been pushed into walls for playhouses, and burned in the stove, and put into pillows; but they always lay even, like none of them was gone. That's a funny thing about pine needles, that you can't use them up or wear them out.

After my oldest girl come up from village school and opened a school down the road, she'd tote over the biggest pine cones and color them bright, and set them all around the wall like new flowers. But the school did poorly and finally them as wanted went to the village and the others back to working.

Will Frankin took Thea to wife when she was about sixteen, and they fell to displeasure right away. Thea didn't hold with forgiving too ready and Will didn't care if she did or neither, so it went poorly for them.

Thea was the only one of them all ever coming home; the rest stuck it out in quietness. But Thea was never like the others in anything; she was my dreaming child and she was the only one of the lot could sing. She used to sing all the time of an evening—songs we knowed and songs that seemed to come up out of her inside, and they were the sweetest songs.

"You sing fairly," my man used to say to Thea of an evening. "You sing fair as a bird," and Thea would snicker, but she wouldn't sing any more for a while.

My man died when he was fifty-odd. That was just after the sawmill come to the village, and nobody was used to its ways yet. I told him he had hands for dirt and growing, but he went off from the patch and down the hill to the village because of the rich wage.

And it looked to me everything knew he had no business there, for the belt threw back a slab of wood the next day that drove his head in.

The rest of the family was coming along behind when they brought him home that late evening, but I didn't feel nothing, not even when he was laid on the pine needles and everybody stood still and waited for me to move someway. I dished them up a supper for their trouble, and the preacher said a service at the burial.

It seemed to me always after there was a sticky place in the needles where they laid him down, and I never walked on that place, not even when it had rained a hundred times.

And even when my sight wasted, I would walk a long ways around, not wanting to set a foot on the place where they laid my man's dead corpse that day.

Will didn't come back hurried, so Thea and her boy stayed on with me awhile. He was growing and after awhile he got so he would crawl around on the floor and he was always getting stepped on. He didn't talk, though, and he got to where he could stay out of the way pretty good.

Thea wasn't much help to my need. She brought in firewood and she swept and cleaned, but she never could cook good.

One day I was walking in the kitchen when the boy took hold of my leg and hung on.

"Get away," I said, kicking at him, "Get away from here," but he just laid on the harder and looked up my leg at me. His hair was already yellow and there wasn't any curl in it; it stuck out all over his ears like a dandelion edge.

When I saw the boy wasn't going to let go, I bent down and took his fingers loose and gave him a spoon to hit things with. But after that he watched me when I went through the house, and if I came near to him he would put out his hands at my skirt and open his mouth with a soft noise like he wished he knew something to say.

Thea didn't care much for the boy and one day she said that he was a heaviness to her account of his face. I used to look at the boy but everything melted to my eyes when I looked, and I couldn't tell nothing but yellow hair and skin color. His hair was like rich butter and I shamed Thea and said he was a fair child.

She still walked about early at night, but the singing wasn't the same; Thea was more than twenty year and she had borne a boy and she made an old woman's singing.

After a year or so, Lack Fitz took to coming over the hill to see her, and she was singing sweet again and they went off in the dark and come back quiet. I knew what they was up to on the hillsides, but I couldn't see shame in it, with Will Frankin off with that Maple Street woman and Thea left by herself lonesome.

The boy was slow in talking and we didn't drive at him; I never talked much myself and Thea neither, so it was quiet where he was.

But when he stood up then he came taller than my knee joint and he fell to calling me Big Woman, talking slow and careful, and all the day he followed right behind me. He called his mama Thea after my own way, but he didn't go to her much.

When it was time for his weaning, Thea painted a face on her tit with berries, so when he came again he was made very scared, and after that he took from a cup. But he didn't cry at the colored face, although it was fearsome, and after that he stayed with me more and didn't go much to his mama.

Wasn't long before Thea said she was going over the hill to keep a house for Lack Fitz and he would be her man now.

"I have his child," she said, and though you couldn't tell it yet, I knew she had to go.

I said, "Will you take the other?" But Thea shook her head.

"Lack doesn't like to look at him," she said, "because of

his mark, and he doesn't want the new one to get it." So I knew the boy would stay with me.

After Thea was gone I pulled the boy's face up close to mine and looked, but it was pale-colored as milk and his hair was like yellow butter and he was a fair child.

He put his hand into my hand and pulled soft at my fingers and said "Big Woman," and I was glad Thea had Lack Fitz's child and had to go live with him.

My sight got worse and worse, so that I couldn't tell but lights and some colors, and the boy led me around and did the tasks. He was a strong one for his age and he learned to laugh. I had to teach him house things before he was old enough to learn because my seeing was past. At seedtime then, he knew already the things apart, and he learned about growing and about the bugs and making the rows even.

He grew up by my thigh, and when I put a hand down I could feel his tallness and then he got hip-high, and he could talk a little more; but he had some thickness in his tongue.

When Thea bore Lack Fitz's girl, she came over and told me; but she said she didn't want the boy with her for his mouth, and he wouldn't come out any time she was there.

When he got bigger, he could sing more fair than Thea with his high sound, but the words were distant and I could not tell them.

Till one day he put my finger up to touch his upper lip, and there was a queer pucker in it that I could not tell about. But I did not care for that; he was as high grown as my heart and I knew his hair grew long and yellow and hung down fairly to his shoulder.

The Very Old Are Beautiful

THE VERY OLD have a unique beauty of their own. It consists, perhaps, in that they have passed beyond the necessity for pretense, and need no longer be bothered with convincing anyone that they are by nature handsome, or clever, or even agreeable. Life has grown puckered and hard around the core of each of them; it has contracted over dried-up little raisin faces; it has sunk deep into the faded eyes.

You have seen them sometimes on public buses, clambering slowly to their seats in complete awareness that their feebleness is an inconvenience to the driver, an affront to the young. They will sink sighing onto the leather seats and then snap their glances around quickly; it is as if their look proclaims without apology: "I am old. I am tired. I have grown ugly and I know that it matters to no one."

And because for the first time in their lives they know something honest about themselves, they possess then their own special beauty, and no one else can touch it or destroy it.

Mama Bower was like that.

She had none of the insipid beauty which the very young like to envision in their grandmothers; there was nothing pale or smelling of lavender; no pastel-blue eyes set about with the gentlest side crinkles, and she wore no fluff of lace at the throat. Lace, Mama Bower maintained, tickled the nostrils.

But there was a certain integrity about her frankly bony old form which seemed to have leaned of a sudden off-center, and the face crossed and crisscrossed intricately with wrinkles, and that jut of a chin that started farther out in front of her than anything else did.

"Mama has her pecker out," the grandchildren would exclaim gleefully when she was displeased, and it *did* seem as if she might go thrusting it forth and sharpening it on anyone who got in her way.

There was something dauntless about Mama Bower, or perhaps there was something merely undaunted, but it was unmistakable; it supported her as a boned corset supported many a less determined woman. Looking at Mama Bower, you had the feeling she had driven covered wagons across a raw continent—or could have—and had managed to cope with almost everything—or could if she had to. This had left her with a faith in herself and with a self-respect that somehow stopped short of being pride; it is a hard distinction to draw—that thin line where self-confidence reaches the point of diminishing returns. But Mama Bower had it; she lived her life in the light of it; and she was suspicious of people who proclaimed too loudly their sense of humility. It was too likely to be an excuse, thought Mama Bower.

Mama Bower was especially contemptuous of that group of human beings who seemed to be living a sort of trial-and-error existence, practicing up for the next time. Despite her religious bedrock, she was convinced that this life was absolutely all a man was entitled to, and she could grow enraged at the sight of anyone who trickled out his days as if there were an eternity more where these came from. This condemnation took in almost a whole generation of lazy and inefficient youth; and Mama Bower was forever clapping her thin lips together in an almost invisible line and putting her chin out disapprovingly to see it.

Her periodical visits to the younger Bowers were hailed with mixed resignation and respect.

Sam Bower would come home with one of her infrequent letters scrawled on tablet paper and toss it into the center of the table where everyone would eye it as they might a copperhead.

"Mama's coming," he would say.

Milly was always casual before the children. "That so?" She would clear her throat. "Jackie, pass Dad the roast," and look across the table at him warningly.

"Tuesday."

Pricilla would then voice everyone's unspoken question. "How long's she going to stay?" and Sam would keep a watchful eye on his wife while he answered.

"She said till we didn't need her."

Milly's retort would be wrung from her like an involuntary moan of sudden pain. "Oh God," Milly would say, slowly and prayerfully.

God, however, was firmly enlisted on the side of Mama Bower, a relationship of many years' standing. When Papa Bower had passed to his reward nineteen years before (out of utter exhaustion, thought Milly grimly and with some sympathy), Mama Bower had been quietly but firmly remarried to the Almighty—to whom she was forever chat-

235

tering underneath her breath, and who seldom got a word of reply in edgewise.

There had been, for instance, Mama's last visit to the younger Bowers. In an attempt to convince her by demonstration that the whole family of souls had not yet gone to the devil through sheer neglect (Mama Bower saw the human soul as something of a garden demanding regular Sabbath pruning and insecticides), Milly and Sam had taken them all to church services. They had made a handsome family group, Milly thought—the two little girls pressed and starched, and Sam looking quite dignified in his blue suit, and even Mama Bower more meek and subdued than was her habit. Then, just as the offering plate passed down their bench, Mama Bower had taken note of the sole quarter dropped in with a clank by the rich widow Martin, and had suddenly called aloud for the Lord to witness such doings, which—Milly had no doubt—the Lord had obediently done, putting up no argument. It gave Milly the unpleasant feeling that the Lord was forever perched on Mama Bower's shoulder—like some disagreeable green parrot—with a brass chain around His leg.

Mama Bower lived alone at the old homestead, a spotless old two-story house on the Lincolnton, N.C., RFD, which Milly and Sam visited once a summer. The walls of the house were nearly worn thin from years of endless scrubbing and whitewashing, and the earth in the front yard had long since given up the unequal task of simply looking like earth—it lay hard and dustless, perpetually lined from Mama Bower's restless broom, and rooting not one unwanted grass seed.

There had been two of the Bower boys, Saumel and

Kiser, and as often happens, Mama had secretly inclined toward Kiser, the younger, a rather worthless but charming lad whose behavior was a constant trial to her. He had somehow made Samuel, who was actually a model of everything that was best in Mama Bower's teachings, seem too sober and too dull by comparison, and for all her tongue clucking and chin jutting and soulful looks to Heaven, she loved him for his very flaunting of everything she said.

The two brothers joined the army together when World War II came, and Kiser died at Anzio. That was all wrong to Mama Bower; Kiser had not gone forth with any big ideals; he was not really fighting *for* anything—it seemed to her that the war had literally robbed him of his life and there had been nowhere any fair exchange, such as Mama Bower would have respected. And on the other hand, Sam came home with only a thin wrist scar from a shrapnel wound and all his thoughts intact, just as he had carried them firmly away to war—nice abstract thoughts about democracy and world peace and the totalitarian threat.

"Is not fair," Mama Bower had muttered. "Is disorderly."

That was her word for anything which threatened to show that all was not well in her universe—it took in nearly all the paradoxes, the unfairnesses; it pronounced finally and completely upon the presence of undeserved pain in the world and the whole gigantic irony of things—this was all so much superficial untidiness to Mama Bower in a world that otherwise, she felt, was run with fair competence. It was as if God were really an excellent housekeeper, but He was having to care for an oversized place, so that here and there something had to slide—some dirt had to go under the rug, and some hall closet had to be jammed with debris, and some woodwork wait around until the spring cleaning. It was all right; God would get around to it in His own time.

Yet she grieved for her younger son in ways that none of them knew; she let herself be immersed for awhile as in some stinging carbolic that would keep the flesh from rot. She insisted on gathering his belongings herself—the little-boy clothes and the high school souvenirs and the battered broken toys—and after a fortnight of mending and glueing, she carried them all to Nigger Hill and gave them away without a tear.

And in the evenings she sat outside where the red crepe myrtles grew: they had set them out together when he was small and came no taller than her thigh, and now they were blooming still when he was gone; it was another untidy note in the Scheme of Things.

Then for a week or so, Mama Bower went way back to the beginning of it—to her youngness when Kiser was only a stirring in her belly—and she thought him along, every single thing she could remember about him: his birth and his babyhood and all the pranks and report cards and un-successful jobs, the injuries and the illnesses and the whip-pings; she thought him all the way up to his army life and the V-mail letters and then to the last letter, and after that she snapped it all shut like a book she had read thoroughly once and digested, and would not read again.

Is all I know about Kiser, thought Mama Bower. If every-day I thought and grieved and wondered, I could not remember any more.

And so she didn't—or if she did, not one of those who knew her guessed it—and when they asked if she would

238

ship his body home to rest she shook her head firmly, and that was an end to it.

Mama Bower had a way of speaking that was almost a special dialect, and people meeting her for the first time felt surely she had come over from the Old Country. As a matter of fact, Mama Bower had sprung from Swedish immigrant stock, but she was altogether an American and her speech habits were entirely her own. She had developed them over a period of years because her husband had been a silent man and she learned early in her marriage that the only way to get answers was to be economical with questions.

It left her with a contempt for pronouns, especially the group which included this and that, and for adjectives and adverbs.

This opinion was strengthened by her close observation (and criticism) of the education her two granddaughters were receiving. During one of her visits they showed her, one evening, how one diagrammed a sentence, and she pounced upon the paper with ill-concealed delight.

"See?" she explained to her son Samuel, pointing with a finger. "The straight road goes here, and the others are side roads which get no place." Having it drawn like that with all the useless adjectives ending in obvious blind ends, and only the vital subject-verb "getting someplace," convinced her that she had long since hit upon some great educational principle, which was even now being discovered in the best schools of the land.

If there was one thing on the old homestead to which Mama Bower was passionately devoted, it was her apple tree, all the more because it was never a very satisfactory tree. It seemed to have some willful caprice of its own, as if it could not be bothered with the times and seasons like any ordinary tree.

When Kiser—then a little boy—first brought the sapling home (there had been a nursery truck overturned on the highway and since the accident was due to the driver's falling asleep, everyone felt that his load was fair game), Mama Bower had been instantly pleased. To steal was one thing, but to remove from inefficient hands a piece of life deserving better care was a noble achievement, and she had always been partial to apple trees anyway.

"Good tree," she had insisted, nodding her head firmly, and it had been planted not in the general orchard but just outside her kitchen window where she could watch it grow, and where in later years, she thought, she could but step outside the door and pick up makings for a pie.

But even from the first the tree had flaunted its independence, putting out blooms long before it was old enough and starting a root that headed maliciously for the foundations of the house.

"Is the soil," explained Mama Bower, frowning, when the tree gave up its first season of fruit—hard streaked apples that were about the same reddish color as the mud in which the tree was rooted. And when those apples rotted on the branches before they could be gathered and jellied in respectable fashion, Mama Bower was emphatic in blaming the heavy rains.

But that was only the beginning. Thereafter the tree blossomed almost always out of season, and was frostbitten and drooped; it gave up sun-yellow apples one year that vindicated all of Mama Bower's faith; and another year it bore no fruit at all, only a crowd of lush green leaves that threw a thick shade against the house.

"But it shuts the heat from my window," Mama Bower defended bravely, and all year long she toted buckets of water and dumped them at the roots, and laid manure about, ignoring the smell which it made near her spotless kitchen.

"Is a good tree," she declared firmly.

They began to look alike, Mama Bower and her useless apple tree—they bent and settled and hardened into firm and stubborn things; the family teased her and she was delighted at the comparison, although she would not have it known. Thereafter she pampered her apple tree even more; she would go out in a windstorm and stand defiantly under the tree, as if she were waiting for one branch to weaken so she might keep it from breaking with her own hands; and she would glare furiously at the whirling clouds above them which were like personal enemies.

And in the springtime she would wait and wait until the blossoms came, and carry a few inside the house, although no one else would have snapped a twig of Mama Bower's tree.

She was always trying to start a second generation by coaxing the apple seeds to grow, watering her pots as if they held priceless orchids and waiting daily for the sprout to show above the soil.

"I am making you a tree," she would say to Sam, who would nod gratefully and try not to look at Milly. Milly had already said she would have no Jonah tree in *her* family, but Mama Bower was so proud that he had not the heart to protest.

241

Fortunately for family peace, the seeds never grew at all
—a circumstance which Mama Bower could not understand. She had always had a very green thumb; things grew
for her which would never grow for anyone else, but the
apple seeds refused her, year after year.

Finally, each year when all hope was gone, she would go
muttering into the back yard and dump her pots angrily;
then she would scrabble through the dirt with impatient
fingers, seeking even the smallest sign that the seeds had
burst and sent out a tendril which had never reached the
top. Usually she could find nothing at all, although once
in a while she turned up hard black balls where the apple
seeds had dried away completely. Then she would be relieved—it was only lack of water, or a bad moon; and she
would smile sympathetically at her apple tree as at a woman
who had miscarried, but would conceive again.

She came to visit Sam and Milly only once a year, but
the thought of her visit clouded all of the other months
except the one right after she had gone. It wasn't that Milly
disliked Mama Bower; it was only that she was driven crazy
every time she came, and when they finally waved good-by
to the old woman at the station, Milly would come home
and fall recklessly across her best chenille bedspread and
sob for an hour or so. This troubled Sam greatly, because it
was almost the only time Milly ever cried.

"But what's the matter, Honey?"

She would bury her head in a pillowcase, heedless of lipstick smears, and give vent to sounds of utter misery. "O
hway," she would order in muffled tones, which to Sam
meant the usual "go away," a meaningless command that

always angered him when he had only been trying to help.

"Is it something Mama said?"

Milly would then lift her head furiously from the pillow, face flushed and hair stringing on all sides—it was rather like a red sea serpent rising from the depths.

"I'm just tired!" she would screech with what seemed to Sam an inexhaustible amount of energy. "Can't you see I'm worn out?"

After that Sam would bang out of the house with his wounded feelings, and every conviction renewed that women were simply the most cantankerous creatures under the sun and furthermore they didn't want to be helped out of it, either. They were ungrateful to boot. And Sam would walk down to the local library and read in the magazine room until supper.

Milly was always fine by then; she would kiss him sweetly when he came grimly in the front, and she said she had been an old bear and how did he ever put up with her —which choked off his lecture before it even reached his tongue—and ended up making him feel like an unreasonable husband who obviously put forth no real effort to understand her at all.

Later, somewhat cautiously, Sam would ask her about it.

"Now really, what upset you so this afternoon? You never cry like that." And Milly would try to explain it.

"It's Mama Bower," she would begin. "It's because Mama Bower is so much herself," which struck Sam as being, at best, a little confusing.

"Well now," he would come in jovially, "she *is* getting on, you know," and then stop abruptly because Milly's face revealed sharply that she had not meant anything like that at all. He would take to a cough or so to relieve some pressure in his throat and earn a little time.

"No, no," Milly would say over his general grunting and harrumping. "I really love Mama Bower. It's when she goes away that I know how much I love Mama Bower."

Here Sam would nod. This seemed reasonable to him; it was much easier to love Mama Bower long distance than when she was firmly rearranging your whole life to suit her.

"And I'm going to be as old as Mama Bower someday . . ." Milly went on. (Sam nodded again; nothing was to be gained by denying the truth of that.)

"Only I don't think I'll be the same, you see?" she would finish triumphantly, and Sam—who was very confused by now—would smoke awhile in silence and then cautiously wonder aloud where Jackie and Pricilla were; and the subject would be dropped until the next time.

If Mama Bower's visits ended the same way, they also began in the same manner.

First there would be the letter announcing her intent, and then the grim days of preparation. All of Sam's clothes must be darned and cleaned, as Mama Bower looked with horror upon a toeless sock, and would stare wide-eyed at Milly for hours after the discovery, more shocked than if her son had married an adulteress.

The bookshelves had to be censored, too, for Mama Bower was an avid reader, and sometimes carried away a new if somewhat garbled education. She had, on one occasion, discovered a book which Milly had been using to answer the sometimes awkward questions of her daughters.

"Amazing!" Mama Bower had proclaimed, staring especially at the drawings of an unborn human embryo. She had later convulsed Sam by showing him a line drawing of the external female sex organs and remarking in all seriousness, "Is not a very good likeness."

In addition to the book examination, the house had to be cleaned and washed and sterilized from top to bottom. This was a futile task, since Mama Bower seemed equally distressed at whatever state it was in, and spent the first week of her visit cleaning happily. Sometimes when Milly had exhausted herself beyond reason for days before a visit in making absolutely sure no crumb of dirt remained, she would grow nearly hysterical at the way Mama Bower manufactured it.

"Do you know what she's doing, Sam?" Millie would be trembling all over from rage and exasperation. "She's on the floor in her room with a hat pin, scraping between the boards!"

A discovery of this sort was apt to send Milly into hysterical tears, and Sam was very gentle with her at such a time. They would go out into the kitchen and brace themselves with black coffee and mutual reminders that Mama Bower was, after all, growing old and childish.

Mama Bower would also turn over to the two girls the job of scraping all the dirt from the cracks in the public sidewalk which ran in front of the house, and then she would go out with a bucket of water and a broom to scour the concrete. This was a trial to Milly because it amused the neighbors. Once Mrs. Kingsley had come out to meet "Sam's delightful old mother" at such a task, and had been informed in laborious and concerned detail that she ought better to be cleaning her own sidewalk, which was deplorable; and her shrubbery would die unless pruned occasionally; and did she know the brick pillars were crumbling on the east side of her house? Mama Bower had then gone back to her work singing (she always sang when she was working at something she enjoyed) and the next day had nodded in silent approval when masons began repairing the Kingsley pillars and the man of the house was seen to be doing a somewhat clumsy job with pruning shears.

Jackie and Pricilla were another problem when Mama Bower announced a coming visit. They must suddenly wear dresses that were not too short and panties that were not too thin (Mama Bower was suspicious of the intentions of the little boys with whom they played) and must speak neither too much nor too little. ("Why so meek?" Mama Bower might demand. "Your Papa beat you too much?"—a question which always embarrassed Sam.) And they must always drop everything else to come when Mama Bower called.

This in itself was not so bad, as Mama Bower brought them fascinating presents from the country, which Milly was powerless to forbid.

"Is a pig's tail," said Mama Bower once, giving them each a hard curled-up thing which they accepted with delighted horror. She had hired a man to kill hogs the week before and it had occurred to her that these poor underprivileged city children had probably never seen a pig's tail, so she brought the two along. They hadn't either. For weeks after Mama Bower left, the possession of these strange objects set them up as royalty in the neighborhood younger set.

Another time it would be a bird's nest, or perhaps a baby chicken which Mama Bower had carried in her coat pocket undetected on the train, and most often, it was apples from her favorite tree—usually not edible.

The two girls never really recovered from the wonderful experience when, on one of Mama Bower's visits, she discovered that caterpillar webs were hanging in one of the back-yard trees.

"We will have a burning," she had announced solemnly, and that night even Pricilla and Jackie had been permitted to hold the burning rags on long sticks underneath the webs, squealing when the worms fell and curled themselves into balls of brown agony, or snapped and popped in the flames and gave off a green ooze.

"They'll have nightmares for weeks," Milly had prophesied, although actually the children had done nothing of the sort and had only remembered the experience as exciting and not as terrible at all.

Finally a crowd of neighbors had come over to see what the fire was all about, and the whole thing wound up as an evening lawn party. Sam had even served a few drinks, but Mama Bower had been the main attraction, dropping a live caterpillar into a cocktail and holding the glass aloft so everyone could see it writhing.

"See?" demanded Mama Bower with her chin stuck out. "Even the caterpillar!"

And then she had offered the drink to a neighbor's wife who laughed weakly and asked for a coke instead.

Before she left from one of her annual visits, Mama Bower would have completely rearranged the house furniture, and written intricate directions in the pages of Milly's cookbooks, and advised Sam to put his money into real estate where there was still a margin of security. Then she would be gone again, her whole journey home brightened by the knowledge that after her absence her house would need a complete overhauling and cleaning; and Milly would come home from the train and burst into those unexplainable tears.

Mama Bower hired Mr. Cagney, who lived a little west on Route Four, to do the heavy work around the farm and to look after things while she was off "helping Milly and Sam." She disliked him outwardly because every summer he would kindheartedly try to give her a bushel or so of apples from his own overloaded trees, and this insulted her beyond description.

"I'll wait on mine," she would snap at him in answer, nodding back at the tree at her kitchen window. She would keep her eyes fixed sharply on his as if daring him to look toward the tree and remark on the bare branches. "Plenty apples," she would add crisply.

In spite of that, Mr. Cagney was very fond of Mama Bower, and since she lived alone in the house he was in the habit of checking on her welfare, noticing at night whenever she lit the lamp and if the chimney smoked in the mornings; and sometimes stopping by of an evening to discuss their mutual and nearly perpetual dissatisfaction with the weather.

That was why Sam knew what it was the night Mr. Cagney called him.

"This is long distance. I have a collect call from Robert Cagney in Lincolnton . . ."

He gripped the phone. "Yes, put him on."

It turned out that Mr. Cagney had waited for the familiar gleam of Mama Bower's lamp; she always lit it promptly at

7:30, no matter if darkness had descended hours before; and when fifteen minutes had passed and there was still no light, Mr. Cagney had had a feeling.

"I think I'll walk down and see about Mama Bower," he said, reaching for his jacket, for it was very early spring and still chilly in the evenings.

"Yes, you'd better," said Mrs. Cagney.

The kids and the three dogs had wanted to go too, but Mr. Cagney knew how Mama Bower would react to such a parade, so he took only the oldest dog Tip, a toothless hound that Mama Bower sometimes fed, grumbling because she had to break up bread in advance and soak it in bowls of milk or gravy.

"Dumb old dog," Mama Bower would mutter. "Outlived your time."

And she would go on breaking the bread into fine pieces for the old hound, which eyed her in speechless devotion.

It was nearly eight o'clock by the time they got down to the Bower place, although the moon lit up everything like daylight. The moon was a bad sign, Mr. Cagney thought, especially when Tip let out a holler at it, and then again as they came up into the yard. When they got to the porch, Tip wouldn't even go up the steps at all, not even when Mr. Cagney kicked his backside, so he knew what was inside. Old Tip just laid down at the steps and put his nose between his paws and snuffled it, so Mr. Cagney had to go in by himself.

Mama Bower was lying neatly across her own bed, almost as if she had laid herself out, tidily arranging the limbs and pulling the skirt down to a decent length. She had evidently fallen asleep after supper and before she woke up again the mainswitch had been thrown and all the strength had just stopped coming in. She looked a little tired, and none of the wrinkles were gone from her face; they seemed merely to have sunk a little deeper and her eyesockets had dropped down the merest fraction. Her mouth was closed with neither smile nor frown, but when Mr. Cagney noticed her chin it seemed to him thrust forth a little bit, as if once she had dimly realized what was happening and had started to summon all her old defiance. He put a coverlet across her and went home to call Mr. Sam.

Sam and Milly and the two girls came by train the next morning, still dazed and bewildered at the news. They had been unable even during the trip to ask each other the unanswerable "But why?" and they had all been remembering with a rush of surprise how old Mama Bower had been; it startled them to realize Mama Bower had been old.

Mr. Cagney had handled the primary things that had to be done—the doctor and the death certificate (a mild heart attack, said Dr. Kane, and she was very old) and seeing the body off in the long black automobile.

So the Bowers had little to do but wander blankly in the spotless house, picking up this thing and that which had belonged to Mama Bower, and turning it in their hands, as if it were the answer to some riddle. If ever there had been a "disorderly" thing in the universe, it seemed to them all that Mama Bower's death was it—as if the Lord had suddenly jammed the whole cosmic gears and done something He had really no right to meddle in.

They could have, perhaps, been reconciled if Mama Bower had been treated like Lot's wife—turned suddenly into a pillar of something, transfixed perhaps with a broom and a dustcloth in her hand—as though Death had called and called; and when he found her too busy even to hear him, had simply snatched her wholecloth from all that she was doing.

But to find that Mama Bower had been lying down asleep, to realize for the first time that she tired like all the others—this was a jar; even the children felt it and fretted and fell to weeping all day long, frightened at what it might mean.

Later in the day when the body came, people began to gather—distant friends and cousins, and dozens of neighbors with their offerings of food and sympathy, and old old people. Sam had never seen so many old people, wizened bent men and women who hobbled around stubbornly, aged females who stumbled through the kitchen making supper, and doddering old men who went with jaws set to see after the livestock.

Sam said once in amazement, "Mama Bower was old," and Milly nodded. That was all they said about it. That was all they knew to say about it.

It wasn't until after supper that Milly noticed the apple tree. The poor old thing had stuck out a bloom or two, puny things that were already withered, and Milly swallowed hard.

Mr. Cagney had seen her glance. "Crazy old tree," he said softly. "It's way too early for blossoms. Tree never knows the right time."

Sam and Milly looked at each other, thinking sharply that for once the tree had known just the right time. It was as if the spirit of Mama Bower, passing by for the last time, had spotted the untidiness of their grief and bewilderment and had fallen upon it with her customary delighted clucking and wiped it all away.

The End of Henry Fribble

HE HAD SPENT his whole life denying any dependence on other people, and now he was old and he was going to die.

This realization came to him abruptly one spring afternoon while he was taking his daily walk (which led across the road and down through Circle Drive where the new houses were being built and then back home again). There was that feeling in the air that was neither warm nor not-warm, but peculiar to early April days; and here and there the trees that he saw flushed green and the Japanese cherries seemed on the verge of popping into bloom, as if they were only holding back from commitment by some violent, desperate effort. Along his customary way stood the new ranch-style houses with their naked windows and their look of having fallen prone upon the ground (there was no grace to houses nowadays); and in the last bare spots of land which remained along Circle Drive, the red clay had already been dug away and the rain water standing in future basements was like thin blood, and gave the whole area the appearance of an open wound, while nearby stood piles of brick and cement blocking that would later become other graceless houses.

I can remember when all of this was woods, thought Mr. Fribble. He had been taking this same walk now every day for years, had seen the first house go up (it was already weatherbeaten now, he thought with some satisfaction) and at first there had been only an unpaved road through pine trees. (An amazing number of cars had driven through at night—some very slow, some stopping altogether.) And then the city had paved the street, and the realty signs were posted, and on Sunday afternoons young couples came to see the lots and to walk about hand-holding, turning this pine clearing into a living room and getting mud all over Sunday shoes.

"It's too damp for a house down there," Mr. Fribble complained to his daughter Sarah. "Water stands all the time."

"Yes, Papa," said Sarah.

"Everything'll mildew," he had prophesied glumly in those days.

But there had been terracing and drainage ditches, and the new homeowners had planted moody grass to keep their back yards from washing away; loads of sand had been dumped on the gummiest places and young women with bare legs had put out shrubbery and rose bushes where the front lawns met.

And now the houses elbowed at each other, crammed onto small squares of land, and there were sidewalks and boxwoods and hydrangea bushes growing. It gave Mr. Fribble a sense of some sort of defilement which was unforgivable.

This was all woods once, thought Mr. Fribble on his daily walk, as if his knowledge of the past could somehow dim the way things were—give them their come-uppance, so to speak.

That was what made him think how old he was (remembering the woods)—not old really, and straight as he ever was and walking unaided, thank you—but he was, after all, past sixty-six. Sixty-seven in October as a matter of fact; he stopped abruptly on the sidewalk; Lena had been fifty-eight when she died and he was younger than she, a year or so. So he had lived ten years more; that was about all you could expect, insurance statistics said, since most women outlived their husbands anyway. Just to show them up, he suspected.

But I feel fine! Henry Fribble told himself firmly, while little nagging aches and pains tugged in his shoulders and under him his legs seemed suddenly to have the strength of strings, and his knees bulged out with every step.

At last his fear mounted and grew until it overcame him, and he completed the walk as fast as his weariness would let him, coming home all out of breath with the blood pumped redly into his cheeks and his heart thudding against his ribs.

He stood in the front door, holding it open with one hand as if he might go out again, and bellowed, "Sarah! Sarah!" until he heard his daughter's voice come back to him from the kitchen.

"I'm back here, Papa."

Mr. Fribble slammed the front door and stalked through the house because he was an old man and Sarah ought to be more respectful.

"I didn't ask you where you were," he said from the kitchen door. "I *called* you."

His daughter turned with a start from the icebox and stared at him so that she was caught in his eye completely for a minute—the blue-flowered dress and the plumpness and the wisps of graying hair. Sarah looks like a cow, thought Mr. Fribble angrily. She watched him without speaking and her glasses magnified the eyes, wide and blue and wet like a cow's, and looking at him now with the same blank patience.

"I *called* you," he repeated accusingly—but weaker, feeling a bit ridiculous at his own rage and at the fear.

Sarah went on staring at him. "I heard you, Papa," she said finally, and turned back to the icebox as if that were the end of it.

Rage swept over him again. He crossed the kitchen and took hold of her sleeve and shook it sharply. "See here!" he said. "See here, Sarah, suppose I'd been ill?"

She seemed for a minute on the verge of frowning but did not, and he dropped the sleeve self-consciously and looked at his feet. "But you're never ill, Papa," said Sarah patiently.

After that, Henry Fribble left the room without another word; that girl was impossible, absolutely impossible! Trembling seized his legs and he sank into his leather chair in the front room and felt the weakness in them; they could not have held him up another moment, he realized suddenly, and he leaned forward and stared down at them— surprised. Somehow he expected something outward to have happened, to be able to see dry rot clinging to the knees or touch the bulge where both shinbones had snapped; but there was nothing—the legs looked the same and the dark blue trousers were the same. He lifted his feet onto the stool with a sigh.

This was all wrong. The process of age was supposed to be a slow deterioration, something a man could feel growing within himself and taking first this thing and then that, or something at least that friends and relatives would see. ("He's slower on the steps, did you notice?" and "Doesn't hear as well.")

He snapped his head up and stared around the room suspiciously as the truth came home to him. That was it! Sarah had seen it coming on for God knows how long, but the process was so subtle that he had missed it until now when it was almost over. But all the time Sarah had stood by and watched with her contented cow-eyes, pretending nothing was wrong, smiling to herself to see first this thing go and then that until now he was only a shell of himself and still she had said nothing.

He clenched his hands—(old hands, he realized, white on top with blue veins bulging as if they were gorged with tired, sick blood)—and Sarah standing back in the kitchen just now as if she didn't see his weakness, hear his heart thudding desperately, notice the flushed face! He let his hands go limp and felt the wet chill on his fingers and he put his head back in his chair and closed his eyes wearily.

He remembered that he had bought the leather chair before Lena died, because it was the sort of thing a man needed to have, and during the years it had cracked and settled until now it exactly fit his body. Mr. Fribble could remember the very afternoon they brought the chair home; he had been very proud and Lena had dutifully agreed that

257

it was a handsome piece of furniture and smiled at him, fluttering her hands because he was pleased with something. Sarah had been quiet that day; that was just after the end of her one so-called love affair, and she was—perhaps—a little angry with him. But it had all worked out for the best, just as he said it would after he sent the fellow away, and you might expect her to be grateful to him now, now that he was an old man and dying.

That was one thing (he remembered now with satisfaction), Lena had been grateful to him for everything; he had planned their whole lives around her realization of all she owed to him. There had been the ceremony every Friday when she would ask him for the household money— all of it written down and carefully itemized—and he would check her list, crossing off the occasional things that were not necessary and adding perhaps the treats he liked, chocolate so she could bake him a pie, or oranges when in season. Sometimes he would say, "A very good list this week, Lena," and she would flush with pleasure at his praise, taking the money and saying "Thank you, Henry"—shyly, like a little girl.

And once in a while he would buy her a flowerpot just to see her pale blue eyes light up and her small underlip fairly trembling with delight, "Henry, how dear! How simply dear of you!"

It was a rare gift, he had often told his daughter gravely, the gift of proper appreciation, and a very comely thing in woman. But she would only look at him; her eyes had not been cowlike in those days but darkly brooding (all because of that silly fellow he had gotten rid of for her), and they rested on him thoughtfully, as if taking in his size and weight and storing the information away somewhere. But it had passed, and she had forgotten it all, just as he always said she would.

Sarah, as if in response to his thoughts, appeared now in the doorway and called him in to supper. He jumped in the chair as if awakening from a dream, and all of it came back —his weariness, the quiet form of fear, and above all the suspicion of his daughter who had known all along and was waiting patiently till he should die.

He went in to supper without hunger or desire, and puttered at his food with only cautious conversation. Afterwards he went upstairs to his room, shuffling from one tread to another as if they were a great distance apart. Sarah, clearing the dishes, wondered briefly if something could be troubling him and shrugged her shoulders. Nothing ever troubled her father.

Henry Fribble had been twenty-five years old when he and Lena Cates were married; he was a law office clerk at that time and doing so well that Mr. Fincannon was sending him to school. And Lena had been a girl that he had once known in grammar school. At least she always said afterwards that they had been in school together and finally he was able to draw up in his mind a picture of a bony colorless little girl, although he was never sure that he really remembered her, or if this were his idea of how she must have been.

He met her again at a party someone gave; there had been a delicate prettiness about her thin face then, and the wisps of pale frizzed hair and her light blue eyes; but mostly he had noticed the admiring way she looked at him, her small lips turned up as if she could not resist the slight pleased smile.

(He had been a fine figure of a man really, not so tall perhaps, but all in proportion and with a head which he thought privately had Grecian lines, and thick black hair.)

After that he had called on her and found her eminently suitable—competent in embroidery and table manners, and from a respectable, if poor, family, and well trained in matters of the church. Whenever he was talking to the young Miss Cates (she was really of spinster age, he realized later) something in Henry Fribble expanded warmly, and he was able to positively beam upon her, and all because of her delicate, worshipful smile.

And so they had been married, quietly and at her church, on an afternoon that threatened rain; and he had taken her to the seashore for their honeymoon. (He could still recall her pleased surprise at the ocean, seeing it for the first time, and the way he had showed her everything with a triumphant sense of pride, as if all of it were of his own making.)

She was, as he had guessed, woefully ignorant of the marriage relationship, and he had known a woman only once before—somewhat as a part of an education—so that part of it was not very successful. Under him she would writhe away with little animal moans, and pressing her hands flat on her face would cry herself quietly to sleep.

(She was so thin and small; he could barely lay one hand on her stomach between the sharp hipbones, and the skin on her sparse buttocks seemed always covered with goosebumps.) It was funny that he should remember small details like these about Lena, especially since he could not

recall her face in later years—only a familiar kind of blur—
and as for what she had looked like dead, he did not know;
but the coffin had been gray and there were satin ribbons.

Still, on their honeymoon and afterwards, she had never
turned away from him, even when little cries of pain
slipped out between tense lips, and later he supposed it had
not been so painful for her, although always—throughout
their married life—he exerted great force, because she was
so small and tight, he supposed.

(That made him think that sex was not so large a part of
life as people thought. He was certain it had been a meaningless process to Lena, and now that he himself had passed
beyond it, he felt no loss that it was gone.)

After they were married, Lena was almost immediately
pregnant with Sarah, and because she was such a small
woman she was especially awkward and almost always off
balance, leaning this way and that, and vomiting ceaselessly.
Her condition had revolted him completely; it was so
grossly physical, and as the months passed the swollen flesh
stretched tight over fragile bones gave her a grotesque appearance, as if any moment the skin might part and the
jagged bones come through.

Lena had sensed the way he felt and she moved through
the house as though in shame, and she hid her monstrous
body from him, swathing herself at night in great shapeless
gowns and sucking her breath in when she felt his eyes
upon her.

When Sarah was born, two weeks beyond schedule, Lena
had nearly died. It was a long slow labor, and Mr. Fribble
was exhausted with the endless waiting; and it ended finally

with the long tearing and Lena's high shrieks that brought him upright from a nap. (Sarah was a big child—the doctor said there must be no others.)

He had thought afterwards that it was perhaps unfortunate that Sarah was an only child; she was so obviously designed to be the inconspicuous middler of a large family. She had no real distinctions either positive or negative— this fat, rather plain child who made a straight series of average marks in school, both scholastically and as a personality, who never got beyond elementary piano, or athletics, or even homemaking, and who never in her whole life was slim, or poised, or genuinely attractive.

Sarah had been a great disappointment to him. At first he had tried everything, thinking impatiently that somewhere she possessed either interest or ability, but so far as he could discover, there was nothing. It was true that had Sarah been very gifted in anything he would probably have detested her and thrown all kinds of obstacles in her path, for he would never have been able to rid himself of a sense of competition.

But even dislike would have served some purpose. It might have given Sarah the notion that he *was,* after all, aware of her existence, and that as a personality she carried a certain amount of importance and counted for something.

However, after the first several years, Mr. Fribble ignored her completely, and she faded into insignificance even before her girlhood, having accepted her role completely and without complaint. She was Lena's daughter; she was a part of the whole system and fabric of Henry Fribble's life; she was the contented wallflower and the placid ugly duckling. (Of course, there had been that one time and the terrible fellow who owned a butcher shop, of all things, but that had passed. "It will pass," he had said to Lena after he had been forced to interfere, and the years had proved him right.)

For the most part, Mr. Fribble's life moved along unperturbed by any disturbance. In the background were always Lena and Sarah, moving quietly through the house when he was home so as not to disturb him, and preparing his favorite dishes, and serving as attentive cars to his long and involved accounts of his law practice. He never stopped to wonder what sort of relationship they had, these two unobtrusive women of his, and even if he had observed them closely, he would probably not have understood.

Actually, mother and daughter were each embarrassed by the other, seeing there a mirror only slightly distorted by the difference in age, and quickly turning away the eyes, not wanting to recognize the image which was reflected there.

This is not to say that they were either of them unhappy —they had found and accepted a certain niche in life and they filled that niche capably, and nothing more. There was only one rebellion for each of them—Sarah's butcher, and Lena's gradual longing for the gratitude that went uncontested to the dead. And where Sarah's butcher was sent safely away, there later remained some question about Lena, so that now when Henry Fribble thought about her last years, there would appear across his nose two wrinkles, and he would wonder about her.

Still, to all outward signs, the two women lived together pleasantly, each serving a similar end, and observing toward each other a restrained politeness which prevented them from being really friends. It was as if each were guest in the other's house, and they made—whenever Henry Fribble was absent—embarrassed small talk, evaluated the weather and compared it with yesterday and the potential for tomorrow, read aloud items from the paper and took—each of them—unwanted afternoon naps, to spare themselves conversation.

The household duties were a great salvation to them both; they seized upon some problem of management with unconcealed delight, and would spend a whole morning clucking and smiling over the dinner lamb chops.

Then the funerals began.

There was nothing really questionable about it the first time; Henry Fribble came home to dinner and found only Sarah, who said that "Mother isn't back from the funeral yet," and the two of them dined alone, without much concern for Lena's absence.

It had been, Sarah explained, some distant friend—Mother had seen it in the papers that morning and frowned and said she supposed she ought to go, and at four that afternoon a cab had called for her, but she had not yet returned.

However, as the evening wore on and Lena still did not come home, they began to be uneasy, and sat in the somber library (full of unread volumes in expensive hand-tooled backs) and waited. Neither of them knew exactly what they waited for; it was more than just Lena's return, it was an explanation. How had she dared to violate the pattern so as to force them into the position of waiting for her?

"When was the funeral?"

"Four-thirty, I think. I don't believe she said."

Outside the wind was blowing with the thin reediness of a pipe organ; it was mid-November (Mr. Fribble was always to remember that later as if it were the important factor), and the fire in the grate wavered when the wind whistled in the chimney.

"She should be back by now."

He stood up restlessly, more angry than anything else, because it was not like his wife to be out past dinner without even so much as a phone call. There were, after all, the waiters and the waited-upons, and Lena by her very nature was a waiter; she was Woman worrying lace curtains and leaving the light on and keeping supper warmed. That was the way she was, and to shift the balance even for one time demanded a vast impudence with the whole scheme of things which Lena did not possess. Henry Fribble moved about, restless from his own anger.

Sarah was watching him from under half-closed lids; the bovine resemblance was already apparant in the cast of her features, he thought irritably. Finally she said, "I suppose she should be back," without much interest or excitement, and plucked vaguely at the pages of a magazine.

He was very angry with her. He had the feeling she secretly supported her mother in this absence and he searched her face for evidence of plotting as he crossed the room, picked up the poker and jabbed it into the fire; turning the bits of coal this way and that so that the smallest ones fell through uselessly and smoldered in the ashes.

He replaced the poker with more noise than was necessary. "No need to pester the fire," said Sarah sensibly.

He did not look at her. "I wish you'd learn to use a more

exact vocabulary," he snapped. "How can one *pester* a fire?"

Just then Lena came in; they heard the front door close behind her and the rattle of wire hangers in the hall closet as she put away her coat. Now that she was home, Mr. Fribble sat in his leather chair and put his feet up, chilling his anger into a quiet disapproval that met her in cool waves when she came into the room. He had just gotten ready to speak to her when Sarah interrupted with a practicality which infuriated him.

"Have you had dinner?" And Lena—unbelievably enough—replied, "I'll have a sandwich," and moved off to the kitchen before he could even say a word. Now he would have to sit still until she chose to come back into the room, or else follow her foolishly out to the kitchen to ask his questions; it put him in a bad light anyway you looked at it. He rumpled several pages of newspaper by turning them too fast and finally went to the kitchen where Lena was eating. (Tomatoes and mayonnaise, he observed with distaste.)

"Where have you been so long?"

Lena looked at him above the ragged edge of sandwich with genuine surprise. "I'm sorry. I thought Sarah would tell you. I've been to a funeral."

"All this time?"

He wanted a glass of orange juice, but he felt to pour it and join them at the table (Sarah was hungry too, she had discovered) would be a concession he could not afford to make.

"Martha Enwright died." Lena munched on the sandwich; her chin was grease-shiny from the mayonnaise. "Lovely service. Husband was distraught with grief."

For the first time in all the years they had been married, Henry Fribble felt he was being in some way ignored. "Surely the rites were over by now," he said with a vague sense of desperation. It was as if something of which he had every right to expect stability, such as the kitchen floor, were suddenly discovered to be crumbling quietly under his feet. He watched her, suspicious of anything she might do or say.

Lena looked up at him again and for one moment he saw a veil come over her eyes and cloud them, covering some secret which—astoundingly enough—shut her off from him. "I walked home," she said simply, and poured herself some more milk.

He *had* to sit down then, so he got the orange juice to supply some motivation. "You walked home, Lena? In this wind? What on earth for?"

He would have sworn that the expression on her face was pure defiance. "I was thinking," she said. "That's all, Henry. I was just thinking."

And just for a minute he was sure her mouth had flickered in a smile.

It was very alarming. He rose without another word and carried his orange juice back into the library, where he nursed it grimly, as if it had been strong drink, and mused upon Lena's strange behavior.

After that night he was never able to understand the whole thing, not even when the first incident had been multiplied into a thousand others, and the same scene had been re-enacted between them over and over again almost in the same words.

At first he thought she must be lying to him, but he checked on her story and it was completely true—Lena Fribble would attend some funeral and then walk slowly home, staring at her feet and seemingly in deep thought.

As time passed, the corpses ceased to be those of friends or even acquaintances, and were picked at random from the city papers. They were always women (he noticed), and neither spinsters nor widows seemed to fit into her weird qualifications; she also preferred ornate church services and had a leaning toward certain of the more impressive ministers. She felt that Berkely and Howard did a better job on these occasions than Rutledge Mortuary, and that the handsomest wreaths were made up by McKinley's Florists.

Usually she carried along with her a small black leather notebook in which she wrote comments which Henry sometimes secretly read:

Mary Markham. 68. Heart attack. Berkely and Howard. Family wreath in white glads (McKinley's). First Baptist. 3 P.M. Dr. McConnell. Husband grief-stricken. Youngest daughter fainted while taking the Final Look. Over 200 present.

Then there would be quotes from the main address, usually something referring to the dead woman's ultimate worth and value to family and community, to how she would be missed, and to the reward awaiting her.

Sometimes at the end of it all there would be penciled in Lena's firm neat hand a comment that was like a gentle sigh of pleasure—"Lovely . . ." or sharply, "Insincere!"

Finally Henry Fribble was forced to admit it; his wife had a portion of her life set aside for something in which he had no part; she had—if you will—a hobby. Where other people went to ball games, flower shows, square-dance festivals, plays or the opera, Lena Fribble went to funerals.

It was not enough that Lena should engage in this completely enigmatic activity, but somehow his daughter Sarah seemed to condone it. She never accompanied her mother to the countless rites or defended her to him, but when Henry Fribble paced angrily through the house awaiting his wife's return, he would sense in Sarah some quiet sympathy for Lena, and this angered him even more.

"You think it's all right, this morbid habit of hers," he would accuse her.

But Sarah only protested weakly, "It does no harm," fluttering her chubby hands awkwardly as he stalked about the room.

"It's not normal," he would declare to her in genuine rage. "It's not the product of a normal mind."

And Sarah would look at him as patiently as any cow, saying nothing in answer to that; and often he would go to bed without waiting for Lena, too disturbed and resentful to sleep, and angrier than ever at her because of it.

Their life did not change in any other way: Lena was always quiet, respectful, admiring; there was the same household list on Fridays; she was still as pleasantly delighted to receive his occasional flowerpot; the house ran smoothly and he was superbly cared for. And yet it seemed to Henry Fribble that life changed in every way, that this secretive part of Lena was an ugly infection in his life that would spread and grow and finally consume him with disease. He was actually afraid to forbid her to continue attending these funerals because he had a strong suspicion that in this one thing she would not obey him, and that he could not have stood.

And that was the way things went for almost nine years, until Henry Fribble was fifty-six years old, and they laid little Lena Fribble away with as intricate a service as she might have wished—Berkely and Howard, and with flowers from McKinley's.

On the morning after the fatal walk when Henry Fribble realized fully his age and his decline, the dawn came with a terrible relentless grayness; it struck him as soon as he was out of bed that the sky was the color and texture of gray satin ribbons and the light seemed sucked out of everything. In the mirror his eyes looked darker; he squinted and peered at them with his nose almost against the glass—it was the darkness of sterile empty rooms and it seemed to him that the hand at his tie was unsteady, although he held it out frowning and could not distinguish a tremor.

He had slept badly that night, his thoughts tumbled and tangled like dank summertime sheets. There had been the memory of Lena, all the way back to the early days of their marriage and up to her funeral, a kind of bird's-eye view of their life together in this house.

Mr. Fribble had a terrible feeling that his whole life was now passing again before his eyes, as before those of a man drowning, and there came sharply the sickening fear of the time when he should have remembered it all up through yesterday, and there would be nothing left. That will be all of it, he thought, and he put his hand out again as if daring it to quake, but it was still. Still as death, he thought, and went downstairs to breakfast.

The whole day passed like those first moments, grinding itself out sluggishly ahead of him like a cinema in which he dangled and was useless. Although he was retired from practice he went regularly to the office to read in the law library, but today was like no other day had ever been. He felt strangely suspended and unreal; when he took a step it would seem to him that the concrete or the tile or the stair had appeared only a second before his shoe came down upon it, and that if he should take courage enough to peer over his shoulder he would find the whole world had disappeared behind him, leaving not even so much as a heap of sand.

It haunted him; he came to a door and it was as if the knob grew forth to fit his hand and went back to nothing after the latch had clicked. He read his books without thought, and had not bravery enough to leaf back through, half-fearful that the pages had gone blank behind his hand.

Lunch was the same; his plate was filled with something tasteless which had materialized from air; he ate it hastily, dreading the moment when he should relax a bit and have to see the morsel on his fork melt off to nothing.

The day wore past, only one second ahead of itself, and Henry Fribble was miserably aware how soon the wall would break and the two moments—the real and the unreal—would rush into each other like water over broken, drowning dikes.

He had never been so tired in his life as that afternoon, riding the bus home through rows of neatly clipped suburbs. The lots and the houses seemed all of a size, so that they clicked into place in the small square of bus window and then clicked out again, like colored slides, and every detail was sharp until it hurt his eye. There was the straight brown line where someone had edged the lawn back from the sidewalk and drawn a border around his plot of land, a tricycle which had fallen on a step and been forgotten there, crumpled crazily in red and green circles against the concrete.

And children playing. It hit him suddenly that he had never noticed the children much before, and now he stared at them with something akin to terror. They played at idle senseless games, and yet there was a precision in everything they did—the insane but somehow logical precision of the Alice fairy tale. Three little girls were playing gravely on the sidewalk at a hopscotch square; he wondered where the game had risen and how it was that all children knew it, in all its endless variations, without ever having heard it from parent or teacher. It seemed to him then that there was some great conspiracy among all of youth which he was incapable of understanding and he drew back from the glass with a shudder and closed his eyes. I shall be mad by dawn, he thought.

When he opened them again he looked straight into the face of a quiet little boy across the aisle—seven or so, he guessed—and the little boy was watching him with a terrible patient hunger that made him tingle in every nerve and turn his eyes away.

When the bus came to his stop, Mr. Fribble almost fell in his eagerness to be off the bus and away, and once he was out on the sidewalk, he dared not turn his head, knowing surely and beyond doubt that the little boy had crossed the aisle and climbed into his seat, and even now was grinning at him slyly through the glass.

When Henry Fribble got home that day, Sarah did not make an answer to his call and he slumped against the coatstand and felt every bone in him sag; Sarah was always there in the evenings; Sarah *always* answered his call. It was too much on top of everything else, that he should come into his own house and call for someone, and only the stillness answer.

Finally he made it into the library and over to the leather chair, where he half sat, half fell into the shape of it, knowing even before he settled back that today the chair would fit strangely to his body, as if it were made for someone else, someone already forgotten. The house was quiet as a tomb; he sat there listening to the stillness until it rang in his ears as audibly as sound, then he would move and wiggle to make the chair creak and shut it out.

I don't really want any supper, Mr. Fribble thought with some surprise. It was as if he had crossed over some line and now had no more need of food. I only want to sit quietly here a little while. And he sighed softly so that the sound it made was as if a wind had gone gently through him without touching.

He must have slept awhile, for when he looked about again a whole chunk had been lifted from the day and the shadows leaned out into the room from behind bookcases and chairs and tables. He grew suddenly afraid, and he started up in his chair and began to call his daughter loudly, "Sarah! Sarah, answer me! Sarah!" But there was only his own voice coming back to him, and he marveled at how little noise it made. He was jarred to know how sure he had been that now she would answer him—(she had always answered)—and the fear in him went to panic until he felt he might cry, the loud vexed tears of a frightened child shut into a strange dark room.

Cars passed outside; he could hardly believe that anything existed beyond these four walls, and laughter bubbled in his throat painfully at the thought of all of it still going on in the same way.

He would have gotten up and walked around and looked for her, but there was that certain feeling of being left here on a small island of existence, and he felt if he should take one step from the chair he would go off its edge into he knew not what, and so he dared not move.

After awhile he began to call for his wife, but his own voice was strange and broken to him. He called her name over and over, "Lena? Oh Lena, Lena . . ." and she came out of the library wall and stood looking at him for a long minute and then went away again. That was when he knew she would not come to him now, and he put his head back against the chair and an ocean washed over him sadly.

When Sarah came in from buying his supper favorites at the grocery store, she found him there in the leather chair, and all around him the room had gotten dark.

$\mathcal{V}$ OICES OF THE $\mathcal{S}$ OUTH